DESPERATE JOURNEY

Recent Titles by Julie Ellis from Severn House

THE HAMPTON SAGA

THE HAMPTON HERITAGE
THE HAMPTON WOMEN
THE HAMPTON PASSION

ANOTHER EDEN
BEST FRIENDS
DARK LEGACY
DESPERATE JOURNEY
THE GENEVA RENDEZVOUS
THE HOUSE ON THE LAKE
A NEW DAY DAWNING
ONE DAY AT A TIME
ON THE OUTSIDE LOOKING IN
SECOND TIME AROUND
SILENT RAGE
SINGLE MOTHER
SMALL TOWN DREAMS
SOMERS V. SOMERS
A TURN IN THE ROAD
A TOWN NAMED PARADISE
VILLA FONTAINE
WHEN THE SUMMER PEOPLE HAVE GONE
WHEN TOMORROW COMES

DESPERATE JOURNEY

Julie Ellis

severn
House

This first world edition published 2008
in Great Britain and the USA by
SEVERN HOUSE PUBLISHERS LTD of
9–15 High Street, Sutton, Surrey, England, SM1 1DF.

British Library Cataloguing in Publication Data

Ellis, Julie, 1933-
  Desperate journey
  1. Romantic suspense novels
  I. Title
  813.5'4[F]

  ISBN-13: 978-0-7278-6661-5   (cased)

All Severn House titles are printed on acid-free paper.

Typeset by Palimpsest Book Production Ltd.,
Grangemouth, Stirlingshire, Scotland.
Printed and bound in Great Britain by
MPG Books Ltd., Bodmin, Cornwall.

For Caren Solomon, a very special lady – whose given
name I've borrowed for this book

One

O n this spring evening of 2005 American Caren Stephens – who like most wives in Iran retained her single name – sat in the living room of her house in the upper-class suburb of Elahiyeh in northern Tehran. The atmosphere tense. Foreboding. Caren geared herself to hear disturbing news. When her husband Marty – as he was known to her from their student days at Columbia University – paced in that fashion, she knew trouble lay ahead.

Marty Mansur paused, turned to her. 'You must understand what I'm about to tell you.' His tone ominous. 'This concerns Danny's well-being as well as my own.' Danny was their eight-year-old son. 'You must do as I say.'

'What are you trying to tell me?' Alarm eroded her effort to remain calm. Marty had become a stranger in the course of the past five years. But they were a family. For Danny's sake, she told herself, they must remain together.

'You're not to drive Danny to school each morning, nor pick him up at the end of the school day.' Their eight-year-old son was studying in his bedroom, as on every evening. 'No more,' Marty emphasized.

'Why?' Her throat tightened in fear. 'Why can't I—?'

Marty held up a hand in a familiar demand for silence. 'I'll drop Danny off on my way to the office each morning. My driver will pick him up at the end of the school day and bring him home to you. My new driver is an experienced bodyguard. A second bodyguard will alternate with him so that at no time,' he stressed with deceptive calmness, 'will Danny or I be without the protection of a bodyguard.'

'What's happening?' Her mind was in chaos. 'Why must you and Danny always be accompanied by a bodyguard?'

'I feel this is wise.' His eyes shut her out. Again, she railed mentally at the lack of communication between them. A situation that had existed for most of their five years of living in Tehran. *Why is it wise?* 'Danny will drive into the city with me each morning.' Marty never drove himself – he used the time to study office material. 'I will see him into his school. My driver will pick him up at the conclusion of the day and bring him home to you,' he repeated. But now Marty's driver would wear a holstered gun beneath his jacket.

'Danny will be upset,' she protested. 'He'll be frightened.' *I'm frightened.*

'Danny will do as he's told.' Marty's eyes were opaque. *What isn't he telling me? He's received threats against his life and Danny's?* 'I'll explain the new arrangement. No problem.'

When Danny was to enter first grade, Marty had insisted on transferring him from the International School to the Orthodox religious school approved by the Administration. She'd driven him there each morning, picked him up at dismissal time. A long commute to central Tehran.

With unnerving clarity she had seen Danny change from a joyous, high-spirited little boy to a somber, introverted small stranger. With each passing day she became more upset at this. She, too, had changed, she rebuked herself. She was insecure, allowing Marty to make decisions that once would have been a joint effort.

'I'm going in to my office.' Marty punctured her introspection. 'I have work to do.' His private home office adjoined the master bedroom – where he'd slept alone the past three years. *'With my insane hours I'll disturb your sleep. You'll be more comfortable in one of the guest rooms.'*

Alone, she made a pretense of reading one of the American magazines to which she subscribed through the years. But her mind was in turmoil. Her precious baby's life was in danger! Who would want to harm an eight-year-old boy?

She glanced at her watch. Time for Danny to go to sleep.

She went to Danny's bedroom, opened the door. He sat on a corner of his bed – crouched over a textbook. As with all children in Iran, most of his waking hours were devoted to studying.

'Time to go to sleep, Danny,' she said tenderly. 'Put on your pajamas, go brush your teeth.'

'I'm not sure I've memorized enough for class—' he worried.

'You've memorized enough,' she insisted and pulled his pajamas from beneath a pillow. What was this frenzy for memorizing the Koran? Let him memorize less and understand more. 'You need your sleep.'

Prepared for the night, he slid beneath the light coverlet, lifted his face for his mother's kiss. Already he was fighting yawns. So sweet, so vulnerable – and now someone threatened his life?

'I love you, Mommie, even if you are an American.'

She froze in shock, fought for composure. 'I love you, too, my darling.' *Doesn't he understand? He's an American.*

She turned on the night light, tiptoed out of the room. He was asleep already. But his last words shattered the floodgates that had held back her alarm at the changes she'd seen in him these past three years.

Her husband, too, had become a stranger. The Marty she had known and loved back in New York had disappeared. Moving to Tehran had been the death knell of their marriage.

Here he objected to her calling him Marty – the Americanized name he'd chosen for himself in their days at Columbia and in their pleasant life in Westchester County after their marriage. Now he was Mohammed Mansur – stern, forbidding. Contemptuous of everything American. Fighting to become part of that small, radical cleric elite that tyrannized the country. Yearning for political power.

How could a man change so drastically in the five years they'd been living in Tehran? How could their lives have changed so drastically?

Marty makes me feel stupid. I'm not stupid.

In the morning Caren stood at a living-room window and watched while Danny was escorted by his father to the waiting car in the sycamore-shaded courtyard. The new driver – an experienced bodyguard, she remembered – sat behind the wheel. She was too distraught – after a night of broken slumber – to be aware of the beauty of the Alborz Mountains on this rare day when noxious smog didn't mask their splendor.

Now the car was driving away. Caren shivered. What had happened to her life and to Danny's that he could say he loved her despite her being an American? For too long she had tried to block out reality.

Face it. She must contrive to take Danny home. Out of this insanity. *How am I to do this? Where can we run and escape Marty's grasp?*

He'd be enraged. Fight to track them down. He'd be determined to take Danny from her. Ruthless. Where back home would they be safe from Marty?

The whole world changed that evening when a phone call from Tehran told them that Marty's father and older brother had been killed in a plane crash. Marty was now the head of the family. Head of the family business, which included a tea plantation in Gilan and an export house that shipped tea to many countries.

Marty had been sent to Columbia – first as an undergraduate, then as a graduate student – to acquire the knowledge he needed to set up an American branch of the family business in the United States. Now he was the sole surviving son, who must take charge of all family affairs.

Her mind raced back through the years – to the early spring of ten years ago . . .

With two hours between classes Caren decided to go to the bookstore across from the Columbia campus. She'd ordered herself to pick up a copy of *Ivanhoe*. In a corner of her mind she could hear Mom's voice:

'Don't wait till you're teaching to read the classics you read in those grades yourself. And remember, you'll see more than the kids will – and it's your task to help them appreciate the fine points.'

After earning her bachelor's degree this year she would go on for a master's in education, like her sister Janis. To Mom and Dad a degree in education was like a trust fund. They'd both taught in the New York school system, expected to retire on pensions that would allow them to live in comfort if not in luxury. But in her junior year at Columbia both had been killed in a senseless act of violence within a few years of retirement. The police called it 'a robbery gone wrong.'

This wasn't an hour when the bookstore was mobbed, she realized gratefully as she found her way to the classic fiction section. She skimmed the shelves. Ah, there was a copy of *Ivanhoe* – on the very top shelf. She stood on tiptoe – stretching every inch of her five feet three, but the book remained beyond her reach.

'Let me get it for you,' a warm, charming male voice said. '*Waverly* or *Ivanhoe*?'

'*Ivanhoe*—' She turned to face him. Tall, dark and handsome – the cliché darted across her mind. *Is he English? He has a faint British accent.*

He brought down the book. His eyes searched hers as he gave it to her with a dazzling smile. 'You look like Rowena,' he told her. 'Lush black hair, blue eyes, exquisite features.' *Wasn't Rowena's hair blonde? But never mind.* 'When I was fourteen, I was madly in love with Rowena.'

'Thank you,' she said softly and chuckled. 'I think.'

It's just the blouse I'm wearing – the medieval 'look', the mosaic colors.

'I read *Ivanhoe* when I was in boarding school near London,' he reminisced.

I was right – he's British. Janis always teases me for being fascinated by British accents. She says I must have been British in another life.

'It was required reading.' His eyes were full of questions.

'I expect to teach eventually – after a master's in education,' she began. 'I'm into a private refresher course on romantic English literature.'

'You're at Columbia!' he crowed, as though making a major discovery. 'I'll have my degree in May, then go back for graduate studies in economics.' His face exuded pleasure. 'Let's go to the cashier so you can buy *Ivanhoe*, then head over to the pastry shop for coffee and something sweet. We have to catch up on all the years we've been apart.'

*   *   *

That was how she began to see Marty – as he was called by American friends. She learned that he wasn't British but Iranian. *Not an Arab, as most people believe – Iran is Middle Eastern but not an Arab country.*

By graduation time Marty was insisting they were meant to spend the rest of their lives together.

'*I had no intention of going to the bookshop that day. Fate sent me there. Caren, we were destined to meet.*'

She was euphoric. She had been plagued by loneliness until Marty entered her life. Her only surviving family – Janis and her husband Ira – lived three thousand miles away, in a small community near San Francisco.

Marty was handsome, bright, warm – and lonely despite a large family back in Iran. He had dreaded leaving her at the end of the semester.

'*I must go home for two months during the summer break – the family expects that. But I'll come back for graduate studies. I've gone through the paperwork – I'll be a legal US resident. When I'm through with the economics program, I'll set up an American office for my father's company here in New York.*'

On Marty's return – after two months of daily e-mails and phone calls – he moved into her newly acquired one bedroom apartment on West 104th Street. They were to be married the day before Thanksgiving – when Janis and Ira could take time off from their jobs and would fly in from San Francisco to be their witnesses.

Janis and Ira had arrived on Tuesday evening. Janis glowing with more good news – she was six weeks pregnant. On Wednesday morning the four of them cabbed to City Hall for the civil marriage ceremony.

She and Marty sat holding hands, Caren recalled. She'd never felt so happy. Her whole little world was here – Janis and Ira and Marty – and the baby Janis was carrying.

They'd waited impatiently for their turn in the small room where the ceremony was performed. In two minutes she and Marty were married. They went for their wedding luncheon – where Ira insisted on picking up the check – at the fabulous Windows on the World. For a moment she mourned for the tragedy that had destroyed the restaurant, along with the lives of almost 3,000 people on that fateful September 11th, 2001.

She and Marty had chosen to stay in the city for the long weekend – to be with Janis and Ira. 'We've already had our honeymoon,' Marty had declared. Janis and Ira had stayed at a nearby hotel. It was such a happy time for the four of them. She'd rejoiced at seeing Marty and Ira as kindred souls. She remembered how Ira had teased Marty.

'Man, why do you insist on being such a perfectionist? We don't live in a perfect world.'

Marty understood – and accepted – that she would never be a Muslim convert. In turn she understood that Marty retained his Iranian citizenship out of respect for his parents. In truth, during the long years of the Revolution and of his schooling Marty had lived outside of Iran. And he'd agreed – then – that their children would be raised in their mother's faith.

Loving Marty, expecting in time to be accepted by his family despite their aversion to his marrying an American – though this never happened, she'd studied the Koran, respected its teachings. There was much similarity, she realized, to the Judeo-Christian teachings.

The Koran declared Jews and Christians shared an alliance with Muslims since they believed in the same God, shared the same moral values. But radical Muslims were interpreting the Koran in a frightening vein. Instead of peace and tolerance radical Muslims taught hate.

'My family isn't Orthodox,' Marty had explained. 'They're all Westernized. My two younger sisters and I were shipped off to boarding school during the Revolution. My brother – he was sixteen years older than I – stayed in Iran, worked with my father in the business.'

'It must have been rough for you,' she'd sympathized. 'To be sent off to boarding school when you were so young.'

'I'm the younger brother – I don't count.' His flippant dismissal didn't entirely hide the hurtful knowledge that as the younger son he was dispensable.

That was the Marty she'd loved. Now a stranger inhabited his body. An obsession for power had driven out that other

Marty. Now he was convinced bodyguards were necessary for his safety and Danny's.

Why do I feel so helpless? I can't be helpless. My precious baby's life – his future – is at stake. I must be strong – I must discover a way to take Danny home.

Two

Staring at the Alborz Mountains in the distance without seeing, Caren was caught up in the past. At intervals she'd tried to track down the change in Marty. Their first months in Tehran Marty was the warm, sweet man she loved. He'd spent long hours each day in trying to organize the business into a profitable institution, had flown back to New York on several occasions until he was satisfied that the New York office could survive without his presence.

'We'll be here a year,' she'd told herself. That was what Marty said when they left for Tehran. Then they'd return to New York. But that hadn't happened. Slowly but insidiously – Marty began to change. He was obsessed by a need to build his father's business into a major operation. To show the family he could surpass his father's efforts. He was conscious of new power. He was intoxicated by it.

She'd been so excited when – early in their second year in Iran – she was offered a teaching job at the UN preschool. She'd waited impatiently for Marty to come home to tell him . . .

'Out of the question!' He glared at her in simmering fury.

She flinched at his hostility. 'Marty, why not?' She was bewildered. He'd been pleased when she had taught in their Westchester community.

'How will it look to my friends? To my business associates? It would appear I can't afford to support my wife and child!'

That wasn't the true reason. Along with his political associates, he'd come to believe that women should be banned from the professions. He loathed Pari – her dearest friend in Iran – for teaching at the university. Neither of his sisters – highly educated – was allowed to pursue a career.

A civil law stated that a husband could prevent his wife from taking employment outside the home. That allowed women to work at home, where many of the less affluent made the rugs and carpets that were a major export.

Caren forced herself back to the moment. She was to meet Pari for coffee this morning before her first class. Thank God for that – she needed to talk with Pari. She was impatient to be sitting across the table from this cherished friend. To tell her of this latest insanity. Pari would understand she couldn't remain in Tehran when Danny must travel with a bodyguard! But how were they to escape?

She and Pari shared their most intimate problems. Pari's ugly divorce, her disillusionment with her own marriage. In the past two years she'd begun to feel as though she was a recluse. Pari brought her out of that.

She glanced at her watch. She wasn't to meet with Pari for over an hour. It seemed an interminable wait. She searched her mind for errands to occupy that period. Oh, she should respond to the invitation to the concert instigated by Pari. The committee expected a confirmation of attendance.

An all-women's concert, she thought derisively – with a woman vocalist. Women singers were allowed to perform only for feminine audiences – and that was a rarity. The ruling clerics considered the feminine voice 'harmfully arousing.'

She went into her bedroom, sat at her writing table and focused on the letter to the concert committee. With the letter written, she reached into her bedroom closet. Impatient for her meeting with Pari.

Here in their exclusive suburb the chador – the long black covering worn by Orthodox Iranian women – was replaced by a long, drab, unlined raincoat plus a headscarf. Essential parts of hijab – the law-demanded Islamic dress code for women. Bright colors were frowned upon – sometimes causing punishment.

On occasion the Komitch – the Morals Police – would approach some woman in violation – but these days rarely was a woman flogged. Instead, a fine was levied or a bribe exchanged hands. At least, this was the practice in their exclusive community.

Tales of violent invasions by the Komitch – in less elite areas – circulated at regular intervals. Dinner parties in modest homes were stormed and people taken away. Some to be flogged, some to pay huge fines, some to escape punishment via bribes. The crime: in the privacy of the host's home the women violated the dress code.

Teenagers from educated, Westernized families – the target of the Morals Police even in Elahiyeh – wore skintight jeans and belly-button-showing tops beneath their manteaus, the unlined raincoats that replaced the hated chador among the more educated. The young often ignored the ban on make-up, wore brilliant lipstick and heavy mascara. Sometimes paying a jolting penalty – but this was their rebellion.

Caren kicked off her sandals. She debated about wearing knee-highs, decided not to tempt fate. Nylon was transparent. The sight of bare feet was not permitted. Black socks, she ordered herself, pulled high. Just last week a total stranger had reprimanded her.

'Pull up your socks – skin is showing!'

Total strangers were allowed to do this at will – and often did.

She'd wear her black designer slacks and a colorfully printed silk blouse, she decided – concealed by her manteau.

Thank God, it wasn't a steamy day. In the summer, when the temperature might hit 106 degrees, she cursed the manteau. But by law only the face and hands of women in Iran could be shown outside the home. Nail polish forbidden.

With her headscarf arranged to show only the allowed amount of hair, Caren left the house and slid behind the wheel of the black Jaguar that Marty considered appropriate for their station in life. When she arrived at the coffee shop on the mall – lightly populated at this hour – she spied Pari at a private corner table.

Pari was speaking on her cellphone. A tall, elegant woman in her mid-forties and, no doubt, smartly dressed beneath her manteau. Even here, Caren thought in recurrent annoyance while she threaded her way to Pari's table, they must sit enshrined in their manteaus and headscarves. Women in hiding.

Pari was proud that she'd contrived to have a career –

when so many Iranian women, even educated women, endured sequestered lives. But Pari loathed the restrictions demanded by the university. The need to observe the dress code even in the classroom. She loathed the constant censorship – what could be taught, what books could be used. Twice Pari had been at the point of being expelled.

Pari finished her cellphone conversation, turned to Caren with a brilliant smile that swiftly evaporated.

'You look uptight.' Her eyes searched Caren's with solicitude. 'Something's happened—'

'Marty told me last night—' Caren struggled for composure. 'I'm not to drive Danny to and from school any more. He and Marty are to be accompanied by bodyguards – wherever they go.'

Pari gazed at her in shock. 'Why?'

'You know Marty. He tells me nothing. But I'm terrified. I suspect he's enraged someone with his political goings-on. Danny's in danger, Pari!' *How do I deal with this? How do I take Danny home to America? Some town where Marty can't find us.*

'Someone uttered a threat in anger,' Pari soothed, but Caren sensed she was unnerved. 'In a few days it'll be over.' But Pari's cajoling smile lacked conviction. This was a country where violence erupted too often.

'I wish I could believe that it was nothing serious.' Caren closed her eyes for a moment, as though to wash away reality. 'For the past three years I've been frightened by what Marty's doing to Danny's young mind. I tried to close my own mind to it. Now this—'

'We live in rough times.' Pari sighed. 'We keep hoping for better days.'

'How can such Iranians distort the true message of Islam?' Caren demanded in a blend of rage and frustration. A religion so close to Christianity and Judaism. And it wasn't solely in Iran. Wherever extremely radical Muslims lived there was chaos. 'The Koran teaches people to be tolerant, to be helpful to everyone. But Marty's instilling hate in Danny. The country is instilling hate in its young. The young should not be taught to hate!'

'No.' Pari's face was taut with rejection. 'Even the toys

preferred for male children are violent. The most prized gift is a toy gun.'

Caren winced in recall. 'I'll remember forever the day four years ago when I was driving Danny to his preschool group on what I was told was the anniversary of the hostage-taking of something or other.' Caren shuddered in recall. 'All those young kids parading and shouting "Death to Americans" and "Down with the infidels!"'

'Caren, you know the Administration creates those incidents. Iranians hate the current American Administration – not the American people. They try to emulate Americans. I know – at some schools the principal lays down an American flag each year for his students to stamp on this day – to show their contempt for Americans. But most students walk around the flag.'

'I look around and see how people throng to American stores,' Caren conceded. 'McDonald's, KFC, Gap, Blockbusters. Especially the young.'

'And they flock to the "cafénets",' Pari added. The popular Internet cafés. 'They're hungry for news of the outside world. They won't find this in Iranian newspapers, on Iranian radio or television.'

All at once Caren and Pari realized the tables around them were being occupied. This private conversation must cease.

'You'll go to the concert with me?' Pari asked. Her tone casual. 'Of course, it's weeks away.'

'I took care of the invitation this morning,' Caren assured Pari. 'I wouldn't miss it for the world.'

Will I be here? Can I manage to leave Iran with Danny before then? Every moment he's out of the house he's in danger! I know – it's illegal for a child to leave the country without the written consent of the father. We would be stopped at the airport. How do I get past this? Where can we run and be safe from Marty?

'Azadeh will come with us—' Pari's youngest sister, now a single mother who worked in a government job and brought her toddler daughter to the office childcare center. 'My mother is considering it.'

'How are things between your mother and you?' Caren's voice was solicitous. She knew how strained relations had become between Pari and her parents since she'd divorced her husband a year ago. In Iran divorce was a social stigma for the entire family. And every male, Pari scoffed, considered any divorced woman fair prey.

'My father remains outraged that I divorced my brute of a husband. Whom they chose for me. My mother—' Pari shrugged. 'To her I've disgraced the family. Still, I'm her daughter. She's proud that I teach at the university.' Pari had a degree from Vassar, earned her doctorate at Cambridge. 'It disturbed her that my ex-husband refused to allow me to pursue a career. I waited a lot of years before I divorced him.' Her tone was defensive. 'You know our divorce laws. The husband – or the husband's family – is by law awarded the children. I couldn't allow that. But now both girls are college age. Even they urged me to divorce him.'

'I couldn't divorce Marty—' Not here – perhaps back home.

'You're in a peculiar position, Caren. You were married in New York – in a civil ceremony.' As so often, Pari seemed to read her mind. 'How could you divorce in this country?'

'In the eyes of the Iranian courts Marty and I are not married.' A situation Marty's mother forced herself to overlook.

'Enough talk of unpleasant subjects.' A warning glint in Pari's eyes. 'My sister Shahla is off on another wild project. She read about this famous orthodontist in London, who's supposed to be doing marvelous work on children's teeth. And she's sure both kids need orthodontia. She wrote for a consultation – with her husband's approval, of course,' Pari added with sardonic humor. 'She waited five months for an appointment. Now she has one for next week.'

'That's a long way to go for orthodontia. And it continues over time. She'll be making a lot of trips to London.' Caren remembered when she and Janis made regular visits to their orthodontist. It had seemed endless until the braces came off.

Pari chuckled. 'I tease her. I tell her she's not so concerned about her children's teeth. She's looking for an excuse to spend a few days shopping in London at regular intervals, a chance to see a few plays. At least, for a while.'

Signals shot up in Caren's head. Her heart began to pound. A trip to London! This could be her escape with Danny! A trip to an orthodontist in London – then a flight across the Atlantic. A move to a distant small town where Marty could never find them.

'Tell me about this orthodontist—' Caren's voice was urgent. Her eyes clung to Pari's. She sensed Pari's instant comprehension.

'I'll ask Shahla to give me all the information.' The atmosphere supercharged. But Pari seemed uneasy. 'At eight Danny is young for orthodontia—'

'I doubt that Marty will realize that.' All Marty cared about was the sales figures from the American office. The state of the stock market, the price of oil. Who held true power in Iran?

'I'll have a two-hour break between classes tomorrow. Meet me for lunch – I'll have all the information.' Pari hesitated. Her eyes troubled. 'You believe Marty will let you take Danny to this orthodontist?'

'Maybe not right away,' Caren admitted. 'But in time.'

I have to believe that. Danny's life is at stake.

Three

Caren paced about the house – simultaneously hopeful and fearful. She searched her mind for the right approach to Marty. Aside from the business – and his soaring obsession with politics – Marty focused on shaping Danny into the perfect Iranian male, as visualized by the radical ruling clerics. Danny was the future of the Mansur family – his sisters had only daughters. Women were second-class citizens – deprived of all civil rights. To be hidden away in their home. Subservient to the men in their lives.

But she had no time to wallow in anger, Caren reproached herself. Concentrate on what must be accomplished. She mustn't rush, lest Marty become suspicious. Drop a casual remark at dinner this evening – if Marty was home for dinner. That would be the first step.

Now she remembered they were to have dinner next week with his mother and widowed sister-in-law and, perhaps, his two younger sisters and their husbands. She had no affection for Marty's domineering mother – but in this situation his mother might be useful. This could be the most important dinner in her life.

Her mother-in-law Mina always made it clear that she and Marty were not to bring Danny to her dinners, though often her other children brought their offspring. In her eyes Danny was not a true member of the family. His mother was an American.

'I realize it'll be past Ari's bedtime – so I'll forgive you for not bringing him.'

Marty's mother refused to recognize the name by which Danny was known at home and – in earlier years – at his preschool group. Neither of the teenage granddaughters appeared at these family dinners. Marty had admitted once that his mother disapproved of their lifestyle. If she brought up the premise that Danny would in time require orthodontia, Caren surmised, then Mina would pounce on this as another imperfection in this youngest grandchild. And – please God, let it happen – Marty would retaliate by trying to correct this.

At the usual time Danny was brought home from school. The bodyguard accompanied him to the door, waited – his eyes averted because Caren was casually dressed in the Western fashion – until she brought Danny into the foyer.

'Thank you for bringing Danny home safely,' she murmured while her mind recoiled from the thought that he might have been in danger. 'Was the traffic bad?' Danny's school was in central Tehran – where traffic was horrific.

'About usual,' the bodyguard reported, eyes still averted. 'We arrived on time.'

'Good. We'll expect you again in the morning.' Now she turned to kiss her small son. 'How was school today, Danny?' Her voice rich with love.

'Fine—' His usual reply. Yet he was so somber, she thought in recurrent despair. At his nursery school and kindergarten with the UN children, he'd been so outgoing, so ebullient.

'Let's go into the dining room. I told Zahra that you were to have a chocolate cookie as a special treat today – along with your milk and fruit.' For a moment Danny's small, expressive face brightened. 'Because you did so well at our math session yesterday.' Despite Marty's contempt for this, she tutored Danny in English and math three times a week – and with her he observed the Christian holidays. English always spoken in the house.

Caren remembered how at first Danny had hated the religious school – so unlike the nursery school and kindergarten he'd attended. But Marty was adamant. His son would go to an Orthodox Islamic school. One that focused on religious teachings. He himself would gain favor with the ruling clerics.

Danny had not faced the unnerving problem of many children starting school in Tehran. He spoke fluent Farsi – Persian – which was the language required in the schools, whereas many incoming students spoke a variety of dialects and too often dropped out of school.

It wasn't that Marty had become an Orthodox Muslim, Caren acknowledged. This facade was tied in with his soaring political ambitions. No one could run for election without the approval of the ruling clerics. Out of the thousand who might apply to run for a public office, perhaps four would be approved.

She was aware of fine, secular schools in their community – with all modern equipment. These schools had parents associations. Parents met with teachers. At Danny's school parents had no part in what happened in the course of the school day, no meetings with the teachers. In both secular and religious schools the teachers were paid less than the average household maid – which she found deplorable.

As a woman she had not been allowed to see Danny's school, but from his initial reaction she knew it was shabby, dark, short of equipment. She knew, too, that religious instruction dominated the teaching. Danny was learning Arabic – so that one day he could read the Koran in the original.

In her soul she rebelled – because Danny was learning the Koran by rote. Memorizing without understanding. She was infuriated and sickened by the interpretations that were being thrust into the brains of young, malleable children.

'Will Daddy take me for swimming class this afternoon?' Danny asked as they settled themselves in the dining room and smiling Zahra – who adored Danny – came in with his afternoon snack and Caren's tea and yogurt. 'He'll remember?'

'I'm sure he will.' Again, with a bodyguard at the wheel of the car. And she would worry until Danny was safely home.

She'd forgot for the moment that this was the day when Marty took time off from his heavy work schedule to accompany Danny to his swimming class. Marty's one complaint about the school – as in all schools in Iran – was that there was no provision for sports. Even to run in the school yard or up the stairs inside was forbidden.

She knew there would be many evenings when Marty would not be home for dinner. Only now would she admit to herself that this was a relief. Once she had waited eagerly for him to return from his business world to her. They'd talked, exchanged ideas.

In their years in Westchester he'd respected her contributions. Now she knew to say nothing about his business operations. He'd dismiss whatever suggestions she made. She was a woman. Stupid.

'What did you learn in school today?' she asked while Danny nibbled with obvious enjoyment at the rarely offered chocolate cookie. Marty's voice echoed in her mind – '*You think you're doing good, depriving him of what every kid wants.*' In earlier days Marty had loved what he'd called her 'health-food nuttiness.' At dinner parties at their Westchester house – which seemed another world – he'd boasted about their driving around half of Westchester County in search of organic food for the table.

'We learned—' A touch of hostility in Danny's voice when he finally replied. 'We learn to be good Muslims.' *But good Muslims don't preach hatred. That isn't what the Koran teaches.*

Danny felt guilty for loving her. Marty was erecting a wall between them. But last night, when she tucked him in bed, he said he loved her. *I love you, Mommie, even if you are an American.* 'I memorized more of the Koran,' Danny added. An almost defiant pride in this. Learned by rote, she thought again with pain – too young to understand the meaning. To recognize the misinterpretations declared by the Administration.

Poor baby – he's so conflicted. He remembers the days at the preschool group and in kindergarten, where he had such fun, had acquired friends – but Marty has etched on his brain that these were bad experiences, that he must learn to be a good Muslim. And, in his interpretation, that means to hate Americans.

Now Caren sat alone in the spacious living room. Danny was studying in his bedroom. The door closed. He'd stay there until Marty – with the bodyguard – arrived to take him for his swimming lesson. Without any real interest she crossed to switch on the TV set. A female newscaster – veiled as prescribed by law – reported what Caren knew was heavily censored news. Nothing negative about the Administration was permitted. Pari said most people hated the endless prayers and readings from the Koran – and were bored by the soap operas that always showed parents focused on finding husbands for their daughters.

'*A lot of people find ways to buy videos – on the black market, of course. We all do.*'

She must take Danny out of this oppressive way of life – where a bodyguard was necessary to protect him. When now she lived in fear each moment Danny was out of her sight. And Danny must not become a clone of Marty. That was not the life she wished for her son.

She ached to be out of Iran. To feel free again. Not to exist in dulling isolation. They had no social lives – Marty had alienated the friends she'd acquired. She was never permitted to socialize with his friends. She lived in a stultifying vacuum.

She stiffened at the sound of a car pulling into the courtyard. Marty – with bodyguard at the wheel – had arrived to take Danny for his swimming lesson. What did Marty fear? A shooting on the road? An ambush? These were common occurrences. How could one bodyguard protect Danny and Marty from that kind of onslaught?

I've heard the terrifying stories of women with small children who try to escape through secret passages in the night. I can't expose my precious baby to that – I must find another way. Somehow, I'll find it. Danny and I are going home!

Four

Caren waited impatiently for the evening when Marty would be home for dinner and afterwards they'd share desultory conversation. The evening she could begin her campaign to fly to London with Danny – 'to see this marvelous orthodontist.' She knew the hazards of trying to flee the country under darkness of night, hoping to buy a safe escape. Graphic stories circulated about tragic results. She couldn't endanger Danny's life by trying that route.

Not until three nights later did Marty come home for dinner.

As usual at the dinner table, Marty questioned Danny at length about the day's activities at school. Caren refrained from joining the conversation until Marty launched into a monologue about the war in neighboring Iraq.

'And when?' Marty exuded contempt. 'When will the Americans decide to invade Iran? But we'll be ready for them,' he said in triumph. 'In how many places can they fight a war at the same time? Already they're having trouble recruiting more soldiers.'

'Must we talk about war at the dinner table?' She struggled to conceal her annoyance.

Marty bristled. 'Danny should know what's happening in the world.' But the subject was dropped.

After dinner Danny returned to his bedroom for more study. A regime followed throughout the country by other school age children. In an hour or so she would go into Danny's room and see him into bed for the night, Caren told herself. Where were the small pleasures of childhood?

Caren joined Marty in the living room, where he watched TV news with meager interest. Now, Caren told herself. Now was the time to talk about Danny's orthodontia.

'I talked with Pari today,' she improvised, ignoring Marty's glare of distaste. 'Her sister Shahla heard about this marvelous orthodontist in London and—'

'We have fine dentists – orthodontists – in Tehran,' he dismissed this. 'Why must educated Iranians feel they have to chase around the world for health care? Our health care system is excellent.' *But outside of the big cities it's primitive. One child in five is said to suffer from malnutrition.*

'Remember, we're to have dinner with your family on Tuesday evening,' Caren alerted him. 'Let's be on time. Your mother is so upset if we show up late.'

Marty grunted. 'My mother lives in a world of her own. But I speak to her once every week,' he said defensively. 'I'm a good son.' He sighed. 'But when will she hire a cook who knows how to serve decent meals?'

'I know—' On this subject she agreed with Marty. 'Iranian food can be delicious – but your mother insists on its being very bland.' *Don't pursue the orthodontist bit – don't rush this.*

Marty didn't appear for dinner again until Sunday evening. Caren waited through a long monologue about the indecency of teenage girls in their community before she tried to introduce the subject of orthodontia – 'something we must consider for Danny.'

'Pari's sister was able to schedule an appointment for her son so soon because of a cancellation,' she fabricated. Foreseeing a supposed cancellation in her future. 'Otherwise she would have to wait another six months. She's so excited. She's read awesome articles about this man's work in several medical and dental journals.' *Marty won't ask to see them – he's too busy for that.* 'They flew to London yesterday.'

She wasn't sure that Marty took any real notice of what she was saying. The soft ring of his cellphone had commanded his attention. But she'd known her campaign would take time, she consoled herself. She refused to accept defeat. A London 'dental appointment' for Danny would be their escape from this insane world.

On Tuesday evening – with Zahra instructed to see that Danny ate his dinner and was in bed at his usual time – Caren and

Marty left for his mother's home with a bodyguard at the wheel of the car, as usual these days. Mina Fatahi – his mother, too, retained her maiden name – shared a luxurious, modern apartment in Elahiyeh with her widowed daughter-in-law, Jamileh. An apartment furnished in the same ornate fashion as the house she'd bequeathed to Marty – as head of the family – and which Caren found oppressive.

'The others are late?' Marty lifted an eyebrow in reproach when they were greeted by only his mother and sister-in-law.

'It'll be just the four of us tonight.' Mina uttered a sigh of martyrdom. This smacked of neglect.

Caren was relieved that the others expected at dinner had phoned their regrets. She and Marty might be able to break away early. But dinner would be endless – seven or eight unappealing courses, all bland. Marty had fortified himself at home by raiding the refrigerator before they left for the dinner party.

As usual, Mina was cool to Caren, effusive with her sole surviving son. Caren suspected that Jamileh accepted sharing her apartment with her mother-in-law as a financial necessity. At his death, her husband's stock in the family business was inherited by Marty as the head of the family.

'Let's go in to dinner,' Mina said after her usual brief questions about the health of each, complaints about the weather – often near-perfect in outlying Tehran, which escaped much of the pollution of the inner city.

Mina had early decreed that Marty sit at the head of the table. He was growing thicker around the middle, Caren noted this evening – despite his efforts to remain trim. His mother's interminable dinners contributed to that.

As Caren anticipated, endless courses were served – with Marty's vocal approval of each. The soup course of *Aash-e Aab Leemoo* – a rich soup with rice, meat, lime juice, sugar and herbs – lacked the necessary herbs. The salad that followed – a blend of cucumbers, tomatoes, onions and mint – was overloaded with mint. And so it went through the main course of *Ghormeh Sabzi* – a usually delicious dish of meat, black-eye beans, potatoes and herbs; side dishes of *Maast-o-Khiar* – a mixture of yogurt, cucumbers, onions, mint, salt and pepper, *Borani Esfanaaj* – yogurt, fried spinach, garlic, and onions.

Caren was relieved that table conversation required little from her. Mina always monopolized the gathering, talked incessantly about her grandchildren – though she asked only perfunctory questions about Danny.

Caren was alert – anxious – for an opening where she could introduce the subject of orthodontia. By dessert time she was fighting frustration. She'd eaten little of each course, but now one of her favorite desserts was placed before her. *Sohaan-e Asali*, consisting of almonds, honey, sugar, saffron and pistachios – though in a corner of her mind she knew it would be overcooked.

'My granddaughter Roya – she's studying in London,' Mina reminded Marty and Caren, 'will be home in a few days for spring vacation. Mohammed, you were at school in London for a time,' Mina said with pride. 'You know London. Talk to her about things to do there. She sounds lonely.'

'She misses her partying here.' Marty smirked. 'These young women today – those in Elahiyeh – have no sense of decorum. They wear make-up, they drive around in their expensive cars, they flirt, they ignore the law.'

'They know what their lives will be like later on.' Marty's sister-in-law's voice was tart, showed unexpected contempt for the lifestyle inflicted on Iranian women. Astonishing Caren, who had seen her as a clone of her mother-in-law. 'This is their rebellion.'

The Revolution had brought women widespread education, with more girls than boys attending universities. But the Revolution had cost women freedoms they'd enjoyed under the ruling of the Shah, Caren recalled. The Shah had abolished the hijab, fostered a Westernized lifestyle – for the elite. But the majority had felt left out of the prosperity Iranian oil provided – and painfully oppressed, with political parties banned, dissent crushed. That had brought on the Revolution. And with it more oppression.

'These girls with their rebellion—' Mina mocked Jamileh, 'they're stupid. Only seeking grief for themselves and their families. Let's talk of more interesting subjects.'

Here is an opening. Take it.

'My friend Pari's sister just flew to London with her little boy.' Caren strived to appear casual. 'They've discovered this marvelous orthodontist there.'

'My children had no need for orthodontia.' Mina responded as expected. Exuding an air of triumph. 'Nor the grand-children – thus far.' Her eyes focused on Caren. 'You anticipate problems with Ari?'

'Just some indications of teeth needing minor read-justment—' Caren sensed rather than saw that Marty was stiffening to attention. 'Nothing serious.'

'It's growing late.' Marty was abrupt. 'I have to see Ari—' He never called his son Danny in his mother's pres-ence, Caren recalled in recurrent annoyance. 'I have to see Ari to his school in the morning. He must be there by 7:30 a.m. As you know, it's a long commute.'

With gritted teeth Caren listened to a discussion between Marty and his mother about the need for bodyguards – which Marty's mother considered outrageous yet required. She felt a surge of relief as she and Marty left the apartment.

The evening was unseasonably warm. Draped in her manteau, Caren frowned in annoyance. She loathed the need for this absurd cover-up – just to leave the apartment and walk to the car.

Still, hope had been given a boost, she told herself. Marty's mother believed Danny might require orthodontia. Marty was annoyed. For all his outward show of obeisance, he was often privately at odds with his mother.

Marty could tell his mother that he'd given her permis-sion to go to London for a few days, Caren improvised. To shop, see a few plays. Marty wouldn't realize that ortho-dontia would require many follow-up visits to London. But she and Danny would fly to freedom on that first visit.

Still, she warned herself, she was in shaky territory. Nothing was certain yet. *Be careful. Don't make a false move.*

Marty was silent on the drive home. Not unusual on such occasions. Caren knew he found no pleasure in family dinners. He considered it his obligation to pretend to enjoy the food, to be solicitous about his mother's endless small complaints about her daily life.

'Put up coffee,' he said as they walked into the house.

'And see what pastry you can find that's fresh and decent.' He grunted in distaste. 'The coffee was foul, the dessert over-cooked.'

Caren pulled aside her headscarf and her manteau, walked to the kitchen, dropped both across a chair in the breakfast area. She was light-headed with anticipation. *Can this be the moment – the first step to freedom for Danny and me?*

She must be canny if Marty appeared to go along. No rush, no misstep. Play this out with care. Danny's whole future depended upon their escape.

It isn't too late. I can bring Danny back to himself again. He can live in safety – no need for bodyguards. He'll find friends, have fun. Be a normal little boy again.

She put up the coffee, checked the refrigerator for pastry. Yes, a pair of the chocolate eclairs she had taught Ziba, the family cook, to make. Marty scoffed at her choice of American desserts – but he relished them.

For an unwary moment her mind shot back to the Columbia days, when so often they'd meet at the Hungarian pastry shop on Amsterdam Avenue. For perhaps the thousandth time she asked herself, 'How could Marty have changed from that high-spirited, warm man I loved into a power-hungry, money-obsessed tyrant in the space of five years?'

She mustn't bring up the subject of Danny's orthodontia again tonight, she exhorted herself while she brought down an exquisite Haviland china cup and saucer and matching dessert plate. Please God, let Marty bring it up.

When she walked into the living room with the tray of coffee and eclair, she was momentarily disappointed to find Marty on the phone – in bellicose conversation with a company employee.

'Don't give me excuses!' he bellowed. 'What counts are results. Call me tomorrow night – at home.' He slammed the phone down. 'Stupid bastard. All the time excuses.' But he glanced at the tray in Caren's hands with approval.

'Ziba made the eclairs yesterday.' *Don't push. I know he's thinking about Danny's teeth not being perfect. Everything about Danny must be perfect.*

'Why do you think Danny needs orthodontia?' he challenged her after biting into his eclair with enthusiasm.

'One little tooth on the right side is pushing against another as it comes in. It'll throw all of his teeth out of alignment.' She forced herself to be casual. 'I should start looking around for an orthodontist in Tehran.'

'Do that,' he ordered, and she was conscious of a surge of disappointment. 'This traveling to London for dentistry is absurd.'

'And Pari tells me this man in London is terribly expensive.' This was a deliberate effort to bait him.

Marty glared at her. 'The cost doesn't matter to me. I want the best for my son.' He paused, deep in concentration now. Caren's heart began to pound. 'If this orthodontist is so great, I should think this friend of yours would have had to wait a long time for an appointment.'

'She'd waited five or six months – then there was a cancellation.' *I told him this before.* 'I suppose some parents realize the cost, then cancel.'

'It's not a one-time visit to London,' he challenged now.

'No,' Caren acknowledged, her heart suddenly hammering. She hadn't expected Marty to think of this. 'She'll fly to London once every six weeks, Pari said. For about a year.'

'It's ridiculous,' Marty brushed this aside now. 'Look for someone in Tehran.'

Caren lay sleepless far into the night. Angry, depressed – but not yet defeated. *What can I do to turn around Marty's thinking?*

At breakfast in the morning Caren was conscious of the way Marty was scrutinizing their small son. His mother's words – her attitude – taunted him.

'Smile,' he ordered Danny when they were about to leave for school. 'Let me see your smile.'

Bewildered, Danny managed to smile. Caren felt a rush of anguish. How rare to see a smile on Danny's face! And this one so contrived – devoid of genuine feeling.

'Find a dentist in Tehran,' he told Caren. 'Someone with top credentials.'

'Right,' Caren agreed – in a flood of desolation. She'd been so simplistic in her thinking. This was not the road to freedom.

At the door – while the bodyguard slid behind the wheel of the car – Marty seemed in some inner debate.

'Talk to your friend Pari—' His face exuded contempt for her. Pari was one of the 'modern women' who flouted Islamic law as the Administration interpreted it. 'See what you can learn about this fancy orthodontist in London. I'm not making any commitment,' he warned. 'Just give me what you can learn about him.'

'He's very expensive—' Caren repeated with an air of anxiety. Knowing Marty would rear again at this.

'Damn it, I don't care about the cost! What can he do for Danny?'

'I'll call Pari and get whatever information she can dig up,' Caren promised. *This doesn't mean victory – I mustn't build up my hopes.*

'This may be just a hype by some shrewd operator,' Marty warned. 'The world is full of them. Show me something concrete.'

'I'll talk to Pari.' Caren strived to appear calm. 'She's sharp about these things.'

'I'm just curious.' Marty's eyes were opaque. 'It sounds like a sucker deal.'

Fighting impatience, Caren waited until a few minutes past 8 a.m. to phone Pari. A respectable time to call. And if Pari had an early class this morning, she'd be leaving for the university shortly.

Pari picked up on the first ring. 'Yes?' A sharpness in her voice.

'Pari, I'm sorry to be calling so early,' she apologized, 'but—'

'Darling, I thought it was my mother. She's on one of her tirades again about how I've disgraced the family with my divorce.'

'I talked with Marty about your sister's orthodontist – and he expressed some curiosity.' Pari would understand that she was being cautious, that she sometimes suspected Marty was taping her phone calls. 'Could you get me the name and address of this man?'

'Let's meet for coffee this afternoon. My class ends at two

– I can be there by two thirty,' Pari said briskly. 'I'll give it to you then. The usual place on the mall.'

Off the phone Caren sat immobile for a few moments. Cold. Trembling. There was no way to know if Marty would allow her to follow through with the London orthodontist. But she must start plotting each move.

Danny will be so upset – at first. I must make him under-stand that the time has come to go home. But not back to Westchester County – that's the first place Marty will look for us.

Where will we live? Where can we go where Marty won't be able to track us down?

Five

Caren arrived at the coffee shop twenty minutes before Pari was scheduled to arrive. She'd felt driven to leave the house, as though to thrust aside the confines of her life. She mustn't rush the situation, she exhorted herself yet again. Do nothing that would arouse Marty's suspicions. But she must plan – be ready to leave at the first practical moment.

The coffee shop was lightly populated at this hour. A handful of women – in pairs – sat at their tables. Enveloped in their headscarves and manteaus. The young and rebellious were beginning to allow hemlines to rise, dared to wear bright colors. Black had long been Caren's choice – as with most women. It was better not to stand out, even in this exclusive northern suburb.

On impulse Caren left her table, sought a public telephone in the coffee shop. Was there a non-stop flight from Tehran to London? At this moment her phone calls to the airlines must be anonymous.

She was impatient with the delays but relieved – at last – to discover there was a non-stop flight via British Airways from Tehran to London. A six-hour flight to a new life.

Pari was seated at their table by the time she returned from her phone calls.

'I didn't believe you'd taken off for London without saying goodbye,' Pari joshed. Again, her eyes said she'd miss Caren. 'I've ordered for us—'

'Marty still hasn't made a commitment.' Caren kept her voice low, though it was unlikely anyone except Pari could hear her. 'Still, he asked for this information.'

'He's not going to run around Tehran making personal inquiries.'

'Not likely,' Caren conceded. 'Not with the hours he spends on the business. But this is for Danny – and anything concerning his son requires serious attention—'

'This orthodontist is tops in his field. People are going to him from all over Europe. Rich people,' Pari added with a cynical smile.

'Whom Marty respects,' Caren reminded. She knew, too, that in the five years he'd headed the family company its worth had soared.

'Of course, Shahla is fascinated at being able to fly off to London every six weeks for the next year.' Laughter lit Pari's eyes. 'But her husband is indulgent.'

Caren knew that Shahla's marriage was one of those rare arranged marriages that was, in truth, a love match. Shahla's parents hadn't realized she'd been secretly seeing her future husband for months before the two families made the usual marriage arrangement. Shahla had been one of the rebellious teenagers who contrived to meet young men outside the family.

Now Pari handed Caren a sheet of paper listing the required information. All at once her eyes were anxious. 'Be careful, Caren—'

'I keep reminding myself this will take time.' *But I won't accept failure.* 'That it will work out as I pray every night.'

'My room-mate at Vassar would say in such moments,' Pari reminisced, 'From your mouth to God's ear.'

Marty didn't show up for dinner – no surprise to Caren. She ate with Danny in the somber near-silence that had become routine. She asked a few questions about the school day, received brief replies. Danny had no friends, no after-school playmates.

The school's decree that studying and prayer should occupy most of their waking hours had become Danny's mantra – as with countless other Iranian children. And always there was the brief tutoring period when she worked with him on the American way of learning English grammar and mathematics.

'I have to study,' Danny said as usual when dinner was over. He frowned, hesitated, his small face reflecting anguish. 'I gave one wrong answer on the test today.'

'Out of how many questions?' Caren asked gently.

'Twenty-five,' he said with an air of shame.

'Darling, that's fine,' she protested. 'To know all but one out of twenty-five.'

'Daddy says I should know all the answers. Every one.' His mouth tightened in self-reproach.

'Daddy's wrong about that.' Caren was firm. *How dare Marty make such demands!* 'I'm very proud of you for doing so well on that test.'

'I have to go study,' Danny mumbled. 'Can I be excused now?'

'May I be excused,' she corrected him gently. 'Yes, you may.'

Caren settled herself in the living room to read the latest of the suspense titles mailed to her each month from a bookstore in New York – an arrangement scheduled five years ago when the three of them left for Iran – for what she'd thought would be a one-year stay. Reading was her escape from reality. What a dull world this would be without books!

At the usual time she abandoned her novel to see Danny settled in bed for the night.

'I love you, Mommie,' he murmured drowsily as she kissed him goodnight.

'I love you, Danny.' *Is it my imagination or is he becoming depressed? It happens with children. It mustn't happen to my precious baby.*

She returned to the living room and her novel, but her mind refused to focus on reading. She and Danny must escape from this unwalled prison – and from the threat of violence that hovered over Danny and Marty. She mustn't fail.

In a corner of her mind she'd been struggling to settle on their destination, once she and Danny flew out of London for New York. And suddenly – this moment – she chose that destination.

They would settle in Primrose, New York – a far upstate town of about 18,000. The town that Lila – her room-mate at Columbia – had talked about with such nostalgia!

Lila had been born there, lived there until she was fourteen – but had never returned because life sent her in other directions.

'It was so peaceful, so beautiful. People cared about one another. They worked together to make the town a better place in which to live. Maybe some day in the future I'll go back there.'

But Lila was a computer specialist living in Ontario the last she'd heard. That was at least eight years ago. By the time she'd met Marty, Lila had transferred to another college. Marty never knew Lila – he'd never heard of Primrose, New York. He'd never think to look there! *We'll be safe in Primrose.*

Now she heard sounds in the foyer. Marty was home. He stalked into the living room. She recognized the tightness of his face. He was about to broach an important subject.

'Did you check around about an orthodontist in Tehran?' he demanded without any greeting.

She felt a surge of alarm. 'Not yet—' She paused. 'You told me to find the name and address of the man in London.'

'I don't like the concept of your running to London on a regular basis,' he began.

'It's not that often,' she said quickly. 'Every six weeks for perhaps five or six appointments,' she shortened her original assumption. *What's he thinking? Discarding it without further discussion?*

'I'm not happy about it – but I want the best for Danny. Write this man. Don't question the financial arrangements,' he warned. 'Just ask about an initial appointment. Make no commitment.'

'All right.' Her heart was pounding.

'It'll probably be months before he even bothers to reply. How long did Pari's sister wait for an appointment?'

'She'd expected a year's wait. Then there was a sudden cancellation. She had to leave in a few days or go back on the waiting list.' *I told Marty this.*

'Westerners have so little ethics – they think nothing of

breaking appointments. I see this every day in the company,' he said with contempt.

'I'll write Dr Tompkins tomorrow,' she told Marty. Her mind charging ahead. *So much to plan. Every step must be handled with care.* 'We should have word within a few days.'

Marty seated himself in front of the TV. He'd watch a newscast – censored to please the Administration – and at the same time he'd be consulting papers he'd brought home from the office.

This was her cue to say goodnight and go to her bedroom. They hadn't shared a bed for three years – though he retained visiting privileges, she thought in distaste. On those occasions she felt like a high-priced call girl.

'Before you go to bed,' he told Caren as she rose to her feet, 'bring me coffee. And when you make an appointment with Dr Tompkins, make sure you're not running off to London the first two weeks in June. I'll be making reservations for us at the same hotel where we stayed last summer. Danny loves the beach.'

I don't love the beach. What woman wants to lie on the beach, covered from head to toe?

Caren lay sleepless in her bed – her earlier drowsiness driven away by the traumatic encounter with Marty. She would write a letter to Dr Tompkins, offer to allow Marty to read it. He wouldn't bother – he had time only for business and politics. But the letter would go out to Dr Tompkins. It might take weeks for Tompkins' office to reply, she fretted. Dare she pretend to receive an early reply? Little chance that Marty would ask to see it.

She would take that chance! It was urgent that she take Danny away from this insane life as soon as humanly possible. She suffered nightmares most nights – visualizing Danny and Marty gunned down by some secret enemy.

Of course she'd encounter problems in making Danny understand what was happening. It would be a shock – at first. He'd be confused, upset. But she would deal with that.

Tomorrow she would write to Dr Tompkins about an

initial appointment. *I won't wait for an appointment six months away. I'll pretend to receive a phone call reporting a cancellation and that I must be in London in one week. I must be away from here before violence strikes my baby.*

With luck on their side she and Danny would soon be in that little upstate New York town that Lila had talked about with such affection. Primrose, New York. Even the name was intriguing.

This coming summer she wouldn't spend excruciatingly dull weekends plus their usual two-week vacation at a posh beach resort at the Caspian Sea – once known as the Persian Riviera. Except that here – under Islamic law – men swam in the morning, women in the afternoon – in swimsuits that covered their arms and legs.

With bitter humor she remembered how Marty had talked briefly about buying a villa in one of the gated communities along the beach. Here residents enjoyed a high-living Western lifestyle – except for occasional raids by the Morals Police. He'd discarded this as detrimental to his image as a devout Muslim.

Her mind darted back to the Westchester years. Each summer Marty had been committed to fly to Tehran for three weeks – both for business and to see family. The first summer after their marriage he'd gone alone. *'It'll be a chance for me to tell my parents what a marvelous wife I've found for myself.'*

The second summer she was pregnant – ever solicitous, Marty had been afraid for her to fly. The third summer Danny had been suffering from some minor infection – no thought of traveling with a sick baby.

But those summers had provided serene, beautiful long weekends in the Hamptons.

'I won't be able to take vacation time off,' Marty apologized that first summer together. 'Not when I'm spending three weeks in June in Tehran. But in July and August we'll take three-day weekends out in the Hamptons. Josh found this great broker in Montauk – Kathy Beckmann – who came up with terrific rentals for us whenever we had long weekends off from school.' Josh was his room-mate through his junior year, lived now in San Francisco. 'You'll love Montauk – it's the "quiet Hampton."'

Each morning in Montauk they sat on their deck and watched the orange-red ball that was the sun rise over the horizon. They were amused by the early surfers. At dusk they'd wait for the exquisite sunsets. They took long walks along the pristine beach.

She laughed in tender recall – visualizing Danny's astonishment at first sight of beach and ocean. The beach the world's largest sandbox. The ocean a pool with no sides. She remembered his delight in playing with the town dogs who sauntered at the water's edge, at times taking forays into the waves.

Marty had been so warm, so charming. How could a man change so quickly? Was that what a little power could do? Now that he was no longer the non-essential younger son but head of the family, he was a stranger to her.

In the morning – as usual – Caren watched Marty and Danny climb into the car, driven by the bodyguard. The car sped away for its long commute to central Tehran. The day was overcast. Pollution would be bad, she fretted. In a small town in the United States Danny would be able to breathe clean air every day. Marty would never be able to track them down in Primrose, New York.

She returned to her room to write the letter to Dr Tompkins. She wouldn't wait months for an appointment. It would happen the way she planned. Marty would come home one evening, and she'd be bursting with excitement. *'I'm absolutely astonished – I received a phone call from London – from Dr Tompkins' office. You know, the orthodontist. His secretary says he has a cancellation four days from now. She can write us in – or we can remain on the waiting list.'*

Marty will be skeptical, she warned herself. Why was she getting such preferential treatment? What about others on the waiting list? The answer leapt into her brain. *'She says the doctor will give us this appointment because Danny will be just his second patient from Iran.'*

She sat at the desk in her bedroom and wrote the letter

to Dr Tompkins. She'd hold up mailing it until tomorrow. First she'd offer to have Marty read it. He couldn't be bothered – he'd wave this aside. It would be weeks before a reply would arrive. By then – with God's help – she and Danny would be settled in a little house or an apartment in Primrose, New York.

Simultaneously elated and fearful, she returned to the living room. Her mind charging ahead. In the usual routine, Zahra brought her a cup of strong black coffee, chatted vivaciously about what Ziba was preparing for lunch and dinner.

'Zahra, this is Wednesday,' Caren reminded. 'I'll be having lunch with a friend. Remind Ziba that I won't be here.'

Every Wednesday she and Pari had lunch at a restaurant near the university. Today she was impatient to confide her latest activity. She'd ask Pari to have her friend Andrea in London – a brilliant university professor who'd escaped Iran and a deadly marriage several years ago – to make a very special phone call. Not right away – time must be allowed for her letter to have arrived in London. Pari would tell Andrea what to say:

'*Dr Tompkins has had a cancellation. We'll expect you at our offices at 10 a.m. next Tuesday morning. If you can't make this appointment, we'll place your name on the waiting list. Dr Tompkins is allowing you this cancellation appointment only because your son will be just his second patient from Iran.*' This explanation in the event Marty was curious about such a swift reply.

She would say 'Yes, thank you. Of course, we'll be there.'

This phone call was necessary because at times, she knew, Marty checked on her activities. Like the detective who'd followed her for weeks last year because Marty feared she would violate the dress code – after she'd spoken with open disdain about this law. Pari had spotted the man right away. If Marty decided to check with the phone company, there would be a record of a call from London.

Once she'd been Marty's adored 'funny American' who fought for causes. Now he was fearful that she might disgrace his family by some rebellious act.

In her mind she visualized Primrose, New York. A warm, friendly small town – where people cared about one another. A perfect place to raise Danny.

Please God, let nothing go wrong. Let Danny and me be aboard a British Airways flight to London within the next two weeks.

Six

In his office at the Primrose Elementary School Brian Woods rose from behind his desk, reached for the stack of papers that sat on one corner and stuffed them into his knapsack. A reminiscent smile of wry amusement on his face. Last week a mother of two of the students had expressed reproach that he preferred a knapsack to an attaché case.

'*It's kind of undignified, Mr Woods. We expect teenagers – the younger kids – to carry knapsacks. Not their principal.*'

So at thirty-four he was the youngest principal ever at the Primrose Elementary School in this area of town. Why did some people resent that? He chuckled as he fastened the clasp of his knapsack, hoisted it into place. He'd been living in this town for eleven years, but to some of the fourth generation families he was an outsider who'd usurped an important position in their public school system.

Today he meant to be home early. He needed to talk to Hannah – his part-time housekeeper – about coming in more than her usual two afternoons a week. He'd stopped by the *Sentinel* this morning on the way to school, placed an ad for the apartment rental, to run for the next seven days.

He'd instructed prospective tenants to call between 1 p.m. and 5 p.m. Hannah's hours twice a week. But the ad meant any day of the week. Hannah must be at the house every day except Saturday and Sunday – when he'd be home. She was free the other three days of the week – no problem there.

His previous tenants had moved out six weeks ago. He'd been so tied up with other things he hadn't bothered till now to think about new tenants. He missed that rent check.

He frowned at the sharp ring of his phone, picked up. 'Hello, Brian Woods—' His voice deep, charismatic.

'Brian, I'm so upset – and furious!' Jill Cramer, with whom

he worked often on town projects. 'I just got off the phone with Phil—' Her accountant husband. 'I'm steaming!'

'What's up?' Jill was one of his favorite people in Primrose. They'd fought together this past fall to introduce the 'special lunch program' for elementary school students unable to afford lunch at the school cafeteria. So most of these kids were the children of newly arrived immigrants in town – they needed a decent lunch. Not all immigrants settled in big cities. The world was changing – even in Primrose, New York. And the wages paid immigrant workers were minimum or little more.

'Phil heard there was a big – secret – meeting at Mayor Davis's house last night.' Jill and her husband shared his contempt for their first-term mayor. 'The mayor and some big city developers. They're discussing a huge, high-rise rental apartment complex – to attract what they call the "over fifty-five crowd", along with an assisted living section—'

'That could create a bunch of jobs,' Brian pointed out. Welcome in Primrose.

'They want to build on about seventy acres along Primrose Lake.' Jill was grim. 'You know the section. Those minuscule little houses that working class families have lived in for the past sixty years. But a water view,' she drawled, 'means they can up the prices like crazy.'

'Wait a minute.' All at once Brian was wary. 'Are you trying to tell me they mean to push out all those people living there?'

'You've got it. Phil says they'll use the old eminent domain bit. The town will pay them what it considers fair market value – and they're out on their butts.'

'Eminent domain says whatever is replacing the land the township takes over must be for public use,' Brian shot back.

'Phil says the high court in this state – and several others – says that private development projects are for public use. The mayor will say that the town needs the additional taxes plus the jobs that will be created. Phil and I are pissed!'

'Why don't I drop by your house this evening around eight? We'll sit down and discuss what must be done.'

'Great.' Brian sensed her relief. *Here we go again. Another local battle.* 'See you around eight.'

Brian headed for the parking lot. His mind racing. Some people in town would go along with the mayor's project because it would mean jobs – for a limited period. Nobody had expected Skip Reynolds – hearty and hard-driving at seventy-one – to close down his factory. In less than a week ninety workers would be preparing to sign up for unemployment insurance. He'd talked to Skip about the situation.

'I have to be realistic – I've been running at a loss for over a year. I can't keep the factory in operation.'

In the past year a dozen small shops had gone out of business – including five on the Primrose Mall. A lot of people blamed it on the big discount store that opened up fourteen months ago. Everybody was looking for low prices. But Primrose wasn't facing rough times alone. The national economy was in a rut.

He opened the door of his nine-year-old Ford, slid behind the wheel. He was getting a lot of teasing because he stalled on trading it in for a new model. But he was ever conscious of the large mortgage on the house. And with a house there was always something in need of repair.

Still, he was glad he'd bought the house. He'd grown up an army brat – living around the world. The house gave him a feeling of setting down roots. He'd bought the house, in truth, in an effort to save his marriage – though by the end of the first year he knew it had been a gross mistake.

Meeting Denise at a Shakespeare in the Park performance in Central Park in New York, he'd been entranced with her. She was beautiful, vivacious, ambitious. And he was so lonely.

His mother and father had died within seven months of each other – three years earlier. He was an only child – he had no other family except distant cousins living somewhere in Texas. He'd never seen them.

Three weeks after he and Denise met, she'd moved in with him in his East Village studio apartment. A month later – when he was hired to teach at Primrose Elementary – they were married at City Hall. He had visions of their having a couple of kids, leading a good life in Primrose.

Denise had loathed Primrose almost from the first day. 'It's boring, boring, boring.' In New York she'd worked as

an office temp – spending time making show business rounds.
Sure a job in a Broadway musical was just around the corner.
Her voice was fair – she'd expected her looks to carry her
through.

He'd bought the house – sure it would be a diversion for
Denise. She hired a housekeeper – which they couldn't afford
on a teacher's salary, went to work as a cocktail waitress to
pay for this.

He was stunned when he finally realized she was into
drugs, refused to consider rehab. Then – eight years ago –
she died of an overdose. Only then did he discover she was
three months' pregnant. He would now have had a son or
daughter who was almost eight.

Arriving at the rambling ranch – after Denise's death he'd
divided it into two apartments – he parked the car and walked
to the house. Opening the door he sniffed the savory aroma
of whatever dinner concoction was in preparation. His dinner
for tonight and tomorrow night.

'Hannah,' he called, heading for the large eat-in kitchen.

'One of these days you'll surprise me and come home a
little past three,' she scolded good-humoredly. 'You need to
get yourself a life.' A wife, she meant. No way, though he'd
been chased since days after Denise's funeral.

'I've got a life. A good one.' His eyes defied her to refute
this. 'I love my work. I love this town.' He considered this
for a moment. 'Most of the time I love it.' There'd been a
fierce battle to approve his dividing the house into two apartments. Howie Bernstein across the road had gone to bat for
him, won the approval. He suspected Howie had twisted
some arms.

Now he explained to Hannah the situation about the ad in
the *Sentinel*. 'Whoever calls, tell them to ring me after
7 p.m. – and they can come over and see the apartment.'
There were few apartments in Primrose – just those garden
apartments in the Rose Hill section. He should be able to
find a tenant.

'I was sorry to see Jack and Harvey move away from
town,' Hannah commiserated. 'They were nice people. My
grand-niece was in Jack Taylor's sixth-grade class – she said
he was the best.'

Brian's face tightened. 'He's a loss to the school. A very creative man. He rearranged his whole classroom, set it up so that a group of five students sat around each of a cluster of small tables. The kids loved him. But a couple of mothers made complaints about his not being the right role model for their sons.' Jack Taylor made no secret about being gay. 'They harassed him. They were behind the ugly article in the *Evening News*. The kids miss him.'

'I hope you don't have to wait too long for new tenants. Nice ones,' Hannah emphasized.

Brian grinned. 'My budget agrees.'

'I get so mad,' Hannah declared, 'the way the government keeps ignoring the way inflation creeps up. Anybody who goes to shop in the supermarkets knows that. I hate the way you buy a box of something – and then you realize where it used to be eight ounces, now it's six. And the price doesn't go down. That's inflation.'

'With the price of gas still soaring, we'll all soon be doing a lot of walking,' Brian predicted. 'And that might just be a good thing for some of us.'

Seven

A s Caren had anticipated, Marty brushed aside her invitation to 'read my letter to Dr Tompkins.' His mind was obsessed at the moment by the coming June elections. He was flagrant in his ambitions to be favored by ruling radical clerics.

Once so liberal in his thinking, Caren recalled in recurrent disbelief, he was now strongly conservative. During their days at Columbia the two of them had joined with other students in distributing free food to the needy in Harlem. Now he had only contempt for the poor and uneducated.

He boasted about the high degree of education in Iran, the fine medical system – without acknowledging that this was available only in the few large cities. Life in the many rural villages was primitive.

In truth, Caren approved, her letter to Dr Tompkins was exemplary. In her insecurity she'd asked Pari to read it.

'Caren, it's time to trust yourself. You're a bright woman. You can carry this through. But, oh, I'll miss you!'

But now came the devious plotting that must take Danny and her out of this hell. She refused to allow herself to consider the consequences if Marty discovered – and aborted – her efforts. But she must take this one chance.

Thank God, she had retained her American passport and Danny's. They were in her possession – not with Marty. Once she and Danny were on a plane lifting off from Mehrabad Airport – flying non-stop to London – she would breathe with some relief.

Still, she feared Marty's efforts to track them down in the United States. He would stoop to any effort to bring Danny back to Tehran, hire top-notch investigators. She must leave no trace. And in this world of advanced technology – where it seemed almost impossible to hide – that would be an unnerving task.

Her American driver's license had elapsed. She must make no effort to apply for another. No record anywhere, she warned herself, of where she and Danny were living. But Primrose, New York was just another small town – unknown to most people. Marty had never known Lila – he'd never heard of Primrose. *We'll be safe there – but for how long?*

She was counting off each day since she'd mailed her letter to Dr Tompkins. Pari had explained to her friend Andrea that proper timing was urgent. The proper number of days must be allowed for Caren's letter to arrive – and to be considered. Andrea was sympathetic, eager to be helpful, Pari assured. Andrea had been through her own private hell before she escaped. *'Don't worry, Caren – Andrea will know when to place the call. Nothing will go wrong.'*

She must pack only enough clothes for Danny and her to need during their pretended stay in London, Caren cautioned herself – lest Marty become suspicious. Since their appointment was presumed to be at 10 a.m. on next Tuesday morning, then they must arrive in London the previous day. She would make hotel reservations at the Dorchester for three nights. Marty would expect to reach them there should he decide to call. But they would never check in.

For the past two years – as though anticipating some emergency – she'd been stashing money away in a garment bag in her bedroom closet. Money changed from rials into American dollars – to be switched to traveler's checks at the right moment. Enough to see them through – along with the sale of her jewelry – for four or five months, she estimated. Until she could find a job.

She'd face no problem in taking her jewelry with her. Marty would expect her to wear her emerald-cut diamond ring and matching earrings – to indicate his affluence to his London cousins, whom she would be expected to visit.

On Thursday afternoon – as planned, Caren received a phone call, supposedly from Dr Tompkins' office in London. Everything on schedule, she told herself when she put down the phone. Her heart pounding in anticipation of what lay ahead.

On the following Monday she and Danny must be arriving in London for a Tuesday morning appointment. She vacillated between euphoria and fear. Freedom was almost within her grasp – but what traps lay ahead that she didn't see?

Danny was in his bedroom – studying, as usual. She paced about the living room, the foyer, impatient for Marty to arrive home. *Let the new act in their lives begin. Let nothing go wrong.*

Later she'd worry about how to cope with Danny, she told herself. Knowing he would be bewildered – and afraid – when he arrived at their true destination. At first he would be upset – he wouldn't understand. But once they were settled in their new lives in Primrose, he'd come to appreciate – love – their new freedom.

Guilt attacked her when she considered his attachment to his father. A demanded attachment. She'd be a single mother, raising her son alone. That wasn't unusual in the modern-day world. Single mothers survived. They raised healthy, happy children. But there would be a rough period, she cautioned herself. She must be prepared for that. She must be strong.

The dinner hour arrived. Marty didn't show. Long ago he'd abandoned phoning to say he would be held up on business. Even Danny accepted his non-appearances at the dinner table.

At the dinner table she tried to involve Danny in cheerful conversation. He was depressed, she taunted herself yet again. Even a small boy could be subject to serious depression. But that would change, she vowed.

After they'd eaten, Danny returned to his bedroom to study again. At the appropriate hour Caren went into his bedroom to tuck him in. She kissed him goodnight, turned off his bedside lamp. He looked so small, so vulnerable. But he would flower in the new environment of an American small town, she promised herself.

She returned to the living room, made an effort to read. She was too wired for this, she thought impatiently. So much depended on how she handled Marty in the next hour or so. Each minute seemed endless. *Please God, let him be in a good mood.*

At last she heard the sound of a car arriving in the court-yard. Marty was home. Struggling to appear enthralled by her afternoon phone call, she hurried into the foyer to greet him.

'Marty, the most fascinating thing happened this after-noon,' she began. Her face exuding pleasurable excitement.

'Later,' he brushed this aside. 'I had the worst dinner with these people from Rudsar.' The people from the tea plantation, she remembered. Marty was working out some business with them, she gathered. 'Wake Ziba and have her bring me dinner.'

'I'll bring you a tray,' Caren soothed. Ziba was up before 6 a.m. She wouldn't wake her now. 'It'll take just a few minutes to warm up.'

Wasting not a moment, Caren heated up a generous portion of Marty's favorite *Abgusht* – lamb stew. Knowing Marty's erratic schedule – and culinary demands, Ziba kept a bowl always available for unexpected late meals. She debated a moment, brought out a portion of *Baagh-lava*. He should avoid desserts, the way he was picking up weight, she thought in a corner of her mind. Back at Columbia, and in Westchester County, he'd run four miles every day. But that was another man.

She waited until Marty had finished eating before launching into her report.

'I was absolutely amazed,' she wound up, 'when Dr Tompkins' assistant called to offer us this appointment. I gather someone cancelled – probably on account of his fees,' she added with a diplomatic smile.

'Why us?' Suspicion in his voice now.

'Because Danny will be just his second patient from Iran. They were very impressed by that. They expect us to spread the word around about his marvelous work.' Under the table she clenched one hand in the other. *Let nothing go wrong now. Let me carry this off.*

'You're sure he's good?'

'Pari's sister said she encountered a member of the British royal family in his reception room,' Caren fabricated. Marty had awed respect for people in high places.

He ruminated for a few moments. Caren's throat tightened in alarm. 'When would you have to leave?'

'The appointment is next Tuesday, at 10 a.m. We'll have to arrive on Monday – which means taking a Monday flight.'

Marty nodded. 'Right.'

She felt a flicker of relief. *Marty's going along with it. We can carry this off.* 'I'll call the Dorchester about reservations.' On those occasions when Marty went to London on business, he always stayed at the Dorchester.

'No,' he said sharply. Caren froze. 'I have cousins in London,' he reminded. 'They're high up in the Muslim community. You'll be their guests. And out of respect for them,' he warned, 'you'll wear your headscarf while you're there.'

'But you're giving them such short notice,' she stammered. 'Wouldn't it be better if Danny and I just went to the hotel?'

'You'll stay with my cousins. They'll send a limo to Heathrow to pick you up. Someone from the family will accompany you to your appointment.' He smiled dryly. 'You'll wish to go shopping. One of the ladies in the family will be your guide.' *Does he suspect this is not just an appointment with the orthodontist?* 'Perhaps you'll want to go to the theater Tuesday evening. I'm sure someone in the family will know what's best to be seen and will acquire tickets.' *And be my official escort for the evening.* 'You'll return on Wednesday. I'll have my secretary order your tickets.'

Caren arranged to meet Pari for morning coffee the next day. Pari was waiting for her at their customary coffee shop on the mall.

'Things are moving,' Pari guessed as Caren sat at their table. Her eyes searched Caren's. 'Don't be afraid – you can handle this.'

'Marty insists I stay with his cousins in London.' Caren took a deep breath. Her head pounding since early morning. 'They're to send a limo for me at Heathrow.'

'You'll miss the limo,' Pari dismissed this. 'Andrea will meet you when you come through customs. She'll have tickets for you and Danny to board a flight to New York three hours after your arrival in London.'

'Oh, she is a good friend.' Caren felt a surge of gratitude. 'But I owe her for those tickets—'

'No problem. You can reimburse her at your convenience.'

'How will she know me?' Fresh alarm welled in Caren. 'We've never seen each other. There may be other passengers traveling with a small boy.'

'I have those snapshots we took last year at the book fair at the university,' Pari reminded Caren. 'I've already e-mailed photos to her. Tell me what you'll be wearing, and I'll pass that along to her.' Unexpectedly she chuckled. 'I know you won't be wearing a manteau and headscarf.'

'I'll miss you,' Caren said with a wrenching sense of loss. 'I'll miss you so much. I won't be able to write. To phone. Not even to e-mail,' she tried for flippancy. Nor would she be able to be in touch with Janis. Just one phone call when they arrived in New York – to let Janis know she was out of Iran, back in the United States. But no other communication – until Danny was grown. *Ten years away.*

'Caren, stay cool,' Pari urged. 'Once you're on the plane at Mehrabad and it lifts off, you've escaped Marty's clutches. You'll be on your way to freedom.' Now she hesitated, seeming to search for words. 'Have you thought about what to tell Danny – when he realizes what's happening?'

'I think about it a dozen times a day. He'll be upset. He'll be angry at me. But once we've settled in and he's in a normal school and making friends, he'll be happy.' She tried for an air of conviction. 'He's excited about flying to London. He has vague recall of our flight from New York when he was three. He'll probably sleep halfway across the Atlantic.'

'One hurdle at a time,' Pari said gently.

'Your friend Andrea – does she have children?' Caren's eyes said what she couldn't bring herself to vocalize. Did Andrea give up her children when she fled from Iran?

'Both daughters – teenagers – were at boarding school in Switzerland. It was a traumatic situation. Her husband brought them home before she could make a move.'

'How awful.' She shivered – ice-cold, though the day was unseasonably warm. How would she survive if she couldn't be with Danny? *But it won't happen – we're going home, together.*

Pari allowed herself a wry chuckle. 'Her husband hates technology – he loathes computers. He doesn't know that Andrea and her daughters exchange e-mails constantly. Andrea knows they'll be joining her soon. They'll be adults.'

'I worry about the limo driver who'll be at Heathrow to meet us,' Caren admitted.

'Don't,' Pari ordered. 'He'll be there with his little card with your name. He'll be watching for an Iranian mother and son. You'll walk right past him – neither you nor Danny fit that description.' Her voice whimsical. 'Not you nor your blue-eyed, sandy-haired son.'

'Nor will I be wearing a headscarf – which Marty tells me will be expected.'

'You'll be met by Andrea,' Pari continued. 'She'll whisk you and Danny off to an airport restaurant, where you'll have lunch. She'll remain with you until you and Danny board your connecting flight.'

'I'll explain to Danny that we won't be going to the ortho-dontist – but on a surprise visit to New York,' Caren plotted. 'I'll make it seem like an exciting adventure.'

But what will be Danny's reaction when he discovers we're not going back to Iran?

Eight

Caren lived in constant fear that some horrific, last-minute move by Marty would abort their 'visit to the London orthodontist.' On Sunday evening she prepared to go to bed at an early hour. Marty warned that they must leave the house by 6 a.m. – though their British Airways flight wasn't scheduled to leave until 9.50 a.m.

'You know what the morning traffic will be like. Everybody ignores the signs, the traffic lights. The forty-minute drive to the airport could take two hours.' He grunted in distaste. 'Then there are the security measures at the airport.'

'We'll have plenty of time, Marty.' She strived to sound casual.

'You'll be flying out of Mehrabad instead of Imam Khomeini,' he grumbled. 'The new airport should have been opened five years ago.' The latest official news about the new airport – expected to be able to handle forty million passengers a year – was that it would be in use next month.

On Monday morning Caren awoke with a start – after nightmare-ridden sleep. Instantly aware that this was The Day. She turned to the clock on her bedside table. The alarm would not go off for another eight minutes.

She switched off the alarm, tossed aside the light coverlet. She must make sure that Danny was awake. Give him ten minutes warning, she thought tenderly. And make sure Marty was awake. He would drive with them to the airport, then head for his office.

She must be cool, pretend to anticipate the trip with pleasure. Conceal the volcanic excitement churning within her. Knowing that six hours after take-off she and Danny would be on British soil – and three hours later would board their flight to New York.

Conscious of their tight schedule this morning, she went into Danny's bedroom.

'Mommie, is it time?' Danny's voice came to her in the darkness. *He's excited – he hasn't been out of Tehran since he was three except for ski trips to the mountains just an hour away or to a nearby beach resort.*

'You have another five minutes,' she said indulgently. A familiar morning ritual. 'Then you must get up.'

Now the house bustled with activity. At Marty's orders, Ziba was preparing a substantial breakfast. He radiated a blend of pride and annoyance. He would boast to his business colleagues about sending his son to a world-famous orthodontist. *'Madly expensive – but I mean for my son to have the very best.'* But he was annoyed at a change in his usual routine.

Caren debated about which of her lovely designer pantsuits to wear, chose black. Perfect for job-hunting. Pack extra blouses, she ordered herself – and extra shirts for Danny. What she packed in her valise-on-wheels, the carry-on bag, and Danny's beloved knapsack would be their wardrobes in their new lives.

No space for the scrapbooks she'd filled through the years, she thought in anguish. Snapshots of Janis and Ira and the kids, photos of Danny back home and at his playgroup here in Iran. Then in sudden comprehension, she removed them from the scrapbooks, slid them into a large envelope that could fit into her carry-on bag.

She dressed swiftly, paused in inner debate. Yes! Add her turquoise and diamond brooch to her lapel. An expensive gift Marty gave her to impress his associates. Selling it later would add more cash to her cache. Once on board their flight, she'd stash it away.

At unguarded moments she worried about how long it would take her to find a job. She couldn't be fussy – she must take whatever came along. She'd been out of the job market since four months before Danny was born. That was scary.

When she returned to the living room, she found Marty on his cellphone – reminding Ayesheh, the bodyguard/chauffeur on duty this morning – that they must leave the house at 6 a.m.

'Not a minute later,' he barked. 'My son and my wife must make a flight to London.'

In deepest secrecy Zahra wrapped two chocolate cookies and slid them into Danny's knapsack. This morning Danny showed a rare vivacity. He was excited at the prospect of flying. He had vague recall of their flight to Iran – with a stopover in London and Frankfurt on that occasion.

Now Danny plied her with questions. The somber small boy who fought so hard for perfection at school, to memorize segments of the Koran was in eclipse this morning. Tears welled in Caren's eyes. Here was a faint glimpse of the Danny who used to be.

Marty made a production of bringing their luggage into the foyer. 'This huge valise?' he clucked, 'for three days in London?' For an instant she was terrified. *He's suspicious.* Then she brushed fear aside. He always complained that she packed too much when they went to the ski resort and the beach hotel. She always gave the same reply – which she parroted now.

'Not that much. If the weather should change, we'll be prepared.'

'I'll deliver you to the airport, then take off. I have a breakfast conference.' He glanced at his Rolex watch. 'Where's that stupid Ayesheh?'

'It's early,' Caren pointed out.

'You're forgetting our insane traffic,' he shot back.

Knowing she'd packed the letter from Marty that authorized her taking Danny out of the country, she opened her Prada purse. Yes, it was there. She loathed this decree which emphasized the deplorable position of women in Iran. Now she checked the passports. Both hers and Danny's in order.

She went to a hall closet, brought out her hated manteau and headscarf. It was essential to be careful in public places such as the airport, where the Morals Police were especially zealous. But after this morning, she told herself in silent triumph, she'd wear neither ever again.

Sounds in the courtyard told them Ayesheh was bringing the car to the entrance.

'Here's the car,' Marty said with relief, and reached for Danny's hand. 'You're to behave yourself in London,' he

ordered for the dozenth time. His Muslim cousins in London
– whom neither she nor Danny had ever met – must be
impressed.

Ayesheh came into the foyer for their luggage, carried it
to the car trunk. Marty prodded Danny and Caren into the
rear seat, sat beside them. Again, he brought out his cellphone, made a call. Danny sat on the edge of his seat.

'Mommie, will the orthodontist – ' he stumbled over the
unfamiliar word – 'hurt me? Sometimes when I'm at the
dentist, he hurts me.'

'He won't hurt you a bit,' she vowed. 'He'll just look at
your teeth and decide which needs straightening.'

Traffic seemed to move well until they were on the
Tehran–Qom Highway. Now they were running into stop-
and-go traffic. Marty scowled, swore under his breath.

'We've allowed plenty of time.' Caren refused to be upset.
'It's only a forty-five kilometer drive.' Thirty miles. She
wasn't sure if Marty was more concerned about missing their
flight or being late for his breakfast conference.

Finally – after a ninety-minute battle with traffic – Ayesheh
drew up at the terminal where their flight was scheduled to
take off. Marty gave Ayesheh instructions about picking him
up, then hustled Danny and Caren into the terminal.

What a dreary place, Caren thought in distaste. Pari had
talked about it on occasion.

*'It's old-fashioned – not at all modern – and it shows its
age. The tarmac is worn out. The restaurants are bad, the
gift shops expensive. And service can be ghastly.'*

'I don't know why the Imam Khomeini International
Airport isn't in operation,' Marty grumbled. 'Mehrabad is
old, too small for a city the size of Tehran.' One of the world's
largest cities at twelve million.

Caren's heart began to pound. A little over five years ago
the three of them had arrived here. Expecting to stay no more
than a year. Just long enough for Marty to pull the business
together, have it running smoothly without his father's presence. That was the warm, bright, affectionate Marty she'd
loved.

She was a bystander as Marty and Danny exchanged
farewells. She knew Marty would make no effort to kiss her

goodbye. To exchange a public embrace – even between husband and wife – was forbidden, could cause an arrest by the Morals Police, who patrolled everywhere.

'My cousin's chauffeur will be at Heathrow,' Marty reminded. 'If he should be late – because British traffic, too, can be maddening – wait for him.'

'We'll wait,' Caren promised. Impatient for Marty to leave. *I'll never see him again. He'll be out of our lives. Please, God, let nothing go wrong now.*

'Call me when you're settled in,' Marty instructed. 'Leave a message if I'm not at home when you call.'

'It'll be late in the day,' she said. 'And remember the difference in time.'

No phone call, she reminded herself. A brief letter, to be mailed from London.

Marty took off in a rush. Caren – one of Danny's hands in hers – began the airport routine that would culminate in their boarding their British Airways flight. The terminal dark, gloomy. A fair amount of fellow travelers on view.

Along with English, a litany of innumerable dialects filled the air. The male travelers in conservative suits, the women – as herself – in drab manteaus that fell to their ankles and headscarves that revealed only the allowed amount of hair. The occasional pair of gloves on view despite the warmth of the day told Caren the owner was concealing nail polish.

She would abandon the headscarf and manteau once they were on board their flight, Caren exulted. Never to wear them again. But now, with boarding passes in hand, she must focus on the computer information screens – in both English and Farsi. She was impatient to be aboard their flight. The first step to freedom so close.

After what seemed an interminable wait, their flight was announced as 'boarding.' With Danny's hand firmly in hers, Caren joined the line of first-class passengers being boarded now. She felt giddy, her throat tight. A tenseness in her shoulder blades that was almost painful.

We're here – it's happening. Let the pilot lift off!

The atmosphere was electric with the drama of take-off. Caren and Danny were escorted to their seats. Caren settled Danny in the window seat. He would enjoy gazing out the window. He seemed intrigued by their pretty stewardess – dark hair in full display, her uniform attractive. A short skirt that revealed lovely, nylon-covered legs.

He gaped in astonishment as Caren pulled off her headscarf, then her coat. In a public place! She saw him stare in growing bewilderment at a woman across the aisle – also disposing of her headscarf and coat. But in the seats before them sat a woman and a small girl – both in black chadors, seldom worn in Westernized, exclusive Elahiyeh.

'It's all right, Danny,' she explained. 'We're leaving Iranian soil. Women don't need to be covered up.'

The seat-belt sign lighted. Caren turned to fasten Danny's seat-belt, then her own. Minutes later the plane moved along the runway, began to lift off. Joy surged in Caren, to be joined an instant later by trepidation. This was the first step in their road to freedom. A long journey lay ahead.

Please God, let all go well.

Nine

C aren had brought along a batch of children's magazines for Danny's entertainment, but he brushed these aside. He was fascinated by the view from their window. Then his attention was drawn to a little girl of about ten, who chattered in high spirits with the stewardess.

'This is Camille,' the little girl told the stewardess, held up a doll. 'She's going back home with me to London.'

'Noisy girl,' Danny whispered in reproach. 'When will she shut up?'

Camille was a Barbie doll, Caren noted. Banned in Iran now. What a furor Barbie and Kenny dolls had created in Iran! It was illegal to sell them now – a shop could lose its license for this. Barbie represented Western values.

Caren's smile was derisive as she recalled the uproar that broke out a few years ago. Announcements were circulated that Iran would produce the 'mullah-approved' Sara and Dara dolls – brother and sister dolls clothed in accepted Iranian garb – to combat the 'corrupt influence of Barbie and Kenny.' But the pink boxes with Barbie continued to be sold under the counter – and Sara and Dara were ignored.

'Mommie—' Danny turned her. 'When will we be in London?'

'It'll be a while,' she conceded. 'Do you remember when we flew to Tehran when you were just three years old?' she asked gently. She'd asked that earlier – and he'd said 'sort of.' It would help him to accept what was happening if he had some recall of those earlier years.

'We went from one plane to another one. Twice,' he recalled.

'That's right. We changed planes in London, then Frankfurt. That's in Germany.'

In a corner of her mind she considered the problems Danny

would face in an American school. The strangeness he would encounter. His English, of course, was flawless. She'd managed – since he'd entered the religious school – to tutor him in math and English as learned back home. Sometimes she suspected he enjoyed these sessions.

In truth, Iranian children had so little diversion in their lives. No play groups, sports, none of the normal recreational facilities. Study filled the hours for them.

Danny's eyes began to close before they were aboard an hour. Caren suspected he'd slept little last night. The stewardess brought a pillow for him. Her eyes admiring.

'Thank you,' Caren said, her smile grateful. Now she managed to settle him in more comfort.

They'd left Tehran behind, Caren told herself in relief. No sudden emergency that would have made the pilot turn around and return to the airport. She glanced at her watch. In five hours they would be at Heathrow. She mustn't be alarmed. They would collect their luggage, go through customs. She would walk with Danny past the chauffeur waiting for them and meet Pari's friend, Andrea.

She hadn't dared to write her farewell letter to Marty at the house. Fearful that some weird incident might bring it to his attention. She turned to Danny. He was asleep. She reached into her purse, pulled out notebook and pen. It would be a brief letter – telling Marty that she and Danny were returning home.

> We'll live in a town in the Midwest. You won't find us.
> But be assured Danny will be raised well. He's an
> American citizen by birth. He'll enjoy an American
> upbringing.

When they were met in London, she would ask Andrea to mail the letter for her. Marty would receive no phone call from London – not from her. It was likely his cousins in London would call this evening – annoyed or solicitous, whatever. But she and Danny would be aboard their flight to New York. Another leg on their way to freedom.

Now the disjointed plans for the days ahead came together in Caren's mind. She and Danny would spend one night in

New York – in an obscure little hotel near Columbia, then head the next morning for Primrose. They would check into a hotel and search for a place to live.

That shouldn't be difficult, should it? Yet she felt some unease. They'd need a furnished apartment – until she had the security of a job and lay out money for furniture. Surely – even in a small town like Primrose – there would be one furnished apartment for rent. Whatever it was, they'd have to take it. Immediately she must start job-hunting. Their funds would go fast. She had her New York state teaching license, but the chances of landing a teaching job were meager. During the Columbia years she'd held part-time jobs – selling in a neighborhood boutique, waitressing. She could do that again.

In Iran she'd pushed away hours each day by reading all the English language newspapers. The conservative *Tehran Times*, the reformist *Iran News*, the *Iran Daily*. Ever conscious of the heavy censorship. She was painfully aware of the tough job market in the United States. Probably magnified by the Iranian media. Somehow, she vowed, she would find a job before their funds ran out. She flinched at the cost of their plane tickets from London to New York, transportation fees from New York to Primrose.

She remembered Lila's talk about her years in Primrose. *'Once a year Mom would take my sister and me down to New York to sightsee and shop. Loaded with shopping bags – Mom adored Altman's – we took the train from New York to Saratoga Springs, then the bus to Primrose.'*

That would be their route – a train from New York to Saratoga Springs, then a bus to Primrose. Lila called Primrose the perfect small town, but then her architect father had spread his wings and taken his family to live in far-off places.

She would allow herself one precious phone call to Janis – from an anonymous public phone. It was agonizing to realize she must refrain from all contact with Janis after this call. She knew that Marty would hire private investigators to search for them. Janis would be besieged.

But Janis would know nothing – only that her sister and nephew had left Iran and would be living in some small Midwest town. Not in a town in upstate New York. No contact with Janis, Caren reiterated in her mind. Painful but essential.

Awakening when the stewardess was distributing food trays, Danny rejected the airline food – which he'd heard his father revile after each business trip. He turned eagerly to Caren.

'Mommie, can I eat the cookies Zahra put in my knapsack?'

'Yes, you may eat your cookies.' Her smile loving, indulgent.

Poor baby, he was in for so many surprises – but it had to be this way. She would tell him in London that she'd thought much about how they had lived in Iran for five years and how it was time to go back to America. She was conscious of a tightening in her stomach as she considered breaking this to him.

Finishing his cookies, Danny kept up a lively monologue about the cloud formations he was seeing from his window.

'That one looks like a man on a bicycle,' he chortled.

It had been such a long time since she had seen him so animated, Caren thought with pleasure. He'd welcome the change in their lifestyle. *Won't he?* He'd miss Marty, she forced herself to acknowledge. For a little while he'd miss his father. But his father wanted to mold him into his own wishes – and that was wrong.

The hours sped past. The atmosphere became electric again when the plane began its descent. Caren dreaded the moment when she and Danny must walk out of customs – knowing the chauffeur bearing a card that read 'Mansur' would be watching for a woman and a little boy. A sign that Danny must not see!

Perhaps when she and Danny walked past the Mansurs' chauffeur – as they must, he would dismiss them as being Americans or British. She remembered the woman and little girl – both in chadors. Perhaps the chauffeur would believe there was a mistake, that he was to meet a woman with a little girl – not a small boy.

Can I carry this off? Am I taking on more than I can handle? No, this is what's best for Danny. I can't let him become a clone of Marty.

Danny gazed out the window – fascinated by their descent. Pelting Caren with questions about London. But they'd see little of London. In less than three hours they would be boarding a flight to New York.

Should she have explained to Danny before they were about to land that they would not be staying in London? No, she reassured herself. She'd explain in Andrea's presence. Make it seem like a wonderful surprise. *'Guess what, Danny? I've decided that we won't go to the orthodontist in London just now. We're going on a great adventure. We're going home for a while.'* So it would be a little white lie. It would ease the situation.

Again – when their plane had landed and they'd disembarked – Danny seemed fascinated by the hordes of people emerging from flights. Others waiting to embark. None of the women in dress demanded by Iranian law – except for an occasional somber figure. The chador-garbed woman and little girl on their flight trailed behind them.

They collected their luggage, emerged from customs. Caren geared herself for the appearance of the cousins' chauffeur. Each breath a straining effort. Her eyes swept the scene. Thirty feet ahead were several people who held cards aloft. Then she saw him, displaying a card that read 'Mansur.' Scanning faces.

I must divert Danny's attention! He mustn't see that sign! He'd call out for sure. Talk to him.

'Danny,' she said with a show of anxiety, 'I think one of the wheels on my valise is coming loose. What do you think?' An edge of desperation in her voice.

Danny stared hard at the wheels as Caren prodded him forward. Past the chauffeur with the 'Mansur' card.

'It looks all right to me, Mommie—'

Keep moving, she exhorted herself. Let the chauffeur not have afterthoughts. Let him not approach them.

'Caren?' A tall, dark-haired woman in a smart suit approached them tentatively.

'Yes.' She felt a surge of relief. 'You're Andrea—' They were being met. The chauffeur would have no interest in them.

'And this must be Danny,' Andrea said, smiling in welcome.

'Yes, ma'am—' Danny seemed startled.

'Danny, this is my friend Pari's cousin Andrea. She teaches at a big university here in London.' Danny had enormous respect for teachers at all levels.

'We'll go to Oscar's at the Hilton. There's a covered walkway from this terminal. We'll have lunch,' Andrea said and chuckled at Danny's air of surprise.

'Lunch?' Danny turned to his mother. 'Didn't we have lunch on the plane?'

'I barely touched it,' Caren told him, 'and you settled for two chocolate cookies.'

'Here in London it's three hours earlier than in Tehran,' Andrea explained. 'In Tehran it's four p.m. Here it's only a little past one p.m.' *And in New York it's five hours earlier than in London.*

'Wow!' Danny was impressed. 'When we go home, it'll be later than here?' He frowned, trying to understand this small miracle.

'That's right.' Andrea exchanged a quick glance of sympathy with Caren. *She realizes I haven't told Danny yet that we won't be going back to Tehran.* 'Would you like to check your luggage while we have lunch?'

'Considering the time involved, I think it would be better to keep it with me.' Caren tried to appear casual. *Pari said we'd have around three hours between flights – but we must be at customs well ahead. She said that security at Heathrow is far more thorough than it is at Mehrabad.*

While they walked to the restaurant, Andrea inquired about their flight. Focusing her attention on Danny.

'Do you like flying?' Andrea asked him.

'It's fun,' he said after a moment. *Poor darling, he's had so little fun these last three years.* 'I like looking at the clouds. I like it when the plane goes up, and then when it comes down.'

They approached the ultra-modern Hilton, walked inside.

'Oscar's is through here—' Andrea directed them. Her eyes sent a message of sympathy to Caren. *She knows this is a crucial moment, that I must tell Danny now we're not going home.*

'Danny, do you like pizza?'

His eyes glowed. 'Yeah.'

'Oscar's specializes in American food. They're open twenty-four hours a day – and they welcome children.' Andrea's eyes met Caren's. *How bright she is – to take us to a restaurant where Danny is sure to be happy.*

They settled themselves, ordered. It was clear that Danny was astonished by the lack of a dress code in London. He stared at a woman diner in a spectacular red pantsuit.

'Pretty clothes,' he said. Almost shy in this comment. And eagerly awaiting his pizza.

'Don't you remember the ladies at the nursery group, before you went to the religious school? They wore pretty clothes, too.'

'But not before other people. I mean, not out in the street,' he blurted out. 'No Morals Police in London?'

'Only in Iran, Danny,' Caren said softly. *This was the time to tell Danny. Now.* 'Darling, I have a wonderful surprise for you. We're not going to the orthodontist. We're going to take another plane and go to New York.'

He gaped at her in shock. 'Why?' All at once he was fearful.

'We've been away from home for five years—' *He's trying to digest that. Home to him is Tehran.* 'You remember our house in Westchester – your jungle gym—' *A foreign language to him.* 'Your swings,' she tried again. 'And your little above-ground swimming pool—'

'Sort of—' His usual reply when he was uncertain. Still, he was bewildered. 'Why are we going there?' he persisted.

'Darling, you were born in the United States – I thought it was time for us to go back and – and live there for a while.' She glanced up with a shaky smile of relief as their food was brought to their table. She and Andrea exchanged a few words with their waitress. *He's upset. That's only natural.*

'Did Daddy say we could go there?' His small face exuded doubt. 'Will he come, too?'

'Danny, sometimes mothers must make decisions.' *How can I make him understand?* 'We'll just take one day at a time—'

'Mommie, Daddy's going to be mad—' His eyes were fearful. On occasion he had witnessed Marty's rages.

'No,' she lied, exchanged an uneasy glance with Andrea. 'A lot of children live with just their mommies at – at one point in their lives. You'll see all kinds of exciting things. You'll go to another school for – for a while.'

'Danny, try your pizza before it gets cold,' Andrea coaxed. 'It looks delicious.'

With an unfamiliar reluctance – trying to assimilate what was happening in his life – Danny lifted the pizza, tasted it. 'It's real good,' he said, diverted for the moment. 'Can I have a soda?'

'Have orange juice,' Caren coaxed. 'Or chocolate milk.' Sodas were banned in their household. 'That's much better than soda.'

While Danny sought momentary refuge in eating his pizza, Andrea slipped an envelope across the table to Caren. 'Your tickets—'

'Let me pay you for them—' Caren reached for her purse. Most of her funds – in American dollars – were concealed in a money belt about her waist. She'd left out what she assumed would be sufficient to pay for their tickets – always ultra-expensive on short notice.

'Not now,' Andrea insisted. 'When you're on your feet again. Please,' she added in a whisper as Caren was about to object. 'We're sisters – escaping an ugly life.'

Caren ate without tasting. At intervals she glanced at her watch – adjusted to London time. She suspected that by now the chauffeur had decided they had not been on the expected plane, would be checking on the next arrival.

Late in the day one of the cousins would call Tehran. Marty wouldn't be home until late – only then would he realize she and Danny were missing. By then they would be high over the Atlantic.

But not until we're in Primrose – leaving no trace behind – will I feel safe.

Ten

C aren and Danny boarded their London to New York flight.
Economy class this time – out of respect for her limited
funds. She was assaulted by conflicting emotions. Towering
relief that they were homeward bound, fearful anticipation
of problems that lay ahead.

Danny must be so tired, she thought with compunction.
Poor baby, he'd been awake since 5 a.m. – except for his
nap on their Tehran-London flight. It was now almost 7 p.m.
Tehran time – and the day had been exhausting for him. He
was confused and frightened and bewildered.

When they were seated and seat belts in position for take-
off, she reached into the carry-on bag for the children's
magazines she'd brought along for Danny.

'Would you like to read one of your magazines?' she asked
him while the plane began to lift off from the runway.

He frowned in rejection. 'No.'

'I think you need a little nap,' she cajoled. 'We can unfasten
our seat belts in a few moments. You can get more comfortable. I'll ask the stewardess for a pillow.'

In five minutes Danny was sound asleep. He'd sleep most
of the way across the Atlantic, she told herself in relief. She,
too, might nod off. But no, that wouldn't happen, she soon
realized. She was too tense to sleep.

In her mind she'd blocked out every step of the way from
London to Primrose. She mustn't allow herself to worry
about unexpected obstacles. She mustn't panic. Everything
would go on schedule.

They'd arrive at JFK, take a cab to that little hotel near
Columbia where Janis and Ira had stayed when they'd come
to New York for her wedding. Inexpensive and obscure. Danny
needed a break before they undertook the train and bus trip.

Tomorrow morning they would head for Penn Station. She'd check on trains to Saratoga Springs. In Saratoga Springs they'd head for the bus terminal, take a bus to Primrose. By evening they'd be settled for the night in a pleasant hotel in Primrose. Far beyond Marty's reach. He would be furious – but he'd have no inkling of where they were.

Still, doubts – fears of her ability to cope – taunted her. But millions of single mothers raised their children on their own. She would find a job to support Danny and herself. Perhaps not in the fashion they'd known of late – but they'd live in a free society.

Danny slept for almost two hours. Then he stirred into fretful wakefulness.

'Mommie, are we almost there?'

'We've got a while yet to go,' she soothed, her mind searching for means of diversion for him. 'While we're in New York, would you like to go to the Central Park Zoo?' Twice during their years in Westchester she'd taken him to the Central Park Zoo. He'd been euphoric. There would be time for a brief visit to the zoo in the morning. 'You loved it when I took you there when you were little.'

'Do they have polar bears?' A flicker of interest now.

'Oh, yes.' He'd been fascinated by the polar bears on those early visits. 'They have a whole Polar Section. You'll see polar bears and penguins – each with a pool of their own.' *He's intrigued. Keep talking about the zoo. Keep him from thinking about Marty, about Tehran.* 'We'll go to the Central Park Zoo in the morning.'

'You promise?'

'I promise.'

From the zoo they'd go to Penn Station, she plotted. By evening they'd be far upstate. In Primrose. Was it still the beautiful small town that Lila had loved?

Lila lived there a long time ago. Maybe it's a depressed area now. So many small towns are in desperate straits – jobs outsourced to the Middle East or India or China. No, stop thinking that way!

Had she jumped too fast in choosing Primrose? No, it probably hadn't changed in all the years since Lila lived there. Yet the possibility that it wasn't the same perfect town

Lila had known nagged at her. They must live in a town where Danny could become himself again.

In Manhattan there would be places that rented computers by the hour. She would search Google – who knew everything! – for information about Primrose. Just to reassure herself. But for now, push bad thoughts out of her mind.

What could she say to Danny that would erase that scared glint she saw in his eyes? She searched her mind with fierce intensity. A puppy! He'd always wanted a puppy.

Up till now they couldn't have a dog because of Marty's allergies. But in Primrose Danny would have a puppy. Her face grew luminous as she remembered how – in the Westchester years – he had adored Snoopy, their next-door neighbor's Labrador retriever.

As soon as we're settled – when I have a steady job – we'll go to the local ASPCA, and Danny will pick out a pup. He'll be ecstatic.

She ached to see Danny become the outgoing, happy little boy he had been before he'd entered the religious school. They'd encountered some problems the previous three years – with Marty's incessant efforts to mold him to his thinking – but the years Danny had spent with the UN preschoolers had been fun for him.

'Mommie—' Danny was gazing about at the other passengers as though in some inner debate. 'All these people on the plane – the people in London – are infidels! Daddy says all Americans are infidels—'

Caren stiffened in shock. The religious school mantra, thrown about by the Administration, reiterated by Marty in these past three years.

'Danny, no! The people here – the people in London and in America – they are not infidels. They live in a freedom that God considers right. In Tehran—' She searched her mind for words that Danny could comprehend. 'In Tehran the Administration is evil. The Koran is misinterpreted – told in an improper way. Islam is a fine religion. It joins with Christianity and Judaism in worshiping one God. Like them, Islam preaches peace and tolerance—' *I'm not getting through to him – he's eight years old.*

'Daddy says that only good Muslims will go to Paradise.

If we don't do what the Imam says – ' a leader at the mosque who leads the people in prayer, as Mohammed did in Medina – 'then we can never go there—' His small face was fearful. 'Daddy says that—'

'Daddy is wrong!' she broke in. 'The Imam at Daddy's mosque says bad things. He says things that are not in the Koran.' *How could Marty do this to Danny? Danny is afraid of him. Terrified that he won't live up to his father's expectations. He's been brainwashed at that school for almost three years.* 'Darling, try to nap again,' she coaxed. 'Soon we'll be in New York,'

'I'm not sleepy.' Danny was reproachful. He gazed out the window. 'It's not even night time yet.'

'It's night-time in Tehran,' she explained. 'You need to get lots of sleep. Tomorrow will be a busy day.' Her smile bright, promising.

A stewardess began to circulate with trays. Danny viewed her with interest.

'I'm hungry,' he announced. Forgetting his father's distaste for airline food.

For a little while Danny was diverted by the arrival of his dinner tray. Caren ordered herself to eat. Her mind troubled by Danny's vision of all Americans as infidels. *Even me. 'I love you, Mommie, even if you are an American.'*

It would require time to bring Danny's thinking back to normal, she warned herself. She recoiled from visions of his reactions at a new school. An American school. But in time she would bring him back to normal. That was her task in life from this point on. Nothing else mattered.

With the trays out of the way, Danny was restless. How to divert him now? With contrived good cheer she launched into more intriguing descriptions of their brief visit in New York.

'I'll show you the place where Daddy and I went to school—' She stopped short. It was a mistake to talk about Marty. 'Daddy was different back then.'

'Mommie, when will we go home?' Danny's eyes were wistful. 'Will Daddy be mad at us?'

'Don't worry about that, darling. Everything will be all right.'

He retreated into silence, gazed out at the passing clouds

– yet Caren suspected he didn't see them. He sat with shoulders tensed, small hands clenched. *What is he thinking?* The hours left before their arrival in New York seemed endless. Painful to survive.

What can I tell Danny to make him feel less frightened?

Eleven

Caren felt a surge of excitement when – at last – the New York skyline came into view. A flurry of antici-pation aboard. Somewhere behind them a toddler was screeching in delight. Passengers began to pack small items into carry-ons.

'Danny, watch,' she urged, reaching to fasten his seat belt as the sign flashed. 'We'll be landing very soon now. Remember, tomorrow morning we'll go to the zoo. You'll see the polar bears and penguins – and lots more!'

Caren was relieved at the speed with which they emerged through customs, with luggage in tow. As at Heathrow, Danny was astonished by the security, by the need for passengers to be patted down, to remove their shoes. They hurried to the line-up of taxis. Caren impatient to be Manhattan-bound.

After a brief wait, they acquired a taxi. Caren gave the driver instructions, leaned back with a huge sigh of relief. *We're home. Marty must know by now that we're not in London. He'll be screaming at the airline's office. Tomorrow he'll receive my letter.*

As the taxi sped along the Long Island Expressway, Caren admired the masses of forsythia still in bloom. She pointed out remembered sites. Then the Manhattan skyline came into view. Oh, how great to be home!

'We'll go through a tunnel soon,' Caren told Danny and reached for his hand. 'Then we'll be in town.' *He's so quiet again. More sights strange to him. But he's with me. Doesn't he trust me to take good care of him?*

Now they were through the tunnel, running into rush hour Manhattan traffic. Caren kept up a running commentary about the passing sights. Despite his bewilderment at what Caren kept calling 'an exciting adventure', he seemed intrigued by the strangeness on every side. He laughed aloud at a bicycle/taxi that rode alongside of them.

'That's something new in Manhattan.' She laughed along with him. 'But there won't be many.'

The cab was rushing up Broadway. 'The hotel is just ahead,' she told Danny with a reassuring smile.

Her mind darted back through the years. Janis and Ira had stayed at this hotel. In the almost three years she and Marty had lived in Westchester, Janis and Ira and the two kids – Diane and Jimmy – had flown out to spend a week with them each summer. She and Marty and Danny had flown to California for a week at Christmas.

At the hotel Caren registered under an assumed name, reported that she would be paying by cash rather than by credit card. The hotel clerk would think that strange, but no matter.

'May I please have a seven a.m. wake-up call in the morning?' She must schedule their travel to arrive in Primrose tomorrow evening. Hopefully, early evening.

Riding up in the elevator, Danny was solemn. In their room he gazed about in disapproval. A typical modest hotel room. A copy of the day's *New York Times* lay across the dresser.

'Mommie, it's so little.'

'We're just going to sleep here for the night,' she soothed. 'And in the morning we'll head right for the zoo.'

Danny gazed at the telephone on the night table between the two beds. 'Mommie, can we call Daddy?' His eyes hopeful.

'I don't think Daddy would like that,' she hedged. 'Did I tell you that once – ' instinct warned against mentioning the occasion – 'Aunt Janis and Uncle Ira stayed at this hotel?' He had vague recall of them – reinforced by a series of snap-shots through the years.

'In this room?'

'Somewhere in this hotel. Danny, it's just a place to sleep—' But he was remembering elegant resort hotel suites where they'd stayed with Marty.

What little unpacking was required could wait until later. 'We'll go down and find a restaurant where we can have

dinner.' She hesitated for a moment. 'And tonight you can
have ice cream for dessert.' In Iran a Sunday night treat.

Danny's face brightened. 'Chocolate?'

'Chocolate.' The two of them were chocoholics.

The streets were lively with people. Again, Danny gazed
about in amazement. Where back in Iran the streets were
drab and depressing with their lack of color, here not only
women but men dressed in bright colors. Danny stared in
shock as a pair of young men strode past in shorts. In Iran
men were forbidden to wear shorts – even short-sleeved shirts.

He gaped in wonder at a cluster of boys about his age
who were involved in high-spirited horseplay. One of the
little boys was carrying a baseball bat. Danny had never seen
a baseball game, never played baseball. Never played soccer,
saw a game only once. He'd never climbed a tree like other
little boys, never rode a bike because Marty disapproved.

Caren was both astonished and amused that so many people
walked with cellphones pressed to their ears. As though, she
thought, these calls were too important to wait until the cellphone owner arrived at home or business. She laughed as
she overheard one caller.

*'I don't know. Should I go out with him again or punish
him a bit for being such a creep?'*

In a pleasant neighborhood restaurant – lightly populated
at this early dinner hour – they ate savory pasta with chicken
strips, then Danny's favorite dessert. Eager to be out on the
street again, Caren signaled the waitress.

'Check, please—'

Caren stared at their check in shock. She'd ordered without
looking at the right side of the menu. She'd become accus-
tomed to the prices in Tehran. In a corner of her mind she'd
been horrified at the cost of taxis. She'd pushed this aside
in her relief at being here in Manhattan.

The cost of living had gone up – not just as she'd noted
in London – but here in New York. The funds she'd brought
with her from Tehran would run out faster than she'd anticipated. She must find a job quickly. The realization was
unnerving.

Caren and Danny emerged from the restaurant into early
twilight, headed northward along Broadway. So many

changes through the years! Some of the mom-and-pop shops were gone. A favorite bookstore was gone.

Fast-food chains seemed to be everywhere – as was happening in Tehran. But wasn't the whole world becoming a fast-food junkie? Even in Tehran it was possible to order in from many fast-food chains.

Caren stood in silence now, gazed across the street at the entrance to Columbia. Assaulted by recall. This had been home to Marty and her for their undergraduate years and the graduate school days. Life had seemed so full of promise then.

She'd been so in love with Marty. She'd thought he'd loved her with that same passion. Those first two years in Iran she'd told herself Marty would change – he would become her Marty again. But that never happened.

Janis would be relieved that she'd left Marty and come home. Her mind darted back to the summer three years ago when Janis wrote that she and Ira along with the kids would be in London for a week while Ira did research at the British Museum. She'd been so excited . . .

'Marty, it'll be so good to see them! It's been so long. It'll be easier for us to go to London than have them come here,' she bubbled. Marty and Ira had been kindred spirits back home. For a moment she'd blocked out the unnerving changes in Marty.

'Not a good idea to bring them here.' He was terse. 'You'll fly out to see them for a few days.'

She was bewildered. 'Why can't you come with us? Maybe just for the weekend—' He'd grown fanatical about the business. About politics.

'Danny and I will stay here. You'll go alone. For three days,' he decreed.

She was stunned by Marty's stipulations. 'But they'll want to see Danny,' she protested. And why only three days?

'Danny will stay here with me.' His smile was contemptuous. 'I remember your brother-in-law's liberal views.' The views Marty had shared. Then. 'Danny's young and impressionable. He'll remain here with me.'

She'd been honest with Janis and Ira. She couldn't understand what was happening to Marty. But this was their life, she'd admitted. Trying to be stoical. Yet already doubts about their future had been invading her at unwary intervals.

Now a sign in a copy shop they were passing captured her attention: 'Computer Rental by the Hour'.

'Darling, let's go in here for a moment. I want to look up something on a computer.'

The secular schools in Iran – in the cities – had computers. Education was deplorable out of the cities. Danny's religious school – attached to a mosque – had no computers, no copiers, only the barest essentials.

She felt a surge of relief as she checked out Primrose on Google. The information was all good. The population was 18,000 at present – the same as when Lila lived there. The schools excellent, employment figures showing some slow-down – but Primrose was not a depressed area. *I'll find a job.*

Three hotels were listed in Primrose. She noted that one was close to the bus terminal, on Main Street. The Hotel Claridge. They'd check in there on their arrival in Primrose tomorrow evening. Then they'd look for a furnished apart-ment. Instinctively she knew there would be few available.

Danny was euphoric when they encountered a woman walking a pair of young pups of uncertain origin. She stopped with a smile at Danny's show of delight.

'Can I pat them?' Danny asked hopefully.

'They'll be unhappy if you don't,' the woman told him.

Danny was enthralled by the presence of so many dogs being walked at the dinner hour. 'Does everybody have a dog in America?'

'Many people.' Caren squeezed his hand. Yes, when they were settled in Primrose, she would go with Danny to the local ASPCA and let him pick out his puppy.

Danny began to yawn as they headed back to the hotel. Caren debated a moment about allowing him to watch a little television before she tucked him in for the night.

'Danny would you like to watch some TV before you go to bed?' She remembered how – all those years ago, before Iran – he'd adored American cartoons.

He gazed at her in astonishment. In Iran he was not allowed to watch television. The occasional moments when he'd contrived to watch a program he hadn't been entranced.

'I'm sleepy,' he dodged the offer.

'All right, you'll watch a bit in the morning.' She'd left a wake-up call for 7 a.m., but they'd have to wait almost three hours before they could enter the Central Park Zoo.

Danny was asleep moments after she turned off the lamps. She suspected that despite jet lag she'd lie sleepless for hours. Tomorrow they would take the train to Saratoga Springs, then the bus to Primrose. Their new life would begin.

Lying in the darkness, staring at the ceiling, doubts began to tug at her yet again. In the early days Marty had teased her about making impulsive decisions – but in those days he'd found it endearing.

Am I making a rash decision to try to build a new life in Primrose, New York? I should have done more research. All I know about it is that Lila had loved it. But that had been eighteen years ago.

Twelve

B rian Woods grunted in reproach when his alarm clock shrieked its message. Without opening his eyes – without moving a muscle – he lay back and considered the day that lay ahead. It was 6 a.m., Tuesday – this evening the parent-teacher association was meeting at 8 p.m. As principal of Primrose Elementary School No. 1, his presence was obligatory.

The meeting would be heated. Controversial. Property owners resented the possibility of increased school taxes – but the schools desperately needed more funds. Couldn't they understand that their children's education was at stake?

Teachers' salaries had remained the same for seven years. Salaries must go up, or they'd begin to lose their experienced teachers. New education graduates were searching around for the best deals – which they weren't finding in Primrose.

Primrose schools needed more computers, new textbooks, routine supplies. He – along with several teachers – had been spending their own money for these. Most of all, they needed bilingual teachers. Minority – immigrant – families tended to be large. Enrollment of little-English-speaking students was soaring.

The Federal Administration talked about the importance of education, but federal education funds were being cut. Some parents were screaming about the cost of hiring bilingual teachers – but they were essential.

Eleven years ago – when he started teaching in Primrose, right out of college – there'd been no language problems. But the whole world was changing. Current immigration changed the school needs. Not just in major cities – in small towns across the country as well.

The second warning of the alarm clock nudged him into action. He thrust aside the light comforter, headed for the bathroom to shower and shave. Personal problems creeping into his thoughts now.

The ad in the *Sentinel* hadn't brought one call for a prospective tenant for the apartment. He was wasting money running it. Drop it, his mind exhorted. The last tenants had come because of word of mouth.

It was a pleasant little apartment, he thought defensively – with its own entrance. The rent helped with the monthly mortgage payments. The month it had sat empty had hurt. Now he faced a second month without a rent check.

Showered, shaved and dressed, he headed for the kitchen to put up his breakfast. He ate with his usual haste – as though every minute of the day was precious. He was on his second cup of coffee – despite his vow to cut back on caffeine – when the phone rang.

It'd be Jill, he guessed, and reached for the kitchen extension. Nobody else would call at this hour. But Jill knew this short period between waking and heading for school was the best time for serious discussion. Last night she had an informal meeting with several members of the school board – to try out his plan to teach English to their immigrant students.

'Good morning—' The sun was streaming in through the sweep of kitchen windows.

'Hi, Brian,' Jill greeted him with her usual voice that said 'no matter how rough things look, they will get better.' 'I didn't buzz you after the meeting because it was past midnight, and you need your sleep.'

'What was their reaction?' A glance at the clock told him he should be heading for school in a few minutes. He made a point of being the first one in each morning.

'We have to consider it's a complete switch-over,' she pointed out and sighed. 'It'll be a tough battle to put in place.'

'Damn it!' He grunted in impatience. 'It's the most practical way to handle the situation. Take the kids who have little comprehension of the language, give them a school year of total focus on English. Forget the other subjects. Kids learn fast – they'll sop it up when it's ladled out full time.'

'Better they should be a year behind,' Jill agreed. 'This so-called social promotion is for the birds.'

Familiar frustration soared in Brian. 'They leave school insecure and unemployable except for menial jobs.'

'I know it, and you know it,' Jill soothed. 'But you'll even find resistance from some of the parents of those kids.'

'I'm working on the presentation for the school board. And I know – we'll hear fighting words all the way up to the mayor's office. How the hell did a nice, fair-thinking town like Primrose vote in an ultra-conservative administration?'

'Tim Davis had the campaign funds and that phoney "man-of-the-people" approach. Too many believed him when he said, "I'm on your side." Just pray we can vote him out in the next election. How're you doing with your rental?' She switched subjects. 'Any action?'

'Not one response to all my ads.' This wasn't New York or Chicago or some major city where young people flocked for jobs – and apartments. Too many left Primrose after college because the job market in town was shrinking and opportunities meager. 'I'm dropping it after tomorrow morning's edition.' The evening paper – the *Primrose Ledger* – had a 'classified' section, but its readers were the local conservatives. His political views were well known – *Ledger* readers would steer clear of him.

'I've got to get breakfast for Phil,' she said hurriedly. 'Talk to you later.'

Off the phone Brian prepared to leave for school. He liked to be at his desk a little past 7 a.m. That provided a full hour or so without phone interruptions.

He collected his knapsack, lifted it in place, and headed for the car. Sometimes – like now – he asked himself why he remained in this town.

His mind told him he ought to sell the house, pay off the mortgage and head back for New York. The city was dying to hire teachers. So he wouldn't be a principal. He'd have a decent salary, a pension – and no cantankerous school board forever breathing down his neck.

Think about it, his mind exhorted. There was life away from Primrose. This wasn't the town it was eleven years ago

– when he'd been enthralled at the prospect of setting down roots away from the harried pace of Manhattan.

For all he tried – along with people like Jill – their school system was in trouble. They needed to reorganize with the times. How to do this without raising property taxes? This was the question that haunted him.

The developers who were fighting to buy the land along Primrose Lake – the eminent domain question being argued by the lawyers – boasted about how this would bring in property taxes but be no burden on the school system. Rentals would be limited to tenants over fifty-five. Never mind they'd be wrecking the lives of sixty-two families.

For the first time in memory a local group was talking about setting up a private school in town – from kindergarten through twelfth grade. The parochial school talked about increasing enrollment. The Primrose school system was slipping in county ratings.

Maybe it's time for me to move on.

Thirteen

Despite her expectation of lying awake most of the night, Caren had drifted into troubled sleep at an early hour. Now she was jarred into wakefulness by the shrill ringing of a phone close by. Aware suddenly of unfamiliar surroundings. Her wake-up call, she realized.

She pulled herself into a semi-sitting position, reached for the phone on the bedside table.

'Thank you, I'm awake.'

'Enjoy the day,' a vivacious feminine voice greeted her. 'It's sixty-one degrees and sunny.'

'Thank you. There'll be no need to call again.'

She turned to the other bed. In the spill of early morning sunlight that seeped through the Venetian blinds, she saw that Danny was awake – solemn and motionless beneath the light, much-washed coverlet.

'Good morning, darling—' She managed a bright smile. *Why did I leave such an early wake-up call? What Marty – the old sweet, warm Marty – used to call my compulsion always to be on time.* 'Have you been awake for a while?'

'I guess so.'

'All right, let's get up and dress.' *It's a sunny day, thank God.* 'We have a date with the polar bears and the penguins at the Central Park Zoo.'

'Can we go now?' A hopeful glint in his eyes.

'In a while,' she hedged. 'Come on, out of bed. I'll set up the shower for you.' At eight he enjoyed showering alone in the bathroom. It made him feel grown-up, she mused tenderly. 'And while I shower, you can watch television.'

She turned on the shower, tested it, waited for his approval while the surge of hot water pounded his back.

'It's OK,' he told her. Seeming less solemn now.

'Be careful not to slip when you get out—' Her normal admonition. 'There's a towel right here – and a little bar of soap.'

She went back into the room, pulled out fresh clothes for Danny to wear, checked the TV page of *The Times*. *Sesame Street* was on Channel 13 from 7 a.m. to 8 a.m. Danny would love it.

When Danny had showered and dressed, she switched on the TV set, found Channel 13.

'Watch the program, Danny, while I shower.' But already his eyes – fastened to the TV screen – were wide with wonder.

Emerging from the shower, she dressed, debated about going downstairs for breakfast or ordering in from a nearby coffee shop. *Have breakfast here in the room, before the TV – it'll be more relaxing for Danny.*

The vivacious voice that had awakened her this morning provided her with the name of a neighborhood coffee shop that would deliver to their room. Danny sat mesmerized before the television set.

Their breakfast arrived. Danny inspected his Belgian waffles and orange juice with momentary interest, but *Sesame Street* was more engrossing. This was a precious little pocket of peace, Caren thought as she ate.

Sometime between now and noon – because shortly after that she expected them to be boarding the train for Saratoga Springs – she must phone Janis. Not from the hotel – where the call could be traced to her. Call from some public phone.

She felt a surge of pain at the prospect of not being able to see Janis – even to be in touch – until Danny was grown and Marty would have no hold over them. She'd call Janis from Penn Station, pray that she was home.

It was urgent that no one could trace their whereabouts. No trace of her to Janis. Marty would hire the best of private investigators. They'd try to track her down through phone calls, letters, e-mails to Janis. In today's world nothing was secret. *We must have no contact. None.*

When *Sesame Street* ended at 8 a.m., Caren gathered their luggage together, prepared to check out of the hotel. She was conscious that, again, Danny was fearful of what lay ahead of them.

'We'll take a taxi down to Penn Station,' she told him with an air of avid anticipation. 'We'll check our luggage, and then go up to the Central Park Zoo.' *Keep talking about the zoo – that's a happy thought for Danny.* 'By then they'll be opening up for the day.'

At Penn Station she'd call Janis. Jimmy and Diane would be off to school. Janis would sit down for a cup of coffee and plan her day's routine. Darling Janis – always so logical, so disciplined.

It would be awful to be out of touch with Janis and Ira and the kids. Diane was nine now, Jimmy seven. Danny was not quite three the last time he saw them. She'd tried to keep them in Danny's memory by showing him the snapshots Janis sent at regular intervals.

She was relieved to find a taxi within minutes. This was rush hour – it could have been difficult. On the drive downtown she talked to Danny about passing sights. Then they were at Penn Station.

Caren moved through the rush of travelers in search of a bank of phones in a less crowded area.

'I have to make a phone call here,' she told Danny at last. 'You watch our luggage and—'

'You're calling Daddy?' His face lighted.

'No, darling.' She avoided his eyes. 'This is to learn about the hotels in Primrose,' she fabricated.

'What's Primrose?' But his earlier enthusiasm about the trip to the zoo was evaporating.

'That's where we're going to stay for a while. Now watch our luggage,' she exhorted and reached into her purse for a handful of quarters, crossed to a bank of phones. Danny couldn't hear at this distance, she assured herself.

With the proper amount inserted in the slot, she waited impatiently for Janis to respond. *She's not answering – she's gone out early.*

'Hello—' Janis's familiar voice came to her on the sixth ring.

'Janis—' She felt a surge of love. 'It's me – I'm in New York—' She paused for breath. Her heart pounding.

'You've left Marty,' Janis guessed. 'Danny's with you?' Alarm in her voice now.

'You know I wouldn't leave without Danny.' Keeping her voice low, lest she be heard by others on adjacent phones. 'I left because of Danny. I couldn't bear what Marty was doing to him. Janis, listen to me. I'm taking Danny to a small town—' she hesitated. Even to Janis, she must lie. 'A small town in the Midwest. I know Marty will send investigators out to track me down. You mustn't know where I am – I can't write, e-mail, or phone you. He'd find me.'

'Oh, my God—'

'When Danny is eighteen, he'll be free. Marty can't touch him.' Her voice broke. 'It'll be horrible not to know how you and Ira and the kids are doing—'

'You'll know,' Janis said defiantly. 'I'll set up a website on the Internet. I'll—'

'That'll take a long time,' Caren broke in.

'Honey, you're forgetting – Ira's in the business. I'll be Carol, who keeps a weekly letter on the website to her sister Barbara – who's a foreign correspondent chasing around the world. Caren, you'll know about us,' she vowed. 'Write down what I'm about to tell you—'

'I have to add more quarters,' Caren warned, reaching into the pocket of her jacket.

She listened avidly while Janis explained the situation, wrote in the notebook she'd pulled from her purse.

'I love you, Janis – you and Ira and the kids.' An edge of desperation in her voice.

'We love you, too,' Janis said softly.

Off the phone, Caren stood immobile for a moment. Clinging to the knowledge that she could go to a computer each week and hear from Janis. She couldn't reply, she exhorted herself. That could be a trail to their whereabouts.

Before leaving Penn Station Caren checked their luggage, then lined up at a ticket window to buy tickets for the New York to Saratoga Springs train. All the while keeping a sharp eye on the time. The zoo would open at 10 a.m. Let them be there moments after it opened.

She was surprised to discover there were only two trains a day to Saratoga Springs. The morning train long gone. The next would leave at 2.45 p.m., arrive at 6.15 p.m. – and all seats were reserved. She made a reservation for two in an improvised name.

As she'd anticipated, Danny was enthralled by everything he saw at the zoo, reluctant to leave though Caren was sure he must be exhausted by the time she decreed they find a restaurant to have lunch.

'We want to find a place before the mad rush,' she said, realizing Danny had no concept of what she was saying. 'Just this once – because this is a special day,' she coaxed, 'you may have a hamburger.' In Tehran he'd been intrigued by the McDonald's that they passed but never entered. 'With French fries.'

'Wow!' Danny's smile was brilliant.

Well before time for their train to depart, they returned to Penn Station. The bright sun of the morning giving way to clouds. Would it be raining when they arrived in Primrose? A dreary welcome to their new home?

Caren retrieved their luggage. They'd arrive in Saratoga Springs at 6.15 p.m., she recalled. From there they'd take a bus to Primrose. How long would they have to wait for a bus?

'Danny, I need to call the bus station in Primrose.' Would there be no bus connection at the time they arrived? Would they have to spend a night in Saratoga Springs? 'There're phones just ahead,' she said, making it sound a happy discovery. 'You watch our luggage while I call.'

They would be able to make a 7.35 p.m. bus from Saratoga Springs. It would bring them into Primrose at 9.50 p.m. Relieved that the layover would be brief, Caren collected their luggage and headed with Danny for their designated gate.

She was suffused with mixed emotions. Relief that they'd covered so much territory, were within hours of their destination. Mounting unease that she had chosen their new home with too little forethought.

Will Primrose be the lovely small town that Lila had loved? How will Danny react to a new school? Will I find a job quickly? At the high cost of living today our money won't last long.

Fourteen

Brian heard the dismissal bell ring. The end of another school day. In moments the halls were thronged with the noisy chatter of students charging from the school building to waiting school buses. But not the end of the day for him, Brian reminded himself.

He had a meeting with a teacher who, he suspected, was suffering from burnout. After that, a mother who insisted on talking with him rather than with Cliff Hanson, their guidance counsellor. One of those women who insisted on 'going to the top.'

'Brian, I figured I should put you on warning—' Cliff strode into the room with an air of apology.

'What's up?' Brian leaned back in his chair. Cliff was good at his job. Laid-back, unpretentious, bright. He'd been with the school almost twenty years.

'We have a seven-year-old from Iraq—' Cliff dropped into a chair opposite Brian. 'The father was killed in Baghdad. The kid's mother fled with him to this country about a year ago. She had family over in Saratoga Springs. She found a job as a domestic here. Hassan is a sweet, earnest kid in a bilingual class. His mother came to me. He's afraid to come to school because he's being bullied by two sixth graders. Every morning she has to fight to get him on the school bus—'

'Do we know who the young bullies are?' Brian demanded.

'Hassan didn't want to talk, but I nailed them down. I have a meeting with the mothers of the two boys tomorrow afternoon.' Cliff grunted in distaste.

'So what's the problem?'

'One of the fathers is on the Board of Education.' Cliff was grim.

Brian whistled. 'That could be a problem,' he conceded. Not every member of the board had approved of his promotion to principal.

'I'll try to handle the situation, of course – but there's a strong chance they'll take the matter up to you.'

'Let's take it one step at a time. Give me a memo about it, Cliff. See what develops after your appointment with the two mothers.'

'The school board member is Jason Harris,' Cliff said pointedly. 'The guy who's been screaming for months about why the hell can't we manage on the school budget. He writhes at the possibility of school taxes rising.'

'We'll handle it.' Brian refused to be perturbed. 'We don't tolerate bullies in our school. No matter who their parents are.'

Cliff took off. Brian sat back, considered the situation. The son reflected the father, he thought with derision. Egotistical, nasty father – bullying son. A father who was furious at what he called 'the invasion of those damn Arabs.'

Ever since 9/11 there had been locals who resented the arrival in their midst of immigrants from the Middle East. He'd thought what had been a rough season right after the bombing of the Twin Towers had subsided. He was wrong.

Fifteen

A s Caren had anticipated, Danny slept most of the way to Saratoga Springs. Leaving the train, they quickly found a taxi. The driver directed them to the proper bus terminal.

'We're in for a real rainstorm,' the friendly driver told them. 'It's been threatening all day.'

By the time they arrived at the bus terminal, rain was pelting the sidewalks. *Why hadn't I thought to leave out umbrellas?*

'Hurry, Danny,' she coaxed, prodding him from the taxi.

Inside the lightly populated bus terminal they settled themselves on a bench. Danny's head on her shoulder. The wait seemed endless. Danny was too sleepy, too exhausted to think about food, Caren interpreted.

Their bus arrived on time. Caren coaxed Danny into wakefulness, and they boarded. Only a handful of fellow travelers, she noted. The bus pulled out of the terminal. The lights were lowered. Along with Danny, Caren dozed at intervals.

Then the bus was pulling into the outskirts of Primrose. An expanse of pleasant houses with well-kept plots lined each side of the road. Warm and cozy inside, Caren guessed, viewing the houses – some already dark for the night. People whose jobs required their rising early.

Further down was a mall, where only a handful of cars sat at this hour. Those belonging to employees, Caren surmised. Then they were passing a section of elegant homes, set on larger plots of land.

The large, sprawling complex of white brick buildings further down, she assumed, was the local school system – or township offices. Her heart began to pound.

Are the schools excellent – as the website claimed? Will

Danny have a rough time adjusting? He's only eight – the young are resilient. Will I find a job before our funds run out?

Now the bus was moving into what appeared to be the downtown business section. Physically – as Lila had described it – Primrose was a lovely town. The main thoroughfare was divided by an island of greenery. The stores seem well-maintained, attractive. The mall hadn't demoted the Main Street shops – there was an air of prosperity about them. Still, there was a vacancy here and there.

When they disembarked from the bus, Caren inquired about the locale of the Claridge Hotel.

'It's just three blocks down, right off Main Street,' a porter told her. 'But the rain's comin' down real hard. You might want to take a taxi. There's one waitin' for a customer.'

The Claridge Hotel was a six-story red-brick structure that rose high above neighboring stores. The lobby small but inviting. Off to one side was a 24-hour coffee shop available for guests, Caren noted.

She registered as Caren Stephens, her single name. She'd been amazed that married women in Iran – even Marty's staid mother – retained their single names. It had seemed so out of character. In Iran women were second-class citizens. Perhaps, she thought derisively, men felt women didn't deserve to share their names.

In minutes the friendly clerk had assigned them a room, summoned a bellhop to escort them there.

'Danny, are you hungry?' Caren asked solicitously when they were alone.

'No—' He was battling yawns, then reconsidered. 'Could I have some chocolate cake?'

'No more sweets today,' she scolded. 'But what about a grilled cheese sandwich – and a cup of hot chocolate?' she added with a placating smile.

'OK—' He sat on one bed – too tired to notice the chocolate mint on a pillow – and curled up in fetal position.

'I'll call down to the coffee shop, and—' She paused. He was already asleep.

Without disturbing him, Caren put him to bed. Food forgotten. She switched off the lamps lest they awaken him, went into the bathroom to read the copy of the *Primrose Sentinel* that had been left on the dresser.

First thing tomorrow morning they must look for a furnished apartment. And then she must find a job.

I can do this. I can raise Danny on my own. Raise him well. For Danny I can be strong.

While Caren and Danny ate breakfast sent up from the coffee shop, she considered the day's activities. Only one furnished apartment listed in the *Sentinel* – and she wasn't to call until 1 p.m. At this point she shuddered at the prospect of raiding her funds for furniture. For now it must be a furnished apartment. And the rent on this one seemed manageable.

The ad read 'close to town.' That was good because her driver's license had expired, and it would be imprudent to go on record as applying for a new license. Not that she could afford a car, she mocked herself.

Unless the apartment was monstrous, she'd rent it. Not much choice. She flinched, remembering the *Sentinel*'s 'help wanted' list. Nothing to which she could respond except for a part-time sales job. But she couldn't go job searching until they had an address and a phone.

She'd be aggressive, she vowed. She was young, strong, with college degrees. Not likely she'd land a teaching job, she warned herself. Whatever job was available, she would try for it.

'Mommie—' Uncertainty in Danny's voice. 'Are we going to live here?' He gazed about their hotel room in rejection.

'No, darling,' she comforted him. 'We're going to find ourselves an apartment. Maybe not today,' she conceded, contriving a bright smile. 'But we'll find a place in a few days – and then you can start in a fine new school.'

He stared at her in shock. 'I don't want to go to a new school!' Rebellion in his eyes. 'I want to go home.'

'We'll talk about that later—' *How do I make him understand we'll never go back to that life? Marty won't find us here. Nobody – not even Janis – knows we're here.* 'Right now you'll have a nice hot shower. The rain's stopped – the sun is shining. It's a glorious day. We'll go out.'

'Out where?' Defiance in his voice.

'We're going to – to the library,' she grasped at this. A glance at her watch told her it was minutes past ten a.m. Does the local library open at ten?

'Why?'

'We – we can't see what may be our apartment until later in the day – and you've never been to a library in Tehran.' Data flashed across her mind: there were fifty-two libraries in Tehran, twelve of which were open twenty-four hours a day. But the censors ruled. 'Once – before we went to Tehran – your nursery group visited a library – and you listened to a storyteller,' she recalled. 'You liked that.'

'I want to go home—' Now belligerence gave way to tears. 'Mommie, why can't we go home?'

Struggling to calm Danny, she enlisted his aid in collecting their luggage. Downstairs – in a moment of optimism – she told the desk clerk they were checking out but asked to leave their luggage for later pick-up. 'We may decide to stay another night,' she explained. *He can't figure us out.*

The public library was open. An inviting white brick building surrounded by masses of spring flowers. The children's room was charming. After a few moments of resistance Danny became intrigued.

'They've got a book about *Sesame Street*!' His eyes glowed.

'Later we'll get library cards for ourselves.' Danny gazed up at her in question. 'With a library card you can take out all the books you like. Take them home with you.' *The librarian wonders why Danny isn't in school. But I can't register him until we have an apartment.*

When Danny at last became restless, they left the library. It was still too early for lunch, too early to call about the apartment. They turned on to Main Street – still without a destination.

'Danny, how would you like a cup of hot chocolate?' she asked with a convivial smile.

'Now?' He was startled but pleased.

'Oh, look just ahead—' She pointed towards an attractive storefront. 'It's an Internet café.' *Could Janis have her website up already? She'd said, 'It'll be a breeze – I'll have my website up in less than twenty-four hours.'* 'I'm sure they'll have hot chocolate.'

'With whipped cream?' Always a special treat.

'Let's go find out.'

This was an off-hour, with only two tables occupied. But Caren could envision it late in the afternoon and well into the night. It would be a hang-out for teenagers and the early twenties crowd, she surmised.

On the other side of the room she noted the line-up of computers. Her heart pounded in anticipation. Maybe – just maybe – she'd find Janis's site up and working.

She waited until a friendly young waitress had brought Danny's hot chocolate – piled high with whipped cream – and her cappuccino. Now she walked across the room to the computers. Janis's domain name darting across her mind.

Her eyes focused on the monitor. Her fingers unsteady on the keyboard. Waiting, barely breathing, for a screen to announce that here was Janis's 'Letter to my sister Barbara.'

Oh dear God, it's here!

Hi Bobbie,

Wherever your reporting takes you now. We're all well here, busy with the garden. You remember my neighbor Nadine – the one whose niece left her husband in the middle of the night and moved with her two kids from Montreal to some little town in Vermont. Well, it's like a soap opera now. The husband has no idea where his wife and kids are – so he has some PI stalking Nadine. A blue Toyota keeps driving around the block – or parking down by that vacant parcel of land that's up for sale. This has been going on for the last twenty-four hours. Nadine thought about calling the police, but Al persuaded her to let it lie. Yesterday the PI came to her front door and asked to see her niece. She told him she had no idea where Beth was – which is true – but the jerk doesn't believe her.

Caren's throat tightened. Marty had a private investigator trying to track them down. Already! The PI was probably making life miserable for Janis and Ira.

But they don't know where we are. I'll make no contact that can be followed up. Marty will never think of Primrose

*– he never knew Lila. I never mentioned Primrose to him.
Did I?*

Fresh fear rolled over her like a tidal wave. But no, she
would have had no reason to mention Primrose. They were
safe here. They'd take roots. Danny would thrive.

She clung to the conviction that Primrose would be right
for them. She and Danny would never go back to Tehran.
But instinct warned her that tough days lay ahead.

Sixteen

Caren returned to the table. Marty's search would keep running into dead-ends. Janis could tell him nothing, would have no word from her that his PI could follow up. *We're safe. We've escaped Marty's control.*

Danny slurped his hot chocolate in momentary bliss. Her mind in high gear, Caren sipped at her cappuccino. Let the advertised apartment be right for them. She couldn't register Danny in school without a permanent address. She couldn't apply for a job without an address and a phone number.

She glanced at the wall clock, conferred with her watch as though hoping the clock was slow. It was too early to call about the apartment. How to waste the interim time?

Go to the little stationery store across the street, her mind ordered. Pick up school supplies for Danny. But he stared at her in sullen reproach when she struggled to interest him in this venture.

She was conscious of a chill darting through her body.

The battle now was to help Danny become his real self again. It would take time, yes – but he would be her sole concern. The young were resilient, she told herself again. He would go to a fine school, make friends. He'd forget the life they'd left behind.

Caren made a point of dallying over her small purchases. Eyes darting at intervals to her watch. All right, it was minutes before 1 p.m. Find a public telephone. Call about the apartment for rent.

A warm, mature, feminine voice responded. 'Hello. Mr Woods' residence.'

'I'm calling about your ad in this morning's *Sentinel*.' She tried to sound casual. 'Is the apartment still available?'

'Yes, it is. Would you like to see it?'

'Yes.' Caren hesitated a moment. 'Could I come over now?'

'Well, Mr Woods won't be home until six o'clock. I'm Hannah, his part-time housekeeper.' She seemed ambivalent. 'I guess it would be all right if I show it to you.'

'Oh, good.'

'It's at Fourteen Cypress Road.' Now Hannah gave specific directions. *She thinks we'll be driving.*

'We'll be walking,' Caren explained. 'Or would it be wiser to take a taxi?' They mustn't hold her up.

'Oh, it's just a ten-minute walk from town. But don't rush – I'll be here for the rest of the afternoon.'

Great! The apartment was close to town. Close to the supermarket she'd noticed earlier. There was sure to be a school bus. They could manage without a car.

'We'll be right there,' Caren said. 'My son and I.'

They moved away from Main Street, turning right on Elm Avenue. Small shops now gave way to what seemed an endless avenue of pleasant, modest houses. They turned right again – per Hannah's directions – on Cypress Road. Here the houses were more affluent – set on larger, landscaped plots. A mixture of colonials, ranches, and contemporaries.

A young St Bernard trotted towards them – tail wagging. Alone – not on a leash, Caren noted with momentary unease. But already Danny was engrossed in patting him. Yes, very soon she'd make sure Danny had a puppy of his own.

Someone must have divided one of these houses to accommodate an apartment, she surmised. Now trepidation invaded her. Would she and Danny be considered undesirable tenants because – at this point – she had no job? Not even a credit card. In today's world everybody had a credit card.

I'll offer to put up four months rent in advance. That should help, shouldn't it?

Now the St Bernard darted off in good-humored pursuit of a squirrel.

'Danny, the lady is waiting to show us the apartment,' she reminded. 'Let's get moving.'

The house – painted fire engine red with white trim – was a sprawling ranch with a deck across the front and was flanked by a pair of tall, spring budding elms. Daffodils lined a flagstone path that led up to the front door. Beds of tulips promised colorful blossoms very soon.

Walking up towards the entrance, Caren noted another door at the far left. That would lead to the apartment, she suspected. She was conscious of a sudden spurt of excitement. Was this to be their home in Primrose?

She pushed the doorbell, waited. *Let Danny not act up – not now.* The door was opened by a fifty-ish, rotund woman with a warm smile.

'You're Mrs Stephens,' she said and smiled at Danny. The 'Mrs' was in deference to Danny, Caren assumed. 'I'm Hannah. I have the key to the apartment.'

They walked to the apartment entrance. Hannah unlocked the door, pulled it open. 'You'll want to look around a bit,' she said. 'You won't mind if I leave you alone for a few minutes. I have chocolate cookies in the oven, about ready to come out. I wouldn't want to burn them.'

'Thank you.' Caren smiled at Danny. He'd heard the magic words – chocolate cookies.

The apartment was cozy, comfortably furnished, Caren decided as she walked with Danny from the living room to the pair of bedrooms. Once this had been one bedroom, she guessed – a wall had converted it to two.

'It's so little,' Danny said, frowning in distaste.

'Plenty of space for the two of us – and even for a puppy,' she added in sudden inspiration.

'We're going to have a puppy?' His face was joyful, almost disbelieving.

'Very soon,' she promised. 'As soon as you get settled in school.' He was frowning again – school meant permanency. That was frightening.

'Let me look at the kitchen appliances.' She pretended not to notice his fast change of mood. 'And the dishes and pots—'

She pretended to be absorbed in this task. She knew she would rent the apartment immediately – if the owner accepted her as a tenant.

'Hello—' Hannah called from the door. 'Have you any questions?'

'No, everything's fine,' Caren told her.

'I thought this little fella might like a chocolate cookie,' Hannah said. 'Is it all right?'

'He adores chocolate cookies—' Already Danny was extending a hand to receive the giant-sized cookie. 'Of course, we only have cookies on special occasions.' Caren took a deep breath. 'I'd like to rent the apartment – and move in right away. Danny and I are staying at the Claridge. I suppose you'll want a month's security in addition to the month's rent?'

'Oh—' Hannah seemed flabbergasted. 'I think I'd better call Brian – Mr Woods – and ask him how he wants to handle this. Excuse me – I'll be right back. Sit down and make yourself comfortable.'

Striving to appear casual, Caren sat down on the sofa while Danny settled himself on a hassock and nibbled happily at his cookie. Had she pushed too hard? *I want this apartment. I want to know we have a place to live – not just for a night but well into the future.*

In a few minutes Hannah returned to the apartment. Her face beaming.

'Mr Woods says you and Danny – ' she seemed pleased at knowing his name – 'can move right in. Give me a check just for a month's rent. No need for security – he never bothers with that.'

'I haven't established a checking account in town yet. Will traveler's checks be all right?' *Something is happening right. We'll sleep in our own apartment tonight!*

'Oh, sure,' Hannah told her and waited while she reached into her purse for her wad of traveler's checks – bought in London in the name of Caren Stephens. 'And if you have any problems, just ring the doorbell on the front door.'

'Thank you.' Her smile warm, Caren gave Hannah the traveler's checks. *Hannah is so nice – that's a good omen, isn't it?* 'We'll go back to the hotel now and bring over our luggage.'

'This is a good town,' Hannah told her. The glint in her eyes said she was curious about their presence in Primrose. 'You'll like it.'

'I was told about it by a friend who lived here many years ago,' Caren explained. Feeling compelled to offer this explanation.

'Oh?' Hannah's eyes bright with questions.

I shouldn't have mentioned that. 'Lila Jackson – that was her name before she married.'

'I remember a family named Jackson. They had two children – a boy and a girl,' Hannah recalled. 'Fine family.'

Caren glanced at Danny. He was at a window – fascinated by a pair of kittens cavorting on the front lawn. 'We've just come home after living in Iran for five years. It's so good to be here—'

She had to mention that, she comforted herself. She and Danny couldn't just pop into town with no explanation. And it was all right to mention Lila. In no way could that bring Marty on their trail.

'I'm sure you'll like living here,' Hannah told her. 'There's a nice young couple with a baby on our right, and a quiet older couple – the Murphys – on the left. They're away right now, visiting a daughter and her family.' Her eyes grew compassionate. 'My, what a change Primrose must be after spending all those years in a place like Iran.'

'It was a bad experience,' Caren said quietly. 'It's so good to be home.'

Seventeen

B rian sat at his desk and stared into space. Why did he feel disturbed about this new tenant? Hannah's words reverberated in his mind.

'*She seems a charming young woman – with a sweet little boy about eight or nine. I'm sure he won't be any trouble.*'

So she was a stranger in town – and she had a little boy. Why should he feel this sudden agonizing pain? But he knew why, he taunted himself a moment later. A little boy would be living in his house. A little boy about eight years old.

Was the baby Denise had been carrying a boy or girl? No one had told him. He or she would have been almost eight if Denise had carried full term. He'd been able to push that loss out of his mind except at unwary intervals. But now he'd go to bed every night – and he would remember.

Why did a woman with an eight-year-old boy just pop into Primrose this way? He should have told Hannah to say that he'd just rented to a colleague. The presence of a little boy beneath his roof would be a constant torment. But it was too late for that now.

Hannah said the woman was American but had been living in Iran for the past five years. Was she running from an abusive husband? People read about such cases. The world knew that life was horrific for women in much of the Middle East. Would the husband be able to trace her here? The town might have an ugly situation on its hands.

The TV and radio news, the newspapers and magazines were full of reports about Iran these days. About terrorists crossing the border into Iraq. An evil, arrogant administration was in power. An administration that loathed the United States. Each time he read of fresh ugliness, he uttered a silent prayer that their own administration wouldn't drag them into another bloody war beyond Iraq.

But be realistic, he reprimanded himself. He needed a new tenant to help meet the mortgage payments. And the demand for furnished apartments in this town was minuscule.

He'd told Hannah – from habit – not to bother asking for a month's security. But what was her financial situation? Would she be able to pay the rent? *I don't want to be in the position of having to evict a mother and child – but I can't afford to allow them to live here rent-free.*

What about the little boy? The son of an abusive father? He'd be coming to this school. Would he be a problem? Would his mother be difficult?

Stop worrying about the new tenant's financial situation. Most likely she left Iran with money. It would be a relief to have the rent money coming in each month, he told himself yet again. He'd been out of his mind to take on such a huge mortgage. Out of his mind to think the house could save his marriage. It never had a chance.

He hadn't missed the romantic undertones in Hannah's voice when she'd talked about the new tenant. Was everybody in Primrose anxious to see him remarried? Why was he blatantly pursued? It would never happen. Once was enough.

In his ageing Ford, Brian turned into his driveway. He felt a rush of caution. Oh yes, his tenants had moved in already. Soft lights glowed in the living room behind the drapes left by the previous tenants. He smiled, remembering how the two men – Jack and Harvey – had added artistic touches to the apartment that would never have occurred to him.

He remembered now that Hannah had said the new tenant – her name was Stephens – had no car. 'I offered her a key to the garage – ' a two car garage – 'but she said she didn't have a car.' Had she ever lived in a small town like this – where a car was essential? Only their small influx of immigrants managed to live without a car.

Out of the car and approaching the house, Brian was aware of classical music filtering from the radio. A Beethoven sonata. Thank God, she wasn't into hard rock. Denise had drawn complaints from the very nice Murphy family living next door because every minute she was in the house hard rock assaulted their ears. He, too, had loathed it.

He walked into the house, headed for the kitchen. More conscious than usual that his house had been divided for double residency. How much trouble could one woman and a little boy be? But he couldn't shake off the suspicion she was running from an abusive husband. An irate Iranian husband, who might trail her here.

Hannah had left two nights dinner for him as usual. He'd heat up this evening's share, transfer it to a plate, eat in front of the TV while he watched the first of the evening news. That was self-inflicted punishment, he jeered at himself. How often was the news good?

With his tea – only in the morning did he take time to make coffee – he'd dig into the batch of chocolate cookies Hannah said she'd baked today. Now Hannah would be back on her two afternoons a week schedule. That would please her husband. He said it made him feel like a poor provider when his wife went out to work – even part-time.

No meeting of any kind tonight, he remembered with a sigh of relief while he stirred his chicken stew lest it stick to the skillet. He'd be able to work tonight on his article for the *Sentinel*. People in town must be made aware of the development Mayor Davis was trying to push through. It was unconscionable to try to throw people out of their homes that way. Most of them senior citizens.

In the living room he set up a snack table before his favorite armchair. He settled down to watch the news while he ate. Like millions of Americans across the country, he thought with wry humor.

The music in the apartment was muted, barely audible. A pleasant background for the news, he told himself. But while he sipped his tea and made a pretense of watching the news, he heard the little boy crying piteously in the apartment. But any little kid crying in the night sounded pitiful.

Five years in Iran, and now the poor little guy must adjust to a whole new life. That could be rough . . .

Eighteen

Caren lay sleepless – assaulted by questions. Finally, Danny had cried himself to sleep in his tiny bedroom while she sat, agonized, beside him. Had it been a mistake to try to move him into a new, strange world? But what kind of life lay ahead for him in Iran? If he survived whoever was out to harm Marty and him.

Each morning when Danny left for school, she'd worried. So Danny and Marty traveled with a bodyguard – what assurance was that of a safe trip? With terrifying frequency innocent people were killed in Iran. She'd been consumed with fear. No, fleeing from Iran had been the right move.

In the morning she would go with Danny to Primrose Elementary School and have him registered. She had his birth certificate and a record of early childhood shots and vaccinations. No school records – but that was understandable.

She flinched as she recalled how the Muslim clerics warned against polio vaccinations. There were wise doctors who provided these in secret. Most Americans considered polio as being eliminated. But now, she'd read, it was spreading among third world nations.

Danny would be startled by many things he encountered here at home, she cautioned herself – fighting anxiety. But he'd have no problem holding his own in the classroom. He was bright and eager to learn. She'd tutored him well.

In Tehran the schools were segregated by sex. Boys in one school, girls in another. At his preschool group there were boys and girls together. His special friend in those days had been a little British girl named Cindy.

Back in Iran she'd made a point in celebrating Christmas – which in early days Marty had enjoyed but later considered abhorrent. This past Christmas she and Danny had set up the Christmas tree in her bedroom again because Marty was nervous about its being seen in the living room.

'Suppose one of the servants reports us to the Morals Police?' he'd demanded. 'This is a Muslim country.'

Their domestic help would never do that, she was convinced. Still, around Christmas time she contrived to keep the household staff out of her bedroom. She remembered Danny's delight while they decorated the tree – with the ornaments brought from the Westchester house.

'Mommie, it's so pretty.' His face transfixed. Each year was the same. Danny was enthralled with the tree decorations, handled each tree decoration lovingly.

'And in the morning you'll open your presents,' she'd promised. An activity Marty ignored.

Her bedroom had become a small sanctuary – apart from the rest of the house. This was where she tutored Danny in math and English – as it was taught in American schools. She was recurrently unnerved that Marty refused to allow her to have a computer. She wrote and received e-mails – always to or from Janis – on Pari's computer.

From the time Danny was three, he'd been exposed to computers at his preschool group. Then the change to the Orthodox religious school. No computers there. Marty had approved of this.

'I don't want Danny to see the obscene material that comes through the Internet. He's a little boy – he doesn't need that filth.' The Internet brought the outside world into Iran. That the fundamentalist Administration tried to block.

She and Marty had agreed before Danny was born that he would choose his religion when he was grown. He was to be raised in his mother's faith, but he'd learn about Islam. By the end of their first year in Iran Marty had trampled on this understanding. His mantra etched on her brain.

'Being a Christian in Iran is dangerous.' Despite the Iranian constitution's declaration that each group had the right to practice its own religion. 'It would wreck my career if it became known my wife and son were practicing Christians. And it's unsafe.'

She knew that both Christians and Jews lived in constant

fear of abuse and arrest. At intervals their homes and places of worship were destroyed. In certain areas Christian and Jewish businesses were required to indicate their religious affiliation at the entrance to their shops or offices.

She recalled the furor several years ago when thirteen Jews were accused of spying for Israel. One a sixteen-year-old boy – because he sent e-mails to someone in Israel. Janis had sent her an eloquent article from the *New York Times*.

The article reported that Iranian Jews – for the most part – felt it wiser to avoid discussion about the matter. But Ira said that Jews had lived in Iran for 2,500 years. A few remained.

For the last three years Danny had been suffocating in his Orthodox religious school, Caren agonized. In time, she vowed, he would learn to love his own country. He'd be a happy little boy again. Nobody smiled, nobody laughed in Iranian schools. Iranians were a somber people. Even Ayatollah Khomeini was said to have declared, 'There is no fun in Iran.'

Exhausted from her first full day in Primrose, Caren at last fell into nightmarish slumber. When her clock alarm shrieked its wake-up call in the morning, she awoke with startled awareness of lying in a strange bed – in a strange room.

Danny could sleep another forty-five minutes, she told herself. It would be wise not to arrive as school opened. Half an hour later, when all the kids were settled in their class-rooms, she decided.

How would Danny react? He'd be scared, bewildered, she tormented herself. But Marty had early trained him to accept what he was told to do. Because if he failed, Daddy wouldn't love him, she thought with fresh rage.

She heard sounds in the other part of the house. Mr Woods was an early riser. Hannah – as she'd introduced herself – said he was the principal at the elementary school. Danny's elementary school, she realized. Would she meet him when she registered Danny? No. She'd learned in a phone call that she was to go to the office of the guidance counsellor to have Danny registered.

She remembered now what Hannah had said about their

landlord: '*Mr Woods is a fine man – you'll like him. He's a widower. Just as nice as he can be.*'

In nightgown and slippers Caren went into the bathroom – where a tub had been an afterthought, she gathered – and prepared for the day. A quick shower this morning – where in Tehran she'd lingered long most days, as though seeking escape under the pounding water.

Out of the shower she dressed quickly. Her wardrobe was limited, she reminded herself. Keep her suit for job-hunting. Casual for around town today.

She settled on jeans and a smoky-blue cotton turtleneck. Wear her suede jacket when they left the house. No jewelry. Certainly not her wedding ring.

She went into the kitchen to put up water for a cup of tea. Standing by to remove the kettle from the flame before it could awaken Danny. At the first wisp of a whistle she reached for the kettle, poured into one of a set of attractive mugs. Let the tea steep for five minutes.

Now she planned her day. See Danny registered in school. Go to the bank to establish savings and checking accounts. She'd noted two banks right on Main Street. Gas and electric were included in the rental. Yesterday, she had spoken with the phone company.

Would the bank demand identity? She felt a moment of panic. What could she show? Her passport, she pinpointed – issued to Caren Stephens. That should be sufficient. If not, then she would manage somehow.

Today she must buy a computer. Again she worried that Danny had not been near a computer since he was almost six. How much would he remember? In this country students from kindergarten on used computers in their classrooms.

The computer would keep her close to Janis and the family, she remembered with a surge of gratitude. Her precious lifeline to them. Marty's private investigators could never track her down through Janis's website. It had been established under a fabricated name.

Yesterday she'd shopped with Danny at the local supermarket right in town. They had food in the apartment for the next three or four days. She dropped two slices of bread in the toaster. She'd have breakfast at the bistro table in the tiny dining area between the closet kitchenette and the living room.

While she lingered over a second cup of tea, she heard a car pull out of the driveway. Mr Woods, going off to school, she assumed. So early in the morning? Or perhaps he was heading for a favorite restaurant for a leisurely breakfast before a heavy school day.

From inquiries she'd made at the newspaper store, she understood there was one large school complex in Primrose with separate buildings for elementary, middle school and high school levels. Additional schools were set up in outlying sections of the town. Hannah had told her that Mr Woods was the principal at the main elementary school. A nice, fatherly figure for their landlord, she thought in approval.

'Mommie?' Terror in Danny's voice. 'Mommie?'

'I'm here, darling—' She hurried to Danny's room. He sat upright in bed. Shoulders hunched in what she recognized as fear. 'Would you like pancakes for breakfast?' Her smile cajoling.

He hesitated. 'With syrup?'

'With syrup. And you must brush your teeth very well afterwards.' Let this seem like a normal morning. 'First, you shower. By the time you're out, the pancakes will be ready.'

With Danny under the shower, Caren returned to the kitchen, began the breakfast ritual.

What is Danny thinking? Does he realize that this morning we'll be going to register him at school? I'll have to explain that at breakfast.

Faster than she'd anticipated, she heard the water stop in the bathroom. Danny had turned off the shower and was heading for the bedroom to dress. She flipped over the pancakes, poured orange juice, brought out the bottle of maple syrup. *Please God, let things go well at the school.*

Danny emerged from the bedroom. Questions in his eyes.

'Sit down and have your breakfast, darling,' she ordered. 'I'm making another pancake for me.'

'Just one?' But he was inspecting his own stack with approval.

'I had toast earlier,' she explained. 'One is about all I can handle.'

'The syrup's good,' he said, digging into the pancakes.

'That's real maple syrup. When I was a little girl, we used to drive up to Vermont for two weeks every summer. Your grandmother used to buy a huge gallon can of maple syrup to see us through the rest of the year.' Mom and Dad would have been such loving grandparents, she mourned for the hundredth time. They would have adored Danny.

She came to the table with her pancake, reached for the syrup.

'Would you like to watch *Sesame Street* before we leave?' she asked enticingly.

He froze. 'Where are we going?'

'Over to Primrose Elementary,' she explained with false brightness. 'To get you registered in school.'

His face was drained of color. 'I don't want to go to school. Not here—'

'Danny, you'll love this school—' Her eyes clung to him. He'd laid down his fork.

'I feel sick,' he whispered. 'I don't want any more pancakes.'

Nineteen

Caren fought against panic. *I knew this would be a traumatic moment. Deal with it.*

'I'll fix you a cup of mint tea,' she cajoled. 'You'll feel better in a few minutes. Then we'll go—'

'I don't want to go to school! I want to go home!' His small face tightened in rejection. His eyes defiant.

'Darling, this school will be a lot like your preschool group.' Only English spoken, no long hours of memorization without comprehension. 'Don't you remember what fun it was? Remember how you liked everybody? Remember your special friend Cindy?'

'I don't want to go to school—' No tears. Just stubborn rebellion.

'You said you'd love to have a puppy,' she wheedled. 'Once you're settled in school, then we can go over to the ASPCA and you can choose your own puppy.'

He frowned in concentration for a moment. 'When can I have a puppy?' he challenged. 'Tomorrow?'

'No. After you've been in school for a month. Then I'll know you're big enough to take on that responsibility.' Caren's eyes searched his. Her heart pounding.

His gaze wavered. She could sense the inner battle being waged in his brain.

'OK,' he capitulated. 'I'll go school. Tomorrow—'

'Today,' she said with a bright smile. 'Just for registration. And exactly one month from today we'll go for your puppy.'

Twenty minutes after the beginning of classes Caren and Danny sat in the office of the guidance counsellor, who handled the registration of new students.

'You have Daniel's birth certificate?' Mr Hanson asked.

'Yes—' Caren pulled it from her purse, handed it to Hanson.

He glanced briefly at the certificate, turned with a warm smile to Danny. 'I suppose everybody calls you Danny?'

'Yes, sir—' *He's trying so hard to accept this. Please God, let him be happy here.*

'Would it be all right for him to begin classes in the morning?' Caren asked. It would be traumatic for him to walk into a classroom now – with a barrage of eyes inspecting him. 'We've had a long trip.' She'd explained they'd come here from Iran. 'Danny still has jet lag.'

'That'll be fine,' Hanson agreed. 'We'll see you in the morning, Danny.' He turned to Caren. 'Bring him here to the office ten minutes before classes begin. Someone will show him around, then get him to his classroom in time. And you'll be briefed on the school bus schedules.' And then came the weekend – two days away from school, Caren reminded herself. That would be good.

Caren and Danny left the school. She sensed his inner misgivings as they walked out into the brilliant morning sunlight.

'Danny, let's go shop for a computer.' Her smile was full of promise. *I must have a computer – it's my lifeline to Janis. A new letter every week, she promised. It'll be like reaching out and touching her. I'll feel less alone – less insecure.* 'Don't you remember using the computer with your preschool group? You thought it was a lot of fun.'

'I sorta remember—' His voice trailed off.

It had secretly infuriated her that Marty kept his computer locked in his home office. Away from Danny – away from her.

The Internet was the Iranians' contact with the outside world, Caren remembered compassionately. Known to the authorities as a 'cultural invasion', along with foreign television.

'Where do you buy a computer?' Danny was curious now.

'In a computer store,' Caren told him, her mind charging ahead. As though living in a hostile world, she jeered at herself, she carried a huge amount of traveler's checks in her purse. 'But first,' she said in sudden determination, 'we're going to the bank and open two accounts. Savings and checking.' Danny gazed at her, trying to comprehend what she was saying.

Dear God, he has so much to learn! When Janis and I were little kids, Mom took us to the bank so we could each open a minuscule savings account. It was part of growing up in the modern world.

'Mommie, what's a savings account?'

While they walked in the direction of a bank she'd noticed earlier on Main Street, Caren explained to him about savings accounts and checking accounts, then told him about credit cards. When she and Janis started college, Dad had arranged for each of them to have a credit card – 'for emergencies.'

She was unnerved when a bank officer refused to allow her to open accounts because she didn't have two photo IDs.

'Sorry,' the woman bank officer said in cool disapproval. 'Your passport alone is insufficient.' *Does she think I'm a terrorist with laundered money?*

Hiding her anger, she marched with Danny to the second bank. Here she belatedly remembered her expired New York driver's license – carried always out of sentiment. She was able to open savings and checking accounts – both in trust for Danny. He listened avidly to these transactions. Curiosity was an offensive trait in his religious school.

A clerk at the newspaper store directed them to the computer shop. Except for e-mails to Janis via Pari's computer, she hadn't used a computer in five years, Caren realized. Pari called her computer 'an antique.' What changes must have developed in the past five years!

A friendly salesman guided her through the purchase. After urgent persuasion delivery was promised in mid-afternoon. Now – with the salesman's guidance – she bought two computer games for Danny.

Will Janis have a new letter on her website? It isn't a week, but these are critical times. I knew Marty would find a way to harass her. I didn't want that to happen – but she understands. Marty knows Danny and I aren't there. Why is his PI hounding Janis?

After a leisurely lunch at a pleasant restaurant on Main Street, Caren and Danny returned to their new apartment.

'The salesman said the computer will be delivered by mid-afternoon,' she told Danny. 'And a technician will arrive shortly afterwards to set up everything for us.' *The computer will be a diversion for Danny – he has the two games I bought for him.* 'We'd better be there in case it arrives a little earlier.'

Keep Danny involved in this. Let him not fret about starting school in the morning.

She was delighted that Danny was so full of questions about the computer.

'In this country from kindergarten on children use computers in their classrooms,' she told him. 'For all kinds of things. And you've got two computer games,' she enticed him.

His eyes widened. 'You'll teach me how to play the games?'

'I promise.'

He's beginning to remember when he played computer games back in his preschool group. They'd had a variety of software, designed for the 3–6 age group.

The delivery man arrived with cartons containing the computer, keyboard, monitor, and printer. Danny gazed at them in wonder.

'All these things for a computer?' he asked.

Minutes later the store's technician arrived. Danny was enthralled as he watched his mother and the technician decide on the most practical area in the small apartment as suitable for a computer station. Then the actual setting up began.

Caren had been pleasantly surprised at how quickly her phone service was turned on. Grateful that the technician would be able to set up and test the modem to make sure she would have no problems accessing the Internet. Unfortunately, she thought wryly, high-speed Internet service was not in their budget.

For a moment she felt a twinge of doubt. But they must have a phone. Marty's investigators wouldn't be able to trace a new phone listing in a little town in upstate New York – especially since she'd asked for an unlisted number.

When they were alone again, Caren piled cushions on a chair before the computer and ordered Danny to sit. As though stepping into a fantastic wonderland, Danny made his new acquaintance with the computer world.

'That's all for today,' Caren decreed at last. 'I'll start dinner. You can watch TV for a while.' She headed for the television set – confident that the local PBS channel would have cartoons at this hour. For a moment she felt as though they'd never been away from home.

Danny would go to sleep early this evening, she told herself while she prepared dinner. Already he was yawning at intervals. So much was happening, so fast!

By 8 p.m. Danny was asleep. Already she tried to gear herself for tomorrow morning. Would the promise of a puppy be enough of an incentive to persuade him to go to school without fresh trauma?

Assured that Danny was asleep, she closed the door to his tiny bedroom and went to the computer. In moments she was at Janis's website. Yes! There was a new letter. Janis hadn't waited a week.

Hi Bobbie,

We're all busy getting ready for Jimmy's birthday party on Sunday. He insisted his birthday cake be chocolate 'inside and out.' I guess chocolate is a family obsession. And the soap opera next door continues. Nadine came over, all excited, last night. They'd been out for the day, and she had the uncanny sense that someone had been in the house. Guess what? The house had been bugged. You know Ira – he's knowledgeable about all that stuff. We went over to Nadine's, and he found, then removed all but one bug. He told her that she and her husband should talk about her niece and the fact that they worry because they don't know where she is. Maybe that'll convince the PI she doesn't know where her niece and the two kids are.

Janis rambled on a bit, to make it appear that the Nadine incident was just one small part of her life. But Caren understood. Marty's private investigator had invaded Janis's house. Wasn't that a felony? But that wouldn't bother Marty.

All right, maybe now the insanity would stop. The PI

would report that Janis had no knowledge of the whereabouts of Danny and her. Maybe – just maybe – Marty would abandon his search.

Dealing with private investigators was time-consuming. He was obsessed by the business and his political ties – he always complained when anything else invaded his life. Yet – deep in her heart – she was sure Marty would persist in trying to track them down.

I must be so cautious. No driver's license. No e-mails to Janis. No trail that Marty's PI can pick up. But this has become such a small world. How safe are Danny and I here in Primrose?

Twenty

Over breakfast Caren kept up a lively conversation about the computer game that had fascinated Danny the previous evening. When they heard a pair of dogs barking close by, she talked about the puppy Danny would pick out for himself very soon now. Terrified that – at the last moment – Danny would fight against going to school this morning.

Poor baby, he's so scared. But going into a new school is traumatic for all small children.

She breathed a sigh of relief when they left the house with no repercussions. A glorious sunlit morning, fragrant with the scent of spring flowers. Unseasonably warm – almost a summer day.

'It's just a fifteen-minute walk,' she told Danny. 'But Monday the school bus will stop for you right at this corner.'

'Suppose they don't stop?' Danny challenged.

'Oh, but they will.' Her smile was reassuring. 'Today I'll pick you up at the school. I'll explain that you won't be taking the bus. I thought we ought to celebrate your first day at your school here. But no more chocolate ice cream until Sunday a week,' she warned. His once-a-week treat since he was three.

'Where will you be?' His eyes were fearful. 'Suppose I miss you?'

'I'll be right at the entrance – where everybody leaves to go on the bus. I'll be there,' she insisted. Her voice softened. 'Don't you trust me?'

'OK.' But he reached for her hand. She felt his anxiety at this first day at a new school.

Twenty minutes later – after seeing him settled in his class-room and being introduced to his teacher – Caren left the school. Danny would be fine, she promised herself. But anxiety tugged at her.

She picked up a copy of the *Sentinel* at the Main Street newspaper store. She debated a moment, walked into the little restaurant three doors down. She'd have a cup of coffee, see what the 'help wanted' columns offered.

Is Danny all right? Is he still scared? His teacher understands the situation – that we've returned home after five years in Iran. That a new school is a terrifying situation.

Over coffee she forced herself to study the brief 'help wanted' column in the *Sentinel*. Again, the job listings were depressing. Nothing to which she could respond. No chance of landing a teaching job in the middle of the year. *Take whatever comes along.*

Feeling at loose ends – constantly worrying about Danny's reaction to his new school – she returned to the apartment, headed straight for the computer. So it was stupid, she chided herself – but she wanted to read Janis's letter again. It was touching base.

The day seemed endless. At ten minutes before 3 p.m. – school dismissal time – she was waiting at the elementary school entrance for Danny. Before returning to the apartment, she decided, she and Danny would go to the *Sentinel* office. She'd place a 'position wanted' ad for the Sunday edition. In a small town like this advertising rates should be low.

Despite her bright smile, her heart was pounding while she waited for Danny to appear. He would be startled by the exhilarated surge of students – boys and girls together – emerging from classrooms. Such high-spirited departures would not be tolerated in Iranian schools.

She was astonished to see a pair of ten-year-old girls wearing headscarves, giggling and exchanging conversation with another student who wore a cross on a chain.

Now Danny – knapsack in place – was walking in her direction with an air of apprehension, then relief as he spied her. *He fits right in with these kids. This is where he belongs.*

'Hi, Mommie—' He reached for her hand.

'How was school today?' *Dare I ask?*

'When can we go home?' His tone plaintive.

'Darling, we've only been here a couple of days. And you want your puppy,' she reminded.

'Two kids laughed when I didn't know how to do what they were doing on the computer.' His small face etched with a blend of anger and humiliation.

'That was very rude. But you'll learn. I'll help,' she promised. *His teacher knows the situation. She seemed warm – compassionate. Should I have a talk with her?*

'You said I could have chocolate ice cream after school.' His eyes were challenging as he clutched at this momentary enjoyment.

They went to the small, colorful ice-cream shop that provided several small tables and chairs and sat down to have this special afternoon treat. From there they walked to the nearby *Sentinel* office, where Caren placed her ad for the Sunday edition.

'Now let's go home—' Her smile reassuring. 'You'll have homework to do.'

'Not much,' he admitted in surprise. 'Nothing to memorize.' He paused, as though unsure about proceeding along this line. 'They don't teach the Koran.' Defiance in his voice. 'They're infidels.'

'Danny, they're not infidels.' She struggled to conceal her exasperation. *How many times must I explain this to him?* 'Here in the United States – and in England and in many other countries – people have the right to practice their own religion. To teach you that anyone not a Muslim is an infidel is terribly wrong.'

She'd managed through the years to teach him a bit about Christianity. He celebrated Christmas and Easter with her. Marty and she had agreed before he was born that their child would follow her religion – but that was tossed aside in Tehran.

Danny was already on another track. He was laughing at the antics of what appeared to be a mixture of collie and golden retriever who was ecstatically kissing his young master.

'Look at him!' Danny glowed. 'I want a dog like him.'

'Oh, yes, he's great,' Caren approved. A safe topic. 'So playful—'

They walked in the direction of their apartment, turned on to Cypress Road. Their apartment just ahead. All at once Caren froze. Her throat tightened. Though the afternoon was unseasonably warm, she was ice-cold.

Who is that man trying to break into our apartment? Tugging at a side window! He knows the people next door are away – he thinks nobody sees him. Marty's private investigator! How did he find us?

'Mommie?' Danny was puzzled that she wasn't walking. That she seemed frozen in place. 'Mommie?' Now his gaze followed hers. 'Who's that man?' Now her air of alarm was reaching out to him. 'What's he doing?'

'He – he's a burglar,' she fabricated, fighting panic.

Danny and I can't stay here – we have to get away. He hasn't seen us. He must be one of Marty's private investigators! But this is the United States – he can't just grab Danny and take him back to Tehran.

'Mommie?' As always in moments of fear, Danny reached for her hand. 'Is he trying to steal our new computer?'

'We're going to the house across the way—' She pointed to a much-glassed contemporary. 'Where the lady is out on the deck doing something with the flower pots. We'll ask to use her phone to call the police.' *The police will come and arrest him, take him away. I'll pack up our things – we'll get out of here. Take the first bus leaving the terminal – no matter where it's going.*

With his hand in hers, she and Danny raced to the house across the road. Her heart pounding. Her mind in turmoil.

The young woman rose from the huge flower pot where she'd been working. 'Hi—'

'I'm Caren Stephens and this is Danny,' she said breathlessly. 'We've just moved into the apartment in Mr Woods' house.'

'Oh, how lovely.' She smiled down at Danny for an instant. 'I'm Kathy Bernstein—'

'Kathy, may I use your phone? It's weird – but somebody's trying to break into our apartment! I must call the police!'

Twenty-One

Kathy gaped at Caren in shock, reached for the front door. 'Go right inside – there's a phone in the living room to the right. I can't believe this is happening in broad daylight—'

'Thank you—' Holding on to Danny, Caren charged into the house.

'Oh, no—' Kathy's voice followed her a moment later. 'Caren, wait!'

Caren paused in alarm. 'What is it?'

'That isn't a burglar,' Kathy said gently. 'That's Brian – he's replacing a screen in a window. Brian Woods, your landlord,' she explained.

Not Marty's private investigator! Caren was dizzy with relief. 'But he's a young man,' she stammered. 'I thought Mr Woods was—'

'You know he's the elementary school principal,' Kathy interpreted, 'and you assumed he was an older man. Brian's thirty-four, I believe.' *And principal of the elementary school? How did he move up so fast?* 'He takes such good care of the house. He probably figured with today so warm you might want to open windows. A screen must have needed replacing. Why don't we sit out on the side deck and cool off with some lemonade?'

'Oh, that would be nice.' Caren forced a smile. 'How could I have made such an absurd mistake?'

'It was a natural assumption,' Kathy comforted, leading Caren and Danny around to the side deck, where a huge umbrella provided shade for the table and chairs beneath. 'I gather you haven't met him yet. Hannah must have handled your rental.'

'Yes, she did.' Caren strived for calm.

'Hannah's a doll,' Kathy said, and Caren nodded in agreement.

The two women chuckled as Danny swooped down on a fluffy white kitten snoozing on the deck.

'Danny, don't bother her,' Caren scolded. 'She's—'

'That's all right,' Kathy broke in. 'That's Daisy. She's seven months old – and adores being patted. She thinks all laps were made for her to sit in.'

'She's beautiful.' *Danny's all involved with Daisy – I can talk freely to Kathy.* 'We've moved here from Tehran—' Kathy's face brightened with curiosity. 'We'd lived there since Danny was three.' Her voice dropped to a whisper. 'It was a terrible environment for a little boy. For anybody,' she added with a shudder.

'I can imagine—' Kathy exuded sympathy. *She's too polite to ask questions.*

'My college room-mate lived here when she was a little girl. She told me it was a wonderful town. I decided on impulse that we'd live here.' *That's my story for anybody who's curious. And it's true.*

'I've never lived anywhere else,' Kathy seemed almost wistful. 'Except for my college years at Swathmore – in Pennsylvania. But let me bring out the lemonade. This is turning into a real summer day.'

Here were moments of beautiful peace, Caren told herself. Sitting on Kathy's deck and watching Danny play with Daisy – awake and eager to be friends. Moments to be cherished.

An SUV pulled up before the house. Two little girls emerged in high spirits. About seven and nine, she estimated. Playmates for Danny, she told herself in a spurt of optimism. He'd had no playmates in Tehran – not since he'd been part of the preschool group.

The little girls were running up to the front door while the driver of the SUV waited to see them home. Moments later Caren heard them in avid conversation with Kathy.

'Let's all go out on the deck and have lemonade,' Kathy was saying. 'And you'll meet our new neighbors across the road. A very nice little boy and his mother.'

Danny stiffened, hurried to Caren's side as the other three

emerged. Kathy introduced her daughters – Laurie and Cindy, then introduced Caren and Danny to them.

'What grade are you in?' Cindy, the younger, asked Danny. *Does he remember his friend Cindy at the preschool group?*

'Third,' Danny mumbled, avoiding eye contact.

'Who's your teacher?' Laurie demanded.

'I don't know her name.' He was almost hostile.

'All right, let's all sit down and have our lemonade.' Tray in tow, Kathy rushed in to lighten the atmosphere. 'What happened in your after-school group?' she asked her daughters, but both were too involved with the newness of Danny to reply.

'There's an after-school group?' Caren's face lighted. That would be a huge help once she was in a job.

'Brian started the after-school sessions about three years ago.' She chuckled in recall. 'He shamed the teaching staff to contribute time to handle this. He said so many mothers work these days an after-school group was essential. He couldn't bear the thought of latchkey kids in a town like ours.'

'That was thoughtful of him.'

'I go in to Howie's office from time to time to help out. He's a lawyer,' Kathy said. 'And even when I don't need the after-school group as babysitter, the girls go there anyway. It took a lot of pushing, but Brian got it through.'

'He's a hard-driving man.' In a good way, Caren told herself. Not like Marty.

'He himself holds an English-as-a-second-language group one evening a week at the public library for adults.' All at once she was somber. 'We've acquired a small community of immigrant families. But not everybody in town approves.'

Caren hesitated, making sure that Danny was involved in playing with Daisy. 'A Muslim community?' *Why am I afraid of that? They'd have no contact with Marty.*

'Oh, it's very mixed. Hispanics, Chinese, one Bulgarian family. We have just four Muslim families. Two are third generation Americans. The other two arrived just in the past year. Very friendly and bright. The two little girls wear head-scarves.' Kathy's smile was indulgent. 'The girls and their parents are becoming very much a part of our multicultural community.' But not everybody approved, Kathy had said. Not quite the town Lila had described.

Danny was becoming restless, unable – or unwilling – to relate to Cindy and Laurie. *He'll have to learn to play with other children again.*

'It's been fun to spend time with you all,' Caren said with a grateful smile. *I made such an ass of myself – assuming Brian Woods was a burglar.* 'But Danny and I should be getting home. Thanks for the lemonade.'

Walking across the road to their apartment – Brian Woods nowhere in sight now – Caren asked herself if Danny had noticed the two little girls in headscarves at school. A jolting reminder of his life in Tehran.

Little girls in headscarves in Primrose, she marveled. Adult English-as-a-second-language classes at the public library. Probably bilingual teachers in the school system. In truth, this was becoming one world.

From habit Danny sat down with his school books, prepared to do his homework in this pre-dinner hour. In the tiny kitchen – just a few feet away – Caren began to prepare dinner. Music from the classical radio station she'd discovered drifted into the apartment.

'Do you have a lot of homework?' Caren asked, fighting anxiety about his coping ability.

'No.' Again he was somber. 'It's easy.' A faint hint of triumph in his voice now. 'It's stuff you taught me a long time ago.' Probably weeks ago, she interpreted – she'd followed third grade classwork in American schools.

'Good,' she approved.

'What was that thing Laurie was wearing about her neck – on a chain? It looked like a funny kind of star.'

'It's a religious symbol,' Caren explained. 'Like the Hand of Fatima that some women and little girls wear back in Iran. Ziba wears a silver Hand of Fatima pendant.' All at once Caren felt a wall slide up between Danny and herself. *Why did I say that? How stupid of me!*

'What kind of religious symbol was Laurie wearing?' His eyes were hostile.

'It's a star of David,' Caren said, striving to sound casual. 'Kathy and her family are Jewish.'

Danny gaped in horror. 'They're bad. They'll never go to Paradise!'

'The Muslims call it Paradise—' Caren sought for words. 'To other religions it's called heaven. And Muslims and Christians and Jews will all go there if they live good lives.' *Why do some clerics in Iran distort Islam?* Again, she reminded herself that the Koran preached tolerance and understanding.

'I never knew any Jews,' Danny said with distaste.

'Darling, of course you have. Your Uncle Ira – he's Jewish.' She winced at his shocked reaction. 'The way you are half-Muslim and half-Christian, Aunt Janis and Uncle Ira's kids – Jimmy and Diane – are half-Christian and half-Jewish. When you're all grown up, you can decide which faith to follow. Muslims, Christians, and Jews all believe in one God.'

'But they won't go to Paradise. That's what Daddy told me!' Danny's face was set in rebellion. 'You won't go to Paradise,' he accused and began to cry.

'Darling, you mustn't think that way—' She deserted the range to rush to his side. 'I'll always be with you, Danny. Nothing can ever separate us.'

With Danny in bed – and clinging to the knowledge that there would be no school until Monday morning, Caren went to the computer. Deriding herself for what she dubbed her nightly fix – a reread of Janis's letter on her website. A sort of touching home, she told herself.

A new letter came up on the computer. She stiffened in alarm. *What's happening?*

> Hi Bobbie,
>   We're still busy getting ready for Jimmy's birthday party on Sunday. More names added to the invitation list at the last moment! What happened to the old birthday cake and ice-cream scene? We're having that, of course, plus pizza – 'with everything' – and a vegetable chili for those who might not like pizza. Remember? That was Jimmy until he was five and went

to a party where pizza was served and he was embarrassed not to eat it. Voila, a convert.

Oh, and the latest problem that's hit Nadine. Her niece's husband is running an ad in local newspapers within a seventy-five-mile radius of here. He's offering a $10,000 reward for information leading to finding his wife and kids. Thank God, Nadine said, he has no photos. Her niece took everything with her. Nadine says they're not to worry. Her niece is nowhere near our area.

Janis closed with casual reports about school activities, what was happening on her job and Ira's. But Caren was shaken. Marty was offering a $10,000 reward for information leading to their whereabouts.

But that was in a handful of small communities at the other side of the country. No photos of either Danny or herself. She clung to this knowledge. She'd taken every snapshot, every photo from the scrapbooks. Marty had none. Janis would say, 'He's spinning his wheels.'

Janis said 'not to worry.' She clung to these words. Janis was cool in crisis situations – she saw everything in a clear light. *I'm impulsive – I jump to rash conclusions. Janis is right. All Marty knows is that Janis and Ira live out there. He doesn't know where Danny and I are living.*

But her heart was pounding as she focused on this new situation. Suppose – just suppose – somebody from Primrose happened to go out there, saw the reward offer? Somebody who'd crossed her path? Unlikely, she derided. But it *could* happen – how was the ad phrased? It would mention her name – Caren Stephens, her single name which she'd always used. And Danny would be Daniel Ari Mansur. He was Daniel Mansur at school.

Nobody from Primrose will see that ad with its reward.

Why did I tell people here in Primrose that we came from Iran? Janis said not to worry, but how can I not worry? I'm scared. I'm so scared!

Twenty-Two

Caren awoke to the sound of rain pounding on the roof – a somber symphony. Janis would say, 'It's great for the flowers.' No alarm woke her this morning. Saturday morning. She turned to inspect the clock on her night table. It was 8.21 a.m. She'd slept late. Sleep broken by nightmares.

All at once she was assaulted by recall. Janis's letter on her website. Marty's ad offering a $10,000 reward. Not just a nightmare. Reality.

In sudden anxiety about Danny, she hurried from her bed to his bedroom door – as though to reassure herself that Marty's private investigator hadn't snatched him away in the middle of the night. Danny lay on one side, arms clutching his pillow. Deep in slumber.

Let him sleep, poor baby. No school today. In an odd way, she reflected, Marty's stern – often brutal – discipline was helping now. Danny had been taught that he must do as he was told. Rebellion was weak.

The morning rain was bringing relief from yesterday's unseasonable warmth. Almost a chill in the air, Caren thought. Under the welcome warmth of a hot shower, her mind traitorously returned to Janis's latest letter.

Suppose Marty grew impatient, decided to advertise in one of the tabloids that hit supermarkets across the country? Her mind darted back through the years to the period when he ran the company branch in Manhattan. In those days he'd talked with her about business, about their advertising campaigns.

'Our line's too classy for the supermarket tabloids – but wow, do they offer coverage!'

She recoiled from the prospect of walking into the local IGA to face Marty's ad in one of those tabloids. But an ad wouldn't run on the front page – it'd be hidden somewhere in the back pages. She found meager comfort in this.

National advertising would be so expensive – but Marty was growing richer by the day. He told her this in odd ways – as though to show her how he'd risen in the world. *To find us he'll spend money – even go into nationwide advertising. No! I won't think like that!*

She showered, dressed. All at once she was aware of sounds in the living room. In soaring alarm she hurried from the bathroom. Barefoot and in pajamas, Danny sat before the TV set. He'd fiddled with the dials until he'd found a morning cartoon program.

'Good morning, darling,' she said and he turned around with a tentative smile.

'You said I could watch TV—'

'Of course you can,' she soothed. Thank God for that diversion. Young children shouldn't watch a lot of TV, she rebuked herself – but in their present situation it would make life less difficult. Later Danny's TV watching would be limited. 'Hungry?'

'Yeah—' But his eyes clung to the TV set.

Kathy's little girls were eager to be friends, she thought with gratitude. Would Danny accept them? Kathy had mentioned that other children on their block were either toddlers or teenagers. She must devise ways to bring the three of them together. Kathy would help.

While Danny avidly watched a cartoon program, Caren plotted their breakfast menu. From their first days as friends Pari had taught her the importance of good nutrition. Marty had derided her insistence on this.

'*Why do you bother with this nonsense? Let Ziba cook what she knows we like.*'

He hadn't been that way back in this country. They'd searched around for organic vegetables, gone apple-picking and strawberry picking in season so as to have the freshest of fruit. Now she suspected he was a steady patron of the American-style fast-food shops – despite his contempt for everything American.

She had noticed the waffle iron on the meager counter space provided in the kitchen. If she used egg whites instead of whole eggs, she told herself, the waffles would be fine. Maple syrup – served in one of the tiny glass barrels she'd admired on a shelf – would be acceptable as their sweet for the day, and a butter substitute with no trans fatty acids. They'd make waffles their Saturday breakfast special.

With some reluctance Danny abandoned TV for breakfast. But he was soon eating with relish. The sound of a dog barking close by earned a broad smile from him.

It was cozy in the apartment, Caren told herself with shaky pleasure. The sound of rain beating on the roof, the aroma of wood burning in a fireplace close by provided an air of serenity. And Danny – intrigued by the newness of television and computer offerings – seemed to be accepting the change in their lives. For the moment, she ordered herself to realize. They had a long way to go.

While Caren cleared the table, washed the handful of dishes, Danny stationed himself before the computer. Last evening Caren had installed the computer game she'd bought for him, showed him how to bring it up. He was enthralled with this new toy.

She walked from the kitchen into the living room, sat in the comfortable club chair flanked by an end table piled high with magazines. Left behind – she assumed – by a previous tenant. Someone with an artistic bent. Little touches about the apartment suggested this.

She started at the sound of the doorbell. Fighting panic. Her instant thought, Marty's investigators have tracked us down!

'Mommie?' Danny was curious. Wary. 'Who's ringing the doorbell?' Her alarm infecting him.

'We'll know in a minute.' Masking her trepidation, she went to open the door.

A youngish, quite handsome man in jeans and a plaid flannel shirt stood there.

'Hi, I heard sounds – I knew you were awake. I'm Brian Woods—'

'Hi.' Their landlord. Not Marty's investigators. The principal at Danny's school. What a charismatic smile! 'I'm Caren Stephens.' *But he knows that.*

'When the weather turned so warm yesterday, I figured I

couldn't stall any longer in replacing your screen at the window there—' He pointed to it. 'If you run into any problems at all, just ring my bell.' He smiled at Danny, who had abandoned the computer to inspect their visitor. 'Hi, you must be Danny.'

'Yes, sir.' Once they were in Tehran, Marty demanded old-fashioned manners from his son.

'I hope you'll like our school.' He turned to Caren. 'I'm the new principal at the elementary school. We're trying out a bunch of new ideas. In these changing times we have to meet new needs.'

'I taught fifth grade back in Westchester County for almost a year – before Danny was born. As a substitute. Even then we had to deal with unexpected needs.' *Why is he staring at me that way? So intense.*

'We have no full-time openings at Primrose Elementary – but we might have some substitute needs from time to time.' A question in his eyes.

'I'll have to settle for a full-time job,' she admitted. *He's a good person. Warm – and compassionate. The way Marty was when I met him at Columbia.* 'But someday I hope to get back to teaching.' *What is this strange connection I feel towards him? But I have no room in my life for a personal relationship. Once was enough. Raising Danny will be my life.*

'Oh, I wanted to tell you something—' He punctured the heated silence between them. 'I know the weather today is rotten for soccer, but every Saturday morning at ten a.m. – weather permitting – there's a soccer game for the young kids on the open lot behind the high school gym.'

'That sounds like fun.' Danny's school had provided no sports facilities. On a few occasions Marty had taken him skiing in Dizin, just an hour's drive from their house. Once he had taken Danny to see a soccer match. The attendance segregated, of course – so she had not been present.

'Do you play soccer, Danny?' *He's trying to be friendly. He realizes Danny will have a rough adjustment coming here from Tehran.*

'No, sir.' Solemn now.

'You'll learn one of these days. We've got a great bunch

of kids playing soccer over there.' *Kathy said he set up the after-school sessions at his school. She said he spends one evening a week teaching English to immigrants. The sort of things Marty might have done if we'd remained in this country.*

'It sounds great—' Caren tried to coax a smile from Danny. 'Danny will be learning a lot of new things now that we're back home.' *Why is Danny glaring at me that way? Because to him Tehran is home.*

'Any problems – either here or at school, you ring my doorbell,' Brian urged.

'Thank you. I'll do that.' *Hannah said he was a widower. What happened to his wife? I'll bet every unattached woman in town under forty is chasing after him.*

When they were alone again, Danny settled himself before the television set, sighed when he could find no cartoons. He returned to the computer, enthralled again by his computer game. He was fascinated by both, Caren thought tenderly. Grateful for their existence.

The rain continued through the day. No chance to involve Danny in playing with Laurie and Cindy.

'Mommie—' Danny sounded distraught. 'The computer's broke!'

'No, darling. You just hit the wrong key—' She saw him stiffen. Marty had made him believe mistakes were intolerable.

She rushed to his side. 'It happens to everybody,' she consoled. 'It happens to me, too.'

Let that be Danny's first lesson. Perfection was not demanded of him.

Twenty-Three

B rian listened rather than watched *Capital Gang* while he ate dinner. Midway through the program he transferred dishes to the dishwasher, switched off the television set. It was time to leave for the meeting at Jill and Phil's house.

Leaving his section of the house he could hear music drifting from the apartment. Old recordings of Peter, Paul & Mary. She had great taste, he approved. Why did she keep invading his thoughts through the day? And the little boy. Danny. Polite, he approved – but troubled.

Hannah said they'd come from Iran, he told himself again. Why to Primrose? Searching for refuge in a little-known small town? Primrose wasn't exactly a strong attraction at the moment.

Again, he worried about the impasse between the teachers and the Board of Education. The board was indignant at the talk of a union. They'd never had a teachers' strike in Primrose – but it could happen if changes weren't made.

Cliff said he'd had a rough time with the mothers of those two young bullies.

'Mrs Harris says her husband will be calling you. Remember, Jason Harris is on the Board of Ed. What a rotten time for this to come up.'

OK, he'd have to deal with Harris. The Harrises were the town's big socializers. Maybe if they spent more time with their son, he wouldn't be bullying a scared little kid from Iraq.

Arriving at Jill and Phil's house, he noted the line-up of cars along the road. They'd have a substantial turnout tonight. That was urgent. Talk leaked out of conferences between Mayor Davis and the developers. Did Davis think he could push through a takeover before the general public realized what was happening?

He hurried into the house – the door left open in anticipation of more arrivals. He was greeted with much enthusiasm. People like these made him feel he belonged in Primrose. After his growing-up years as an army brat, moving from place to place, country to country, he yearned for roots.

As usual he was swept up into the planning.

'Come on, Brian – how do we tackle this craziness?' Jill demanded.

In his usual low-key fashion, Brian outlined a campaign they would launch against the takeover of those modest lakeside houses. But in the midst of their impassioned plotting, he was unnerved by the way his mind took off in another direction at truant moments.

That little boy living in the apartment. Danny. So troubled – so vulnerable. And why had he jumped to the conclusion that his mother was running from an abusive husband? Jumping to conclusions again, he rebuked himself.

Danny isn't happy here. Is it because he wants to go back home? Or is it just that he hasn't had time to adjust to a strange new world? I'll have a talk with his teacher. He'll need a lot of help.

His mother – her name was Caren, he recalled – said she wouldn't be available for substitute teaching. She needed a full-time job. That meant financial problems. She, too, seemed so vulnerable. Desperately afraid of something.

This was hardly the time to be job-hunting in Primrose – with several small shops closing and now Skip Reynolds closing up his factory. Ninety employees headed for the unemployment office.

Not the time to be job-hunting unless she's willing to work for seven or eight dollars an hour at the discount chain on the mall. And most of those are part-time jobs – without benefits. She won't be able to support herself and Danny on that.

Such a sweet little kid – that Danny. I might have had a son – or a daughter – his age. Denise was a bad scene – but I should have watched her more carefully. I knew she was into drugs. I let her kill my child along with herself.

*   *   *

After another restless night, Caren awoke to a dreary Sunday morning. No rain, she noted, but the sky hinted that more would follow. A clammy chill in the house – not sufficient to require heat, enough to cause discomfort.

She heard the sound of church bells in the distance. This would be a town where most families went to their respective houses of worship on Sunday, she guessed. It would be a quiet, peaceful day – but around the world people were dying in battle. American men and women were dying – or being maimed.

The Revolution in Iran and the Iraq–Iran war had been over by the time she and Marty and Danny arrived. But Pari had been most eloquent about those years:

'*Saddam Hussein wanted the Iranian oil fields – and for eight years the Iraq–Iran war waged on. Almost a million people died. And the war allowed the leaders of the Revolution to inflict all kinds of deprivation on us. We had to fight the enemy in every way possible.*'

Pari had talked much about the Palestinian–Israeli situation, Caren recalled. Pari was convinced that the world would continue in conflict until its youngest generation was taught not to hate.

The Iranian government strived to make its children believe that everyone not following the radical Muslim line was an infidel. The enemy. The Palestinian children were taught from birth to hate every Israeli. Proper education, Pari insisted, was the road to peace.

'*Not until children around the world are taught true tolerance – to love, not hate – will we know peace. In our education systems lies the salvation of our earth.*'

Danny would sleep late, Caren surmised. She'd allowed him to remain awake long beyond his normal bed time last night. They'd watched *Jurassic Park* on television. She'd remembered that Pari's sister had said her kids had been entranced by the clandestinely acquired video she'd let them watch.

Danny had done his homework yesterday. 'It's real easy,' he'd declared again – in a blend of relief and triumph. Caren recalled with wry humor Kathy's report that some local parents were concerned that the early grades were being inundated with homework – beyond what they considered acceptable. In Iran homework was a major part of their children's lives.

Caren walked about the tiny apartment on slippered feet. It was good that Danny was sleeping late. She'd been concerned about keeping him diverted from the realization that tomorrow was a school day. Something to be endured.

Close to 10 a.m. the local radio weather forecaster predicted the rain was over. Sun began to creep through the clouds. More church bells rang around the town. Such a serene sound, she thought.

Gazing out the window she saw Cindy and Laurie hurrying out of the house and to the family suburban. A man leaned out the window. That would be Howie, their father, 'Come on, kids,' he beckoned to them. 'You don't want to be late for Sunday school.' Now she remembered driving past a synagogue when they first arrived in town. A lovely building – almost Moorish in design.

Tomorrow morning – when Danny boarded the school bus – he'd see Laurie and Cindy there. Familiar faces. That would be good. And she was betting that the two little girls would involve Danny in conversation. That, too, would be good.

She and Danny would have a late brunch, Caren plotted – hearing no sounds from his bedroom. Then they'd go for a long walk. Danny – and she – needed the exercise. Soon – with a little luck – she'd have Danny active in school sports. Maybe soccer or basketball.

They'd stop in town so she could pick up a copy of the *Sunday Sentinel*. She'd read the 'help wanted' columns. Let there be a job listed that she could fill. Or with a little luck someone would reply to her ad in the 'positions wanted' columns.

Brian Woods had been so friendly when he came to the door yesterday morning. He really cared about people. He talked about bringing new ideas to the school.

All at once she was self-conscious. She was mistaken in thinking he was drawn to her. He was just being neighborly. But there were moments – when he looked at her with such intensity – that she felt as though a whole new life was about to open up for her. For Brian Woods and her. Stupid!

She and Danny would encounter dogs along their walk, she guessed. Moving into more comfortable territory. Maybe a couple of kittens. Danny would stop to play with them. They'd come home. He'd watch TV while she prepared dinner. After dinner, let him have a go at his computer game. He'd be tired, ready to go to bed early.

All at once screams – punctuated by incoherent outcries – emerged from Danny's bedroom. She rushed to his room. He was thrashing about on his bed. He was having a nightmare.

She pulled him into her arms. 'Darling, it's all right – you're just having a bad dream.' He was coming awake, sobbing convulsively. 'Danny, Mommie's here with you. It's all right.'

'I was so scared!' He clung to her. 'I dreamt we were home and Daddy was awful mad. He said I couldn't leave the house for a whole month – I could never have ice cream again. He said I was a terrible disappointment—'

'You're not a disappointment,' she crooned. 'You're a bright, brave boy. I'm very proud of you.'

She rocked him in her arms while his small body shivered. His tears became less convulsive. They still had a long way ahead, Caren acknowledged – but she would fight with all her strength to bring Danny into a normal, happy childhood. That was her mission in life. She mustn't fail.

Twenty-Four

Caren had warned herself that Sunday would be a rough day. All those hours ahead when she must keep Danny's mind away from the old life. At the moment – while she prepared brunch – Danny was sleeping again after recovering from his nightmare.

In Iran so much of the children's time was consumed with homework, the endless memorization, learning by rote. They struggled beneath the stern dictum that nothing less than perfection was acceptable. Not just Danny – most schoolchildren.

She heard a door close, then moments later a car pulled out of the garage. Brian Woods taking off for some morning activity.

Hannah had mentioned that he was a widower – she hadn't said how his wife died. She would have been young. Brian must have been devastated.

Involuntarily she thought about his determination to introduce fresh ideas in the Primrose school system. Like Pari at the university – though her chances were dismal. He'd be horrified at what happened in Iranian classrooms. He'd empathize instantly with Pari.

In tender recall she thought about Pari's impatience with the rules at the university.

'*How awful to hide behind hijab in the classroom! To see our students afraid to present new ideas.*'

Pari was proud that women students outnumbered men in the universities. That many chose math or science as their majors, despite the general assumption that women were lacking in the ability to learn these skills.

At disturbing moments – while she prepared for a late breakfast – Caren remembered what Janis had written about

Marty's ads in their local community newspapers. She tried to thrust aside the alarm his $10,000 reward had set off in her. Her bright, realistic sister felt this would go nowhere. Cling to that thought.

With the making of spinach omelets in a bowl, frozen bagels defrosting in the oven, Caren debated about waking Danny. While she vacillated, he hurried from his room and straight to the computer.

'Hi, Mommie,' he said dutifully while he turned on the computer. So proud he'd learned to turn it on and bring up his game, Caren thought with a surge of love.

'Breakfast in five minutes,' she warned him. 'You can play on the computer later.'

While they sat at the table and ate breakfast, Danny talked about last night's TV watching – a whole new experience for him.

'Wow, it was scary. But good scary,' he added, lest future such occasions be denied him. 'The dinosaurs were so big!'

He peppered her with questions about the computer. A once-hidden treasure now at his disposal.

Marty had no patience with questions, she remembered. He didn't understand that curiosity in a child was good. It was a learning process. Marty hadn't been that way when they lived in Westchester – he'd relished Danny's constant, 'But Daddy, why?'

The sun came out with startling brilliance, poured into the apartment. It was amazing how sunlight could change the mood of the moment, she thought with pleasure.

'I'll do the dishes, then we'll go out for a walk,' she told Danny. 'I suspect there's a little chill in the air. Go get your windbreaker.' His wardrobe was limited. Monday she must take him shopping for more clothes.

'Why are we going for a walk?' His voice betrayed unease.

'I want to pick up the Sunday newspaper,' she told him. 'And walking is great exercise.' Soon, please God, let him be getting the normal exercise of an eight-year-old. Playing with other kids. 'And who knows?' she said, striving for lightness. 'We'll probably meet some dogs along the way. None of them on leashes out here,' she reminded him. 'Now go get your windbreaker.'

Again, she remembered how – when they'd first arrived in Tehran – dogs were shot or 'disappeared' because the government considered them 'unclean.' That time was supposed to be over, but incidents of harassment popped up at intervals. People were instructed to keep their dogs out of public places. Oh, yes, Caren conceded, it was difficult to keep a pet in Iran.

Four years ago, she recalled, a dog show was held in Ghazvin, the first in the Islamic Republic of Iran. But the focus was not on the winning points of the dogs but on the ability of their trainers. Last year there'd been a dog show in Tehran. Marty had rejected her plan to take Danny – who adored anything on four feet – to see it.

'Why waste time on a creepy dog show? Better Danny spends that time in studying.'

With Danny in his windbreaker, they walked out into the Sunday serenity that seemed to deny the horrors that affected segments of the world. They were the lone walkers. Not surprising, Caren mused. In thousands of small towns across the country the car was the usual means of transportation. Yet it was lovely to walk in the sunlight that caressed the area. It was like being told, 'The world is good.'

'Doggie!' Danny approached a friendly collie in a surge of joy, reached to pat him. 'Oh, what a good boy!'

Caren stood by while Danny romped with the collie. A sole jogger rushed past them, waved a hand in greeting.

'Lucky!' a teenager yelled from a doorway. 'Come!' The collie seemed ambivalent. 'Lucky, get your butt over here or you'll stay home by yourself.' With a backward glance at Danny, Lucky trotted towards the doorway.

Further along the road they encountered a pair of black Labradors. Again, Danny stopped to play for a few moments. This time the Labs took off in chase of a rambunctious squirrel.

In town Caren picked up the *Sunday Sentinel*. Eager to check the 'help wanted' column – but that would have to wait until they returned home. Now doubts began to tug at her. On almost any job today computer skills were required. She'd been away from that world for five years – except for her e-mail forays on Pari's computer.

The moment she opened the door to the apartment, Danny headed for the computer. Caren sat down to check the job offerings. A meager listing – only one of which might have possibilities for her.

She marked the ad with a pen, reread it. The requirements not too demanding, she comforted herself. But her throat was tightening in the telltale way she'd come to recognize. This was the only ad to which she could respond. And that was frightening.

She hadn't expected to find a job the first week in town, she rebuked herself. They could survive for three or four months without her bringing in a paycheck. Still, what she saw was discouraging. The *Sentinel* editorial bemoaned the growing unemployment rate in Primrose. A factory was closing – laying off ninety employees.

At 9 a.m. tomorrow morning she would be at the office at 418 Main Street to apply for the receptionist/administrative assistant job that was advertised. Applicants were to appear from 9 a.m. until noon – with résumés. The ad didn't give the name of the hiring organization, stated only that this was a temporary receptionist/administrative assistant position. No salary mentioned. The job would last from six to nine months.

The technical requirements were minor, she reminded herself with relief. She could handle the computer skills requirement with some minor brushing up. She would have no trouble handling telephone calls – which appeared a major part of the position.

If the salary was low – and the job was offered to her, she'd accept. It would be a beginning. Six months of security. That was to be respected.

I won't think about Marty's ad in those community newspapers. If Janis talks about its becoming a worse situation, then Danny and I will move on. Maybe to Canada. I won't let Marty win this race!

Twenty-Five

Not until Danny was in bed for the night – with no talk of school tomorrow morning – did Caren allow herself to go online. Not expecting another letter – but with a need to feel herself in touch with Janis.

Startled, anxious, she saw a new letter come up on Janis's website. Forget the once-a-week deal.

> Hi Bobbie,
>
> Much excitement in Jimmy's class on Friday. His teacher gave them a special assignment: to find an e-mail pen pal somewhere around the world. Remember when we went through that scene? And you know Ira is a news junkie, always talking about world politics. So-o Jimmy will try to find a pen pal in Iran – because Ira is forever carrying on against the Administration's tough attitude towards that country. Not the time to expand the war. And Jimmy poked around on Google and discovered there's a popular Iranian newspaper published in English. Thank God for Google – it knows everything! I've sent an e-mail to the *Tehran Times*. It'll be exciting to read a newspaper from a country like that.

Meaning, Caren interpreted, that they might see some news item in the *Tehran Times* that mentioned Marty. That happened every once in a while – since he became involved in local politics. But the *Tehran Times* wasn't likely to mention Marty's search for his wife and son.

Now she faced the task she had been avoiding all day. To apply for the position advertised in the *Sentinel* she must arrive with a résumé. This presented a problem. For all her bravado about being able to fill an office job – telling herself she was young, well-educated, and bright – her lack of business experience was unnerving.

The crucial moment was here. She must sit down at the computer and build a résumé. Instinct warned her not to mention the eight months of substitute teaching in Westchester schools. The jobs she'd held during the college years. Marty's investigator – more likely, investigators – would follow through on those jobs. The trail could lead back to Lila. To Primrose. *Careful, Caren. Careful.*

Her throat tightening, a tenseness between her shoulder blades, she sat at the computer, willed herself to build a résumé that could lead Marty's investigators nowhere. Use Pari, her mind ordered. They wouldn't bother checking a reference in Iran. If they did, Pari would back her up.

She'd say that she was employed for five years as an administrative assistant to Pari, with English the language in use. Fake a letter of recommendation. The ad mentioned a college degree would be a plus. How could she deal with this? She mustn't mention the years at Columbia, she warned herself again. List Janis's college – they won't check it out. Say that she worked part-time during the college years as a receptionist in a law office.

Go in with confidence, she commanded herself. Discuss her computer skills – not great, but adequate for an uncomplicated office. Stress experience in handling phones in a busy law office. *I can do that.*

Despite the coolness of the evening, she was perspiring as she focused on setting up a résumé. Again, she told herself the company wouldn't check out facts on her résumé – not for a temporary job lasting from six to nine months. But that would be six to nine months of financial security.

She sighed with relief when – after several attempts – she completed a résumé that seemed plausible. The printer was noisy. She'd print it out in the morning to avoid waking Danny in his bedroom – so close in their tiny apartment.

Suspecting sleep would be slow in coming, Caren settled herself in bed to read the *Sunday Sentinel*. She'd read the front page, the classified section, and the editorial page – that was all. *This is where Danny and I are to live. Let me learn about our town.*

The *Sentinel* was not a conservative newspaper, she noted in approval. They reported in depth about the rising unemployment in town, the imminent closing of a local factory. She read a heated article about the need to improve the town's school system.

This was her sort of town, she told herself in a flurry of satisfaction. Then reality intruded. *Was* this to be their town? Or would some word come from Janis that would send them on the run again? Next stop Canada? How would she explain this to Danny? *He's so confused. So much has happened so fast.*

Concentrate on the newspaper – don't think about tomorrow morning, she ordered herself. How would Danny feel about taking the school bus? Would they encounter another impasse? But Laurie and Cindy would be there. Friendly faces.

Far better to travel a short distance to school on a school bus with other young students than to drive – an hour and a half each way – in a private car, accompanied by a bodyguard. No matter how Marty had tried to convince Danny that the bodyguards were their chauffeurs, he must have been aware that the guards wore holstered guns.

On Monday morning Caren awoke well before her alarm clock was scheduled to go off. Instantly conscious of what lay ahead. First, she must see Danny off on the school bus. Then she'd go to the storefront at 418 Main Street to apply for the job advertised in the *Sentinel*. *Don't be turned off if a line of applicants are there ahead of me.*

All right, get up, prepare for the day. An important day. Danny's first trip on the school bus. Her first effort at landing a job.

She tossed aside the light blanket, slid into slippers and headed for the bathroom. Out of the shower, she focused on what to wear. Not a major decision, she derided, considering her limited wardrobe. A quick check on the weather via the radio news told her the temperature was already in the mid-60s. She could wear her black silk pantsuit.

Although she realized this was unnecessary, she pressed the slacks. Her one outfit suitable for job hunting. Great that the previous tenants had left a steam iron when they moved out. One less item she'd have to buy.

She flinched as she recalled the inflated prices of everything in this country. From the moment they'd checked into the hotel in New York, she'd realized her bankroll would not last as long as she'd anticipated. Unless she found a job soon, she'd be searching for a place to sell her jewelry. She would have liked to hold this for some future emergency. A safety net.

She geared herself to wake Danny. Please God, let him go to school without another battle. She'd hoped that over the weekend there would be some playtime with Laurie and Cindy, but that hadn't happened. Kathy, too, was eager to see her girls with a neighborhood playmate. It was a matter of time before the three of them played together on a regular basis. Until he'd been enrolled in the religious school – with no time allowed for this – Danny had loved playing with small friends.

At the last possible moment she awakened Danny.

'Rise and shine,' she ordered ebulliently. 'It's a beautiful day – and guess whom I saw playing out on the Bernstein's front lawn this morning?'

His face lighted. 'Daisy? Is she still there?' He pushed aside the comforter – eager to see the appealing white kitten.

'No, but she'll be out again.'

Caren kept up a lively stream of conversation revolving around Daisy and the friendly pups they'd encountered yesterday. Let Danny keep thinking about the puppy he himself would have in less than a month. That was crucial. Last night she'd been excited when he'd suddenly remembered Snoopy, the little dog in Westchester that he'd liked so much.

I won't consider our not being here when it's time for Danny to pick out his puppy. I'll be realistic – like Janis. The chance of Marty's discovering our whereabouts is minuscule.

But she was tense, fearful, until Danny and she were at the school bus stop at the corner. Laurie and Cindy were there already. Danny seemed OK, she told herself in relief. He wasn't hostile when Laurie talked to him.

'Daisy likes you,' Laurie confided. 'She doesn't like everybody. Sometimes she—'

'Here comes the bus,' Cindy interrupted.

'After school you take the bus back home,' Caren reminded Danny. He'd been briefed on this. 'I'll be on the deck waiting for you.'

She watched Danny climb on to the bus, with Laurie still chattering away to him. He would be fine, she promised herself. He was beginning to adjust.

The bus was pulling away. She saw Danny turn in his seat to seek a last glimpse of her. No, he wasn't fine, she rebuked herself. He was obeying orders – as Marty had taught him to do. But he was still – except for brief intervals – bewildered and frightened of this new world.

Twenty-Six

Caren returned to the apartment when the school bus was out of sight. She was haunted by the poignant vision of Danny – staring out the window for a last glimpse of her. Feeling so insecure – scared – at venturing away from her side.

She poured the final cup of decaf from the carafe on the coffeemaker, sat down with it. The apartment seemed so empty. So desolate.

Stop being melodramatic, she rebuked herself. Danny had gone off to school every morning in Tehran – this was the same. Except that she didn't have to worry about his being attacked on the way. They couldn't be together every moment. It was time to settle down to normal living again.

She'd wait until a few minutes before 9 a.m. Then she would walk into town to present herself as a job applicant. Not at 9 a.m. sharp, she warned herself. She mustn't appear too anxious. Be casual, confident.

At five minutes past nine – by the clock in a luncheonette window – she was approaching her destination. Again, comforted by the air of serenity about the town. And then she stopped short in astonishment. Unnerved by the long line of women waiting before the door of 418 Main Street.

A sign in the window indicated this was the offices of Loveland Development Corporation. Why hadn't the name been mentioned in the ad? Venetian blinds masked the interior of the storefront. What were they developing here in Primrose? Another shopping mall? A new housing complex?

Caren struggled for calm as she joined the line. Aware that those already in line were inspecting her. As they'd inspect each newcomer, she understood. Competition.

Her heart was pounding. Already more than twenty applicants stood in line, she noted uneasily. Most of them in their early twenties. One appeared to be about eighteen – probably fresh out of high school. A pair of women close to retirement age – both appearing uncomfortable.

Why must they wait outside the storefront? An unusual way to treat job applicants. And then she heard the sound of pounding inside. Construction work on the interior, she surmised.

One twenty-ish blonde with crimped hair halfway down her back clutched a paperback Danielle Steel romance novel and read avidly while she waited. Another sipped from a bottle of water – the seeming requisite of modern-day Americans. Were they all afraid of dying of dehydration? One of the older women pulled a cellphone from her purse, frowned as she punched in numbers. Her face lighted as someone responded.

'Honey, don't worry. I'm sure I'll be able to pick up Deedee at her nursery school. If it looks close, I'll just forget this stupid job.'

Caren was aware of furtive glances among those waiting, which betrayed their aura of high spirits. She remembered the article in the *Sentinel* about the high local unemployment. She recalled stories she'd read in the newspapers in the course of their traveling about age barriers. Startling stories.

In Hollywood writers over twenty-nine – with impressive credits – were considered past their prime, denied jobs. TV shows were designed to cater to the eighteen to twenty-five age group. The world had entered a period where youth was king.

I'm thirty-two. Will Loveland Development consider me too old?

Her pantsuit didn't look young, she reproached herself. Smart but not youthful. Those ahead of her – except for the two older women – were of a younger generation. To them thirty-two was probably over the hill.

All at once there was a rustle of excitement. A man was pulling up the Venetian blind on the door, opening the door. Hands reached into purses or totes to pull out résumés.

'Relax, ladies,' he urged. 'We'll interview one at a time. Please be patient.'

Only the interviewee was to be allowed inside, the others realized with – here and there – a show of annoyance.

'Even at McDonald's you're allowed inside,' the teenager among them grumbled. 'You can sit down and wait.' She squinted in thought. 'I'll go try McDonald's,' she announced to the others at large. 'At least I won't have to stand in line like at a soup kitchen.'

Two of those in line tuned out of the tense waiting period via their iPods. The one reading a Danielle Steel novel seemed to cut herself off from the rest of the world. Others chattered as though waiting for admission to a special club. One of the two older women left after the first applicant emerged with an air of impatience.

After a forty-minute wait those in line were restless.

'They know it's hard to get a job these days,' the young woman in front of Caren whispered to her. 'They figure we'll wait. I'll bet the salary's like a little over minimum.' But her shrug was philosophical as she reached to pull off her three-inch-heeled sandals.

Caren was conscious of the glances of passers-by. This was clearly an unconventional approach to job hiring in Primrose. She was startled to note contempt as a couple of people read the sign on the window. Not everybody welcomed the new Loveland Development Corporation to Primrose.

Her smile was strained by the time she was summoned inside.

She'd tried to interpret the expression of each applicant emerging from the storefront. Nobody seemed enthusiastic.

Only a pair of desks and a barrage of telephones were in sight. A 7-foot high folding divider concealed the rear of the store, where construction was in work.

When the door opened, those waiting could see a man in an expensive business suit sitting behind one desk. Another man sat behind the second desk, occupied by computer, monitor, keyboard, and printer. He was engrossed in something on the computer monitor.

At last Caren was summoned inside.

'Your résumé, please,' the man at the other desk demanded

with an air of boredom. But he was tallying up the cost of her designer suit, her Prada purse, she noted. Wondering why she was here applying for this job.

Her smile cordial, she handed over her résumé. Already tense with the anticipation of rejection.

He frowned, glanced up at her. 'Your experience is mostly in Iran?'

'Yes.' She struggled for poise. 'Except for jobs while I was at college.'

'How long have you been back in this country?' he asked. *What a silly question! The résumé gave my last working week as last month.*

'Just a week—' *Why should that matter?*

'You mention familiarity only with Microsoft Word and Word Perfect,' he quizzed, then shrugged. 'But that's sufficient for us. You'd have no trouble with handling phones—' It was a statement rather than a question.

'None at all.' She waited for him to continue.

'You realize this is a temporary position – for six to nine months?' he probed.

'Yes.' *Is he hiring me?*

'For the right person it can develop into a permanent job – at a much higher salary.' He paused, mentioned the starting salary. Shocking her.

'That's low—' Her heart pounding, she was determined to negotiate. It was obvious she was offering something the others were not. Something he wanted.

'All right—' His laugh was indulgent. 'Add another twenty-five a week. You'll start a week from today.' *I have the job!* 'But you must keep this confidential. The town will expect us to interview for the full week. The job is yours, Caren.'

Twenty-Seven

Caren walked out of the storefront, avoided any eye contact with those still waiting to be interviewed. Guilty that she knew the position had been filled, that their interviews were just a pretense.

She'd be working for the man who had interviewed her. Carl Watson. The CEO of Loveland Contracting. It would be her job to keep away callers he wished to avoid, to reply to unwanted callers from a prepared script. His words ricocheted in her mind now:

'There'll be some filing, routine office work. Also, you'll handle some correspondence on your own.' She suspected this had been a decision of the moment.

No health insurance, she warned herself – not as long as she was on temporary status. Even if she could afford this, she'd worry about Marty's investigators looking at insurance companies for new applicants. *Am I being paranoid? No. I must be super-careful.*

Her mind charged ahead as she strode away from the storefront. Even with strict budgeting, she realized, she and Danny couldn't live on her salary. She'd have to dig into her reserve fund. But Watson had talked about a permanent job – at a higher salary.

She would start next Monday morning. That meant by then she must arrange for care for Danny from after school until she got home from the job. She winced at this added expense. But wait! Kathy Bernstein had talked about after-school groups at the school – instituted three years ago by Brian Woods.

'It's great. The hours are from immediately after school until five thirty. And one teacher hangs around until six o'clock, to make sure every child has been picked up. And

if some parent is held up on the job, there's always a mother who'll see that child home.'

She'd talk with Kathy about the after-school group. There must be something that Danny would enjoy. Maybe a music or art class – or there might even be a soccer or basketball group.

At the apartment – after a brief stop at the in-town IGA – she put away the groceries she'd bought, settled herself at the computer. She knew Kathy wasn't home – the garage door was open and both cars were away. She was anxious to talk with Kathy about the after-school groups.

She jeered at herself for checking Janis's website several times a day – but it was almost like talking with her. Now she sat before the computer, brought up Janis's website. Another letter! Fighting off fresh alarm she began to read – scanning the first segment because, as usual, it dealt with everyday happenings in their lives. Now she read more slowly.

> As you can imagine, Nadine is still a nervous wreck about those ads. But Ira – such a sweet, compassionate guy – used his multitude of contacts to learn that her niece's husband had contracted for the ads to run for two weeks. So he quick told Nadine. Her niece's husband is focusing on this ad campaign for close to another fourteen days – and he'll have to wait for possible replies. That's kind of a respite.

So for the next couple of weeks Marty would be watching for results from the ads. Nothing else would happen. Nothing would come of the ad campaign. But what would he try next?

Caren watched at nervous intervals for some sign that Kathy had returned to the house. No need to panic, she told herself. She had several days to make arrangements for Danny's care from the close of the school day until she was home. Office hours would be 9 a.m. to 5 p.m. – and the after-school groups could solve her problem.

Ten minutes before the school bus was scheduled to stop

at their corner, Caren settled herself on her segment of the deck to watch for Danny's arrival. She heard the boisterous noise of a vacuum cleaner in operation in Brian Woods' segment of the house. Hannah was here this afternoon. Somehow, Hannah's presence was comforting.

Right on schedule the yellow school bus appeared at the corner. Caren rose to her feet, watched while the children emerged from the bus in high spirits. Several early teenagers, then Laurie and Cindy.

There's Danny. Don't run down to meet him – let him come up to the house on his own. Setting a routine.

Laurie and Cindy were running up the path to their house.

'Mommie,' Cindy called as they reached the front door. 'We're home.'

Danny was a small, somber figure as he approached the deck. Knapsack on his back. Holding a sheet of paper in one hand. Something he'd done in class today?

'Hi, darling—' Now she rushed to embrace him. Enjoying this moment. 'What's this paper you've brought home?' she asked with tender curiosity.

'We have an art class on Mondays,' he explained, showing her the paper.

He'd drawn a rough image of the house in Tehran, she realized. All at once tense. A few lines beside the house were meant to be the tall sycamore he'd once tried to climb. Only once because Marty had punished him for that.

'You were supposed to draw everything in black?' Caren drew him into the apartment for his after-school snack. As in Tehran. It was important to follow routines, she told herself. 'No color crayons?'

'Yeah—' Danny was defensive. 'I didn't feel like using colors.'

'Oh, I have news,' she told him with an air of pleasure, while she poured a glass of milk to accompany his fruit salad. 'I have a job. Starting next Monday.'

He froze. 'You won't be here when I come home from school?'

'I'll be here,' she reassured him. Unnerved for the moment. *Later I'll explain about the after-school groups.*

Cautiously Caren questioned him about activities in his

class – as though to consider this a delightful adventure. His replies were brief, dispirited.

'Can I go on the computer now?' he asked when he'd finished his snack. No rush to homework as back in Tehran, Caren noted in shaky approval. He was learning there was life away from the school books.

'Sure. But it's so nice out,' she cajoled. 'Wouldn't you like to—?'

'Danny!' A young feminine voice called from the deck. Laurie, Caren recognized. 'Danny, don't you want to come out and play with Daisy?'

Danny's face lighted. He turned to his mother in silent questioning. Computer forgotten.

'Go on out and see Daisy,' she encouraged. Bless Laurie!

'Come on, Danny—' Laurie was impatient. 'Mommie's got oatmeal cookies for us—'

'Go on with Laurie,' Caren ordered with an indulgent smile. 'You like oatmeal cookies.'

It's beginning to happen, she told herself in soaring relief. He was less fearful. He was relating to playmates.

But how long before Marty tracks us down? Before Danny and I have to run again?

Twenty-Eight

Caren sat on the deck and watched while Danny cavorted with the two girls and Daisy on the Bernsteins' front lawn. She'd heard Danny say – while he rushed from the apartment to join Laurie and Cindy – 'I'm gonna get a puppy soon. My mommie promised!'

Earlier Kathy had come out of the house to dispense oatmeal cookies. She and Caren had exchanged waves. Caren debated about going over to talk with Kathy about the after-school groups, dismissed this. Let Danny play over there without her presence. Danny on his own – making friends. They'd talk later.

'Now isn't this a beautiful day?' Hannah came out of the house with a tray in tow.

'Oh, lovely,' Caren agreed.

'I'm taking a bit of a break. I thought you might enjoy a cup of fresh-ground coffee.' Hannah placed the tray – with two generous-sized mugs, sugar and creamer – on a white plastic table, pulled it close to where Caren sat. 'Nothing like when you grind the beans yourself.' She chuckled. 'That's something I learned from Brian.' She reached to bring a white plastic chair close.

'I haven't done that in years – ground my own beans,' Caren added. 'That used to be a Saturday morning special when we were living—' She hesitated. Always careful about giving out background details. 'Before we moved to Iran,' she finished. Now she understood how people living under the Witness Protection Act must feel. Always on guard.

'I see Danny's playing with Laurie and Cindy. That's nice.'

Now Hannah filled her in on local events. The Firemen's Lunch the following Saturday, the Book Fair on the village green on the Memorial Day weekend, the basketball game between competing high schools in the county in mid-May.

'I've filled your ears with enough,' Hannah said when both women had drained their mugs. 'And I've still got the kitchen to do and a casserole to prepare. Enjoy the day because we're promised rain for the next three days.' They exchanged wry smiles. 'But then the weather people are wrong a lot of the time.'

Alone again, Caren strained to hear the sounds from the Bernsteins' front lawn. Daisy curled up asleep while the two little girls appeared to be teaching Danny to skip rope. She was on the point of dozing off in a rare moment of relaxation when she heard the sound of a car turning into the driveway.

Brian was arriving home. He was leaving the car in the driveway, she noted. He'd be going out later. *Why am I interested in that?*

'A gorgeous day, isn't it?' he called out, walking towards the house.

'Beautiful.' She was conscious of a tremor of excitement at his presence.

'Everything OK in the apartment?' He paused on the deck, gazed at her – again with an unnerving intensity.

'Fine,' she told him. 'We're settling in.'

'Remember, if there's anything I can do, just call—'

'There is something—' She hesitated. *I'm out of my mind.* 'It's about Danny, actually—' Her voice uncertain now.

'Hey, he's one of my kids—' He moved closer. Concern in his eyes. 'What's the problem?' He dropped into the chair that Hannah had earlier pulled on to her segment of the deck.

'It's about the after-school groups—' She sought for words. 'I landed a job this morning – I start next Monday. But there's the problem of Danny needing supervision from after school until I get home from the office.' *Don't sound as though you're flirting with him. This is a parent–school principal problem.* 'Kathy Bernstein told me there were after-school groups. Are all students at the school eligible to attend them?'

'Oh, sure. There are art and music groups, a basketball group—' Unexpectedly he chuckled. 'That's a co-ed group of seven-to-nine-year-olds – and it seems to be working out great. Oh, and we've just started a new group – games playing. They start with checkers, will move up to chess. What do you think will interest Danny most?'

She felt a surge of confusion. 'I don't know,' she confessed. 'He loves his computer games—'

'Come in and talk with our guidance counsellor,' Brian advised. 'Cliff Hanson. He's great at digging out what kids will enjoy. Any problems, ring my doorbell.'

She hesitated, ambivalent. 'Danny's spent the past three years at an Iranian religious school. Very strict, heavy on memorization. I tutored him in math and English because I knew—' She struggled for composure. 'I knew that, somehow, I had to get him back home. I married young – and the marriage was dead—' *Why am I talking this way?*

'That can be a bad scene.' His smile was rueful. 'I married straight out of college—'

'So did I. But Marty changed – he became another person.' *Why am I telling this to a stranger?* 'I didn't think it was possible.' She gestured her shock and disbelief.

'After a while we see things in a different light.' His eyes glowed with remembered pain. 'I think half the town knew before I did that Denise was into drugs and alcohol. I tried to push her into rehab – she laughed at me. She died of an overdose – when she was three months pregnant.'

'How sad,' Caren whispered in shock.

'I hadn't even known she was pregnant. The baby would be eight years old if he – or she – had lived.'

That's why he looks at Danny with such tenderness.

'Congratulations on finding a job so fast—' He was making a determined effort to switch the conversation to happier ground. 'In this era job-hunting can be a rough situation.'

'I was worried,' she admitted. She was relieved that they were moving away from deeply personal subjects. 'I read the *Sunday Sentinel* – and there was just one ad I could reasonably follow up. I couldn't quite make it as a short order cook or a mechanic's helper.' She tried for lightness.

'All it takes is one—' His eyes were full of questions. *I shouldn't have talked the way I did.*

'It's a temporary job – for anywhere from six to nine

months.' *Why is he looking at me that way? Why do I feel so drawn to him? Because he's being sympathetic?* 'I'll be an administrative assistant at Loveland Development Corporation. A new firm in town, I gather.'

'Yes.' His face tightened. He glanced at his watch. 'I'd better get cracking. I have an early meeting this evening.'

She watched as he strode across the deck and into his share of the house. What had suddenly turned him off? Something about Loveland Development Corporation? *Why didn't he say what he was thinking?*

Brian tried to appear interested in Hannah's report of her husband's positive response to new medication for his arthritis problem.

'I mean, it's so confusing – the way the drug companies keep throwing all those television commercials at you. I tell Bill – the drug companies shouldn't be prescribing medication. That's the doctor's job.' She frowned. 'Of course, Bill always worries about all those side-effect warnings that come with his prescriptions. He says these days patients have to use their own heads, too – in what he calls assembly line medicine.'

'If prescription drugs were banned from TV advertising, the ad agencies would be in bad shape.' He could carry on a conversation, Brian taunted himself – but Caren's words assaulted his brain:

'I'll be an administration assistant at Loveland Development Corporation.'

It was absurd to be upset because Caren was going to work for those creeps. She couldn't possibly understand what they were trying to do to those families living by the lake. To Hannah's sister and brother-in-law. She was just happy that she'd found a job. But he foresaw an ugly, vicious battle between Loveland and the caring portion of Primrose. Instinct told him she would be upset.

'The salmon-rice casserole is warming in the oven,' Hannah reported, preparing to leave. 'It's loaded with mushrooms and French-cut string beans – the kind you like. You should have salmon at least twice a week,' she reminded. 'That's what the nutritionists keep telling us.'

'You cook it and I'll eat it,' Brian promised.

Hannah left. Brian went to the range to boil water for tea. A cup of tea, his refuge in moments of stress. Then he'd consider an early dinner. He was meeting again tonight with Jill and Phil and the group they'd brought together to fight the town's threatened condemnation of those houses by the lake.

All of a sudden I feel like a teenager suffering over his first crush. What do they call it these days? Forget it! I can be helpful, sympathetic – but there's no room in my life for any woman.

Twenty-Nine

The following morning Caren spoke with Cliff Hanson about the after-school groups, arranged for Danny to attend the Friday seven to nine ages basketball group because Kathy had said Laurie was part of it. Let him start on a day when Laurie would be there with him.

'The coach will have him observe at his first session,' Hanson explained. 'Then he'll participate the following Friday. He'll need shorts to play.'

'He'll have them,' Caren promised.

She and Danny would watch a basketball game on television, she plotted. His one exposure to sports – other than three or four skiing sessions with Marty – had been the soccer game he'd seen with Marty. He'd talked about it for days afterwards, she remembered. A big occasion in his young life.

Fighting insecurity, Caren registered Danny for groups on the other four days of the week. Was this what some Americans called over-scheduling? she asked herself uneasily. But it was necessary if she was to hold on to her job at Loveland.

Danny seemed to be fitting into their new lifestyle, she told herself. Wanting to believe this. He wasn't asking about when they'd 'go home.' Thank God for television and computer games – and for Laurie and Cindy across the road. Yet at intervals in the course of each day she was attacked by fears of Marty's next move to track them down.

She saw Danny off to school on Friday with special trepidation. This was the first day he would be part of the after-school program. Kathy – bless her – had confided she'd told Laurie to 'look out for Danny' at their after-school group.

Thus far, Caren remembered, there was no school bus

program to bring the kids home from the after-school sessions. Kathy had volunteered to bring Danny home along with Laurie and Cindy on the three days a week they were attending now. She'd go straight from work to pick him up the other two days.

Today seemed endless, Caren fretted. So much depended on Danny's accepting the after-school program. This was one of the days Kathy would pick him up, along with Laurie and Cindy.

'*I do some work from home – one or two days a week I go into Howie's office.*' Kathy had been almost defensive. '*But I worked only at home until both kids were in school full time.*'

Only then had she realized that Kathy, too, was an attorney. She'd met Howie their second year in law school, married right after graduation. But their marriage was a good one.

Caren filled the mid-afternoon with cooking. Something that had occupied little of her time in the past five years. She'd checked Janis's website twice already today. No more until bed time.

A chicken – along with yams – was in the oven, the timer set for 6 p.m. Salad in the refrigerator. Low-fat frozen yogurt in the freezer – a small celebration for Danny's first day at the after-school session.

Had Danny been happy in his group? Was his attendance there going to be a problem? No, think positive. Danny will love the after-school activities.

By 5:10 p.m. she was on the deck – flipping through a magazine. Her mind reproaching her for being fearful that Danny wouldn't be picked up. She was self-conscious at being probably the only single mother in Primrose without a car. Outside of major cities a car was an accepted necessity.

She straightened up, magazine sliding to the deck, when she saw the Bernsteins' suburban coming down the road. Her heart pounding. So much depended upon Danny's accepting the after-school session.

The suburban stopped before turning into the driveway. Danny emerged. Laurie's voice calling after him.

'Ask your mom if you can go to the soccer game with us in the morning—'

Caren rose to her feet with a welcoming smile. She tried to decipher his mood. He was walking fast. Was he glad to be home? Or was it just that he was hungry?

'Hi, Danny—' she called out cheerfully as he approached. 'Have fun after school?'

'It was OK—' He was non-committal.

'Come up on the deck and tell me all about it,' she coaxed.

As though this was obligatory, Caren told herself anxiously, Danny reported on the after-school activities. Another car was approaching, turned into the driveway. Brian.

'Hi—' He waved as he headed for the deck. 'How'd you like the basketball group?' *He'd bothered to follow up on Danny.*

'OK.' Danny was polite but wary.

'You didn't get to play yet?' Brian's tone was sympathetic. 'You will next week. You ever play before?'

'No.' *He's scared, afraid he won't be good. That damn 'I must be perfect' deal.*

'I have an idea.' Brian radiated enthusiasm. 'Why don't I set up a basketball hoop on the front lawn here? I'm sure I have a spare somewhere in the basement – and a basketball. I'll set it up in the morning – you can help me. Then you can practice over the weekend. Would you like that?'

'Yeah—' Danny seemed surprised at Brian's offer. 'OK.'

He can't figure out why Brian is being so friendly. It's because Brian likes children. He must be a fine principal.

'We've got a date,' Brian told him. 'See you right after breakfast tomorrow.'

All through dinner – while Danny talked about his home-work with a self-conscious air of triumph – Caren thought about Brian's warmth, his compassion. He saw a little boy in a strange, sometimes frightening situation, and he wanted to help. *I mustn't read anything else into his helpfulness to us.*

After dinner – of his own volition – Danny settled down to do his Monday homework. Then he stationed himself at the computer until he began to yawn.

'Bed time,' Caren said. 'Remember you have a date with Brian after breakfast tomorrow.'

Not until she was sure Danny was asleep did she go to

the computer to check on Janis's website. She was becoming compulsive about this, she scolded herself. She'd reread the last letter just four hours ago.

But she was conscious of a warm feeling that she could reach out and almost touch Janis this way. In moments the website was displayed on her monitor. A new letter! She stiffened at attention.

In her usual fashion Janis wrote about everyday activities.

Caren skimmed, knowing a new letter meant more news. Here it is!

> Nadine came over a little while ago. She's furious. Her niece's husband discovered her e-mail address. He wrote that when the ads in her community complete their two-week cycle and if there are no results, he's placing ads in newspapers in every major city in the Midwest. That's where he suspects she's hiding with the girls. He's swearing she can't keep hiding from him. I don't know if she is in the Midwest – as I gather she said in the letter she left – but I'm betting he won't find them.

Caren was cold with fear when she turned off the computer. Next Marty would hit all the major cities in the Midwest. Maybe up the reward. He'd come up with nothing. But he was tenacious – and furious. He wanted Danny back – no matter what the cost.

How long before he ran ads in one of the tabloids that were sold in supermarkets across the country? Back in their Westchester days he'd talked about them with such contempt – but he'd been impressed with their coverage. She felt sick as she envisioned walking into the Primrose IGA and discovering Marty's ad in the current issue of one of those rags.

When will Marty move into advertising in the supermarket tabloids? How much longer can Danny and I remain in Primrose?

Thirty

From habit Caren awoke early on Saturday morning. She lay against her pillow with eyes closed. Rejecting the new sun-brightened day. Conscious first of a draining tiredness – the result of restless, broken slumber. Then all at once fully awake. Janis's website report ricocheting in her brain:

'He wrote that when the ads in her community paper complete their two-week cycle and if there are no results, he's placing ads in newspapers in every major city in the Midwest.'

So perhaps for another three weeks – possibly four – they were safe from Marty, she assessed. But if he had no success in those two areas, he'd move on to something with greater potential, she tormented herself. The supermarket tabloids.

'Mommie?' Danny – pajama-clad and barefoot – stood in her doorway. 'Do you think Brian is—?' He halted, insecure in using Brian's given name.

'You may call him Brian away from school,' Caren stipulated. Instinct told her Brian would approve.

'Do you think Brian is ready to put up the basketball hoop?'

'It's early in the morning,' she scolded gently. 'No school today. Brian's probably sleeping late.'

'Oh—' Dejection in his voice.

'We'll be ready by the time he comes out to set up the hoop,' she promised.

'He said I could help,' Danny reminded, hope shadowed by doubt.

'Of course you can. We'll be ready for him.'

In record time Caren and Danny showered, dressed, were sitting down to breakfast. Danny's eyes traveled at regular intervals to the door. Marty had never enlisted his help in any venture. Brian understood it was important to Danny to be part of setting up the basketball hoop.

No sounds came from Brian's part of the house. Danny grew anxious. Then a car turned into the driveway. Danny darted to a window.

'It's Brian! And he's got a basketball hoop – and other things!' Danny turned to Caren. 'Can I go out now?'

'Go—' Her smile indulgent. 'I'll wash the dishes and be right out, too.'

Her face luminescent, she listened to the outdoor sounds while she washed the few dishes, stacked them in the rack. Brian had gone somewhere early this morning and collected whatever he needed to set up the basketball hoop, she surmised. He was involving Danny in the whole project. Oh, that was good!

A few minutes later she was on the deck to watch the operation in work. Brian in jeans and red corduroy shirt. Danny in jeans and red-checkered flannel shirt. To strangers driving by, she thought involuntarily, they might be father and son.

At intervals she joined in the lively conversation.

'It's all set,' Brian announced at last. Grinning in satisfaction. 'OK, Danny, take the ball and try it out.'

Danny hesitated. 'I might miss—'

'So you miss,' Brian shrugged this off. 'You'll keep trying until you get the hang of it. No law says you have to score on the first try.'

Caren watched with mixed emotions. This was so right for Danny – but how long could they stay here?

Across the road Laurie and Cindy hurried out of their front door.

'Hi!' Cindy yelled. 'We're going to the soccer game!'

'Danny, you wanna go with us?' Laurie called to him. 'My mommie said we could invite you.'

Danny gazed from the two little girls to Brian, to his mother. Torn between such richness.

'Caren, he can go to the soccer game, can't he?' Brian turned again to Danny. 'You can play with the hoop later.'

Kathy emerged from the house, called to Caren. 'We're going to the soccer game. What about taking Danny with us?'

His face radiant, Danny swung to face his mother. 'Mommie, can I go? Can I?'

'Sure, darling. You'll have fun.' So little fun in his short life. 'Thanks, Kathy,' Caren called back. 'He'll love it.'

In a flurry of anticipation Danny darted across the road. Kathy was bringing the suburban from the garage. In moments the three kids were piling inside. The car pulled away with three pairs of small hands waving goodbye to Caren and Brian.

'Would you like coffee?' Caren asked Brian after a moment of awkward uncertainty.

'Great,' he approved. 'I'm lazy – I usually settle for boiling water and a tea bag. Coffee's a treat.'

'I'll bring it out on the deck.' She hesitated. *Does he think I don't want to be alone with him in the apartment?* 'This is too beautiful a day to stay indoors—'

'Days like this I wish I was at my little place in the mountains.' His smile was wistful. 'It's just a rundown little cottage that belonged to my parents. I tell myself I should sell it – but the taxes are minuscule and the upkeep low. It's the place I run to when I need resuscitation.'

'That's very precious,' she said quietly. 'But let me go make our coffee.'

With mugs of coffee in hand they sat in the pair of chairs that flanked the deck's table and talked on safe topics. The after-school groups he'd set up at Primrose Elementary. His conviction about the best way to utilize the school's bilingual teachers. Then all at once – knowing she was acting on impulse again, yet feeling this was required of her – Caren moved into a more personal topic.

'I suppose people in town are wondering why I moved here – straight from Iran.'

His smile was wry. 'They're too polite to ask questions—'

She took a deep breath, forced herself to continue. 'Danny and I are on the run—' *I'm out of my mind to be talking this way.*

But she was conscious of an urgent need to explain their presence to him. Her words tumbling over one another, she explained about their rigid lives in Iran, her rebellion against the way Danny's mind was being manipulated. Her fear that Danny would be killed in some attempt on Marty's life.

'For a long time I knew I must bring Danny home. I knew his father would never agree – and I couldn't risk trying to sneak out of the country with him in the middle of the night. I'd heard many stories about the tragic results of such attempts. It was too dangerous – too traumatic for Danny.'

'But you managed.' His eyes were gentle. Admiring.

'I had help from two wonderful Iranian friends,' she admitted and told him about Pari and Andrea. *Why am I telling Brian this?*

'If you're right, and Danny's father eventually runs ads in newspapers that will be read in this town, I suspect no one would betray your presence. An American woman and a little boy running from a harsh Iranian husband? From a suffocating lifestyle.'

She stared at him in skepticism. 'The reward will be high – someone will be greedy.' She took a deep breath. 'I want so much to stay here—'

'You say your – husband – is running ads in newspapers in your sister's area?'

Caren nodded. 'And if nothing develops – and it won't – he'll move on to ads in major cities in the Midwest. In my letter to him I said that's where Danny and I would live.' She took a deep breath, exhaled. 'From there he'll head for a supermarket tabloid,' she guessed in anguish.

'Caren, you don't know that,' he objected. 'After a few weeks of getting nowhere – with ads in the California newspapers and in the Midwest – he'll back off. And if the investigators should track you down to Primrose, they'll get nowhere. You and Danny are both American citizens. They can't forcibly take Danny away.'

'I wish I could believe that—'

'Caren, this is the United States. Investigators – no matter how well they're paid – won't try to kidnap Danny.'

'If Marty knows where we are, he'll send over thugs from Iran.' *Brian's so decent – he doesn't understand Marty's capabilities. That Marty will resort to anything to get Danny back.* 'I'm scared.'

'Don't be,' Brian insisted. 'If there's the slightest chance that he knows you're here, then we'll arrange for protection. This isn't Iran,' he emphasized. 'Nobody is going to kidnap Danny and take him back there.'

'Janis always says I overreact.' Caren forced a weak smile. *I mustn't let Brian know I'm plotting our next move. I'll just disappear one day.* 'Sometimes I let my imagination go berserk.'

But she remembered the three years when Marty was working to set up the company's branch in New York. He'd studied advertising in such depth. Try the least expensive markets first, he'd said, then move up the ladder. She visualized his excitement when the company's first commercial appeared on TV, even while he winced at the cost. His father had protested – until he saw the rise in sales.

'The man's running a long-distance battle,' Brian pursued. 'Very soon he'll see it as futile. But at any sign of trouble,' he emphasized, 'we'll bring in the police.'

Local police? she asked herself. Not enough. But bodyguards would be expensive. How long would her funds hold out? Was this the time to run to Canada?

I have our passports. Danny and I could go to Canada with no trouble. But I don't want to leave here.

Thirty-One

Caren was grateful that Kathy was involving Danny in weekend activities. He returned from the soccer game to announce that Kathy was having a picnic dinner on their deck around six o'clock. He was invited.

'Can I go, Mommie?' He glowed in anticipation of this festive occasion. So new to him.

'Of course you may,' she agreed.

'Can I go early?' he pursued. 'Kathy said we could watch *The Lion King* on their DVD player before dinner.' Caren doubted that he quite knew what *The Lion King* was – but it was sufficient that Laurie and Cindy were eager to see it.

'Only if you give me a kiss before you leave,' she stipulated in an effort at lightness. 'But let's go inside now and have lunch.'

Later – with Danny at the Bernsteins' house – she sat alone on the deck and tried to grapple with the problems that lay ahead. Was it possible to divorce Marty here in New York state – where they'd been married? But to do this, she warned herself, would lead Marty here. He would have to be notified of the divorce proceedings.

She gathered the children were inside the Bernstein house watching *The Lion King*. Kathy was bringing dishes out to the picnic table that sat on the deck while Howie was preparing the outdoor barbecue grill. She remembered similar occasions in Westchester – but that seemed another lifetime now.

She felt a flicker of excitement when she saw what Brian called his antique Ford swing into the driveway. It was just that she felt so grateful for his helpfulness, she told herself – and he was only responding to a small boy in trouble.

Nothing more. But she knew that was a lie. His eyes told her differently.

Brian left the car in the driveway, walked up to the deck. 'Where's our basketball player this afternoon?'

'Across the road. Kathy invited him to watch *The Lion King* with Laurie and Cindy.' She managed a festive note. 'And afterwards he's having dinner with them on the deck.' *Why do I react this way each time I'm with Brian?* 'I feel deserted.'

'It's such a gorgeous day – why don't we have a picnic dinner on our deck? I'm sure I can rustle up something—' He seemed exhilarated at the prospect.

'Do you have a picnic table?' For a little while forget the problems facing Danny and her. 'I can dig up the food if you can provide the table.' Dinner demanded more than the coffee table here on the deck.

'I can,' he said in triumph. 'My last tenants – two great guys who moved back to New York – left a bistro table and two chairs they'd used on the deck in the warm months. I'll run down to the basement and bring them up.'

For a little while, she promised herself with a touch of defiance, she would pretend this was a casual Saturday afternoon. They'd have an early picnic dinner, and she'd forget – for a little while – the ugly days ahead.

Brian hurried off to his basement. She went into her kitchen, brought out the salmon steaks meant for dinner for Danny and herself, salad makings, gnocchi. A quick but satisfying meal, she approved. Low-fat frozen yogurt – Danny's once a week treat – for dessert. Oh, and put up more coffee.

Busy in the kitchen, Caren was aware that Brian was bringing up the table and two chairs. Now he was going into his apartment, emerged minutes later with a tablecloth and napkins. Caren brought out silverware, then plates of food and a salad bowl.

'Wow, that looks good,' he approved while they settled themselves at the table – both determined to be casual. But despite their efforts, table conversation turned intensely personal.

It was as though, Caren thought, that Brian was unleashing all the ugliness of his marriage. They were two people who'd married too young and in haste. Who'd strived to make their lives acceptable – when there had been no chance of this happening.

'I haven't talked this way to anybody—' His eyes held hers – saying far more than he'd allow himself to put into words. 'I know you'll understand.'

'Yes—' Her voice unsteady. This was happening too fast. *What can there ever be for us?*

'So—' She knew he was making an effort to dispel the mood that gripped them. 'On Monday you start your new job.'

She nodded, managed a shaky smile. 'I'm hoping that Danny won't fight going to the after-school sessions.' The familiar tightening in her throat now.

'He handled yesterday's session OK,' Brian reminded with an encouraging smile.

'I'm keeping my fingers crossed. This is all so new to him.' How ironic, to run from hell with Marty to what could be heaven with Brian – and knowing this can never be.

'He's a bright, sensitive little boy. He's going to be all right here,' Brian said with conviction.

Will he? How do I handle this if Danny balks?

The weekend sped past – with Danny spending much time at the basketball hoop, accompanied by Laurie and Cindy – for which Caren was grateful. Again on Monday morning she geared herself for seeing Danny off to school. *He's accepting this. Why am I so fearful?*

She watched from the deck while he ran down to join Laurie and Cindy at the bus stop. Moments later the yellow school bus lumbered down the road, stopped at the corner. In avid conversation with Laurie, Danny climbed aboard. Caren exhaled in relief.

She hurried back into the apartment, sent anxious glances at her watch. She mustn't be late her first day on the job. Change into her black suit, she ordered herself – but wear a different blouse from the one she wore at her interview. She'd brought along a second suit – with changes of blouses. That would have to do for now. But she flinched in sudden realization. Summer wardrobe would soon be necessary. For both Danny and her. More expenses to handle.

Ten minutes later she left the apartment. Fighting insecurity. Marty had long ago eroded her self-confidence. She could handle this job with no sweat. Nothing difficult about it. *I can deal.*

She glanced at her watch. In fifteen minutes she must be at the Loveland Development office. No problem there. Still, she strode with a sense of urgency. The lone walker.

Again, she was invaded by doubts. Could she handle this job? She'd been so confident at the interview. *Are my computer skills adequate? Will I be able to handle the phone calls? What do I know about this field? I hate being brusque with people – but I'll have to get rid of unwanted callers.*

The work wouldn't be complicated, she tried to comfort herself. It was a development company – they must build houses. And all at once she understood Brian's odd reaction when she said she'd be working for Loveland. That article in the *Sentinel*! The reporter was talking about Loveland Development!

She struggled to recall the exact words of the front-page story. A just-formed group in town – headed by Brian – was fighting the efforts of a builder to win approval to construct an apartment complex in Primrose. New jobs in town, a help for a sagging economy, they proclaimed. But this entailed ousting – via eminent domain – the owners of sixty-two very modest houses. Houses that had stood there for thirty or more years.

The article hadn't named Loveland as the offending organization, yet instinct told her this was the case. But she would be a lowly cog in the Loveland machinery, she told herself defensively. If she rejected the job, they'd just hire somebody else.

I need that weekly paycheck – even if only for six to nine months. If Danny and I can stay here that long.

Not until she arrived at the office of Loveland Development did she realize how fast she'd been walking. Faintly breathless, she opened the storefront door at 8.51 a.m. and walked inside. Fighting guilt – because this was the kind of operation she'd fought while in college, in the brief years they'd spent in Westchester.

The divider that had been in place when she'd been here

for the interview had been removed. A half-dozen small cubicles were set up at the rear and occupied by employees she suspected had been brought in from out of town. Carl Watson sat at his oversized executive desk – in volatile telephone conversation.

Within minutes she was about to embark on her first day's assignment. Watson explained this was to be a huge mailing extolling the benefits of the proposed development. He gazed at her in speculation. She tensed.

'This letter was done in rough,' he said with an indulgent air. 'Are you equipped to clean it up a bit?'

'Yes—' This she could handle.

'Do it.'

While she sat at the computer – editing as she typed the two-page letter, she heard Watson in conversation with Mayor Davis. Not one of Brian's favorite people, she recalled.

'Let's have dinner tonight,' Watson was urging. 'I have the figures you'll want to study. This is a fantastic deal for the town.' He listened to the voice at the other end. 'Oh, come on, Tim, you can handle those guys. This is progress – the twenty-first century. And you'll be well taken care of,' he purred. A pause again. 'Sure, seven o'clock will be fine. I'll meet you there.'

A few moments later Watson approached Caren. 'Some time before noon call the Coleridge Inn in Langley and make a dinner reservation for me at seven p.m. A reservation for four.'

'Right.' Langley was a community about thirty-five miles from Primrose, Caren recalled. Kathy had talked about a high school basketball game there next week. Dinner in Langley, Caren interpreted – because Watson didn't want to be seen dining with Mayor Davis. 'I'll do it right away.'

Should I tell Brian about this? What Loveland is trying to do to those families is despicable. If I tell him, it could leak back to me. I need this job – if Danny and I can stay here. How can I gamble on losing it?

Thirty-Two

Caren left the Loveland office at a few minutes past 5 p.m. She was exhausted. Not from the work required of her, she realized – from the strain of this first day on a job. She sensed that Carl Watson was pleased with her. But at regular intervals in the course of the day she was attacked by guilt. She was working with the people unmasked in that article in the *Sentinel*.

The *Sentinel* must have been talking about Loveland, she told herself yet again. Ruthless business executives hungry for the dollar. Not caring whom they hurt. Like Marty, she thought, and felt encased in ice.

Would it help the group fighting to save those houses if they knew Carl Watson planned a secret meeting this evening with Mayor Davis? *But how can I tell Brian? I'm the one who made the reservation – Watson will remember that. I could lose my job – or even worse.*

She strode away from the storefront office as though to escape ugly repercussions. She glanced at her watch. Danny would be home shortly from his newest after-school session. Had he liked it? Would he go again tomorrow without a battle?

This was one of the three afternoons when Kathy would be driving Danny home along with Laurie and Cindy. Kathy had said that if she was a little late in coming home from the office, then Danny would remain with her and the girls. How wonderful to meet people like the Bernsteins and Brian.

She turned the corner on to Cypress Road. Birds were carrying on a cheerful symphony. She spied a brilliant red cardinal – a male, she told herself, because the female cardinal's color was more subdued – speeding from one tree to another. A pair of squirrels scampered down the road. Brian said that on occasion deer would dart across the lawns.

'That's why I gave up on planting hyacinths and rose bushes. The deer cut them down in the middle of the night. Their favorite food. But we mustn't begrudge them,' he'd added. 'This was once open country – their country.'

She sniffed the exquisite scent of grass being mowed. A large truck stood at one side of the road while a crew of workmen pushed noisy, mechanized mowers over wide sweeps of lawn. For a moment she was swept back into earlier days.

The spring when she was eleven and Janis thirteen, they'd persuaded their parents to pay them to mow their lawn with an old-fashioned hand mower they'd discovered in the basement of the house. A relic of earlier days. One try and they'd resigned. What Dad called 'the pros' were called in as usual.

Twenty-one years ago, Dad said, 'We're living in a fast changing world. When I was a boy, I mowed lawns for spending money. A lot of kids did.' What would Dad say if he was alive today? And again, she felt a rush of sadness because Danny never knew his grandparents on her side. Grandparents who would have adored him.

Nearing the apartment, she heard the rumble of another lawn mower. Brian was mowing their lawn. She glanced across the road to the Bernsteins' driveway. The garage door was open. No car sat there or in the driveway. Too early for Kathy to have picked up the kids.

'Hi,' she called, walking up the path to the house. 'You're on your second job—' It was a pleasant spring day, but Brian's face glistened with perspiration.

He grinned, waved. 'I need the exercise—'

She went into the apartment, changed into slacks and a lightweight sweater. The sounds outside stopped now. On impulse, she called out the window to Brian.

'Would you like a glass of fruit juice? Apple or orange?'

'I'd love anything cold. Just let me put this away – I'll be right there.'

She brought out a pitcher of apple juice and two tall glasses. Moments later Brian joined her on the deck.

'Oh, that looks great.' He reached to take a juice-filled glass from her, gulped in obvious appreciation. Now he gazed at her with the disconcerting intensity that said what neither of them would put into words. 'So, you survived your first day on the job.' His smile was quizzical.

'Not much required of me.' Her shrug was casual – but her mind was in high gear. 'When I mentioned my being hired by Loveland, you seemed startled.' She paused. 'As though you were trying to hold back disapproval.'

He frowned. 'I didn't mean that—'

'Later I thought about it. And I remembered that article in the *Sentinel*. About your working with a protest group. The article didn't name Loveland – but that's the company involved.' Her eyes searched his. 'Isn't it?'

'Right.' He seemed to be reaching for words. 'We're building up to moving into an open battle. It's a ghastly thing they're trying to do. To throw low-income people out of the modest little houses they've lived in for thirty or forty years. Their mortgages finally paid off. Hannah's sister and brother-in-law live in one of those houses. They sweated through long years to make their mortgage payments. They love their house.'

'I don't understand a law that allows them to lose their homes.' Caren was bewildered. 'I know about eminent domain – but I thought this dealt with property that was necessary for the common good.'

'The interpretation now is that these new apartments – with soaring rents,' he added contemptuously, 'will provide housing for more people. For the common good.'

'A huge mailing is going out—' She hesitated. Somber. Uncertain. 'To a list of local residents—'

He stiffened to attention. 'What's its message?'

'That the housing complex they're prepared to build will create a lot of jobs, bring in more tax revenue. That it'll be great for the sagging economy.'

'Temporary jobs!' Brian scoffed. 'The demand for services will escalate. And what about those sixty-two families who will be destroyed?'

'I know,' Caren said softly. 'The law should not allow this.' She hesitated a moment, then rushed ahead. 'This evening Carl Watson is meeting Mayor Davis – and two others – for dinner at the Coleridge Inn in Langley. I assume they don't want to be seen together in Primrose.' She took a deep breath. 'I overheard a conversation between Watson and Davis. Watson hinted that Davis would be – rewarded.'

Brian's face tightened. 'You're sure about this dinner meeting?'

'I made the reservations. For seven p.m. this evening. Reservations for four.' Now she was uneasy. 'I had to tell you – but how can you use that without its leading back to me?' *I acted on impulse again. When will I learn better?*

'We won't let that happen, Caren.' He clutched the glass of apple juice as though seeking support, squinted in thought. 'We can handle it!' he said in relief.

'How?' Caren's heart was pounding. *I shouldn't have told Brian – yet how could I not?*

'Jill and Phil Cramer will have dinner at the Coleridge tonight,' he plotted. 'They'll be celebrating their wedding anniversary. Jill will have one of those disposable cameras to take a snapshot of the occasion.'

'And she'll take a photo of Mayor Davis and his party—'

Brian nodded in satisfaction. 'Tomorrow morning's *Sentinel* will carry a front-page photo of Carl Watson and Tim Davis – and the other two in their party. It's time to split this story wide open – and here's the fuel for it. Thanks, Caren, for making this happen.' His smile was a warm caress.

'Carl Watson won't know I told you—' Caren sighed in relief.

'We have lawyers who'll refute the use of eminent domain in this situation. And it'll be clear that Loveland is conspiring to woo the mayor to play on their side. And it's clear the mayor is willing.'

Caren lay sleepless far into the night. Her mind warned her it was time to pack up and run again with Danny. They were fighting against time. Marty was running his revolting ad for two weeks in Janis's area. The days were running past – and he'd go on to the large Midwest cities – the way his investigator told Janis. Another two weeks respite – which would reveal nothing. And then he'd hit the supermarket tabloids.

I know Marty so well. That'll be his next move! He used

to ridicule the power of the supermarket tabloids – but now he'll use it.

Brian is logical. He's sure the thugs Marty hires can't kidnap Danny and take him back to Tehran. But we live in an illogical world. Why can't I bring myself to pack up now and run? What miracle could occur to make that unnecessary? I don't believe in miracles.

Thirty-Three

Caren allowed herself a deep breath of relief as she left the Loveland office on this overcast Friday afternoon – the conclusion of her first week on the job. A week that had seemed almost uneventful – though the threat of a dangerous turn never left her mind.

She was leaving twenty minutes later than normal. And each minute had seemed an hour, she admitted to herself. But no real problem. This was a day when Kathy picked up the kids at the after-school center.

Still, she must explain to Carl – who insisted on first names within the office – that on Tuesdays and Thursdays she couldn't work past five thirty at the latest. A teacher remained on duty until 6 p.m. She could walk there in fifteen minutes. But she must make Danny understand – no need for panic if she was a little late.

The only walkers in Primrose other than herself, she thought with an effort at humor, were the immigrant dayworkers. She saw them dragging bags from the supermarket to their living accommodations – basement apartments in rundown houses, where two or three families lived in three rooms. Often illegal rentals, Kathy had told her. Sympathetic to their plights.

She could understand the immigrants' need to flee their poverty-stricken, dictatorial home towns. Like herself, they were eager to live in freedom. She remembered Brian's compassion for the immigrant children. He'd talked about the little second-grade boy from Iraq who had been bullied by two sixth-graders from two prominent local families.

'The father of one of those creepy kids is on the Board of Ed – and disciplining them creates problems. But damn, this isn't some third world country ruled by a dictator! That little

boy from Iraq must be shown that this is a democracy. In a democracy such crap isn't tolerated.'

She felt satisfaction when she was able to supply Brian – and his group of protestors – with useful information about the activities at Loveland. The whole deal was out in the open now. It would be a major factor in voting Mayor Davis out of office, Brian insisted.

This was like old times in Westchester – when she and Marty had fought for the good things. Like the years at Columbia. She had no way of knowing then that Marty campaigned with her because he believed this was a way to win favor in her eyes. He was almost ignored by his family. Lonely. She was a safe haven. But once they were in Iran, that had changed so fast.

This week had been good, she thought defensively. No questions from Danny about when they were going back to Tehran. This was pushed back into a corner of his mind – along with his fears that 'Daddy will be so mad.'

He liked the school and the after-school groups. He reveled in having Laurie and Cindy as friends. He adored Daisy, talked to Laurie and Cindy about the puppy he would soon have.

But I must not wear blinders. Our days in Primrose are numbered. We must move on, outrun the tabloid with Marty's ads. Check on cities in Canada. Forget the small town scene – it'll be easier to lose ourselves in a large Canadian city.

Go online – check out Canadian cities on Google. The dollar is worth more in Canada – an advantage. Figure out the best transportation – the least expensive.

But the prospect was unnerving. Danny was settling in here – he had friends. So quickly Brian had become import-ant in their lives. She didn't want to leave this new life in Primrose.

Approaching the house, she saw Brian weeding the flower beds. He tried to come home early now – before Danny arrived, so that each afternoon they could talk about what was happening at Loveland. He filled her in on what his protest group was planning, talked about his fight with the Board of Ed for more funds, more autonomy in the elementary school.

Always there were the unspoken messages his eyes sent

to her. He knew – she was certain – that his feelings were reciprocated. Yet she kept a shaky wall between them. At unwary moments she remembered that her mother and father had known each other only six weeks when they were married – and theirs had been a fine marriage.

Brian knows my situation. That I'm married – and unlikely to be able to divorce Marty. That I'll run with Danny to keep Marty from taking him back to Tehran. But he doesn't realize Danny and I could be running again very soon.

'Hi—' Brian rose from his haunches to greet her. 'Hannah put up coffee for us before she left. I'll bring it out.'

'Oh, that sounds lovely.' Hannah the romantic, she thought tenderly. Now she ordered herself to thrust reality away. Savor the hours and days with Brian.

By the time they settled themselves on the deck – for coffee and the cookies Hannah had supplied – the clouds in the sky had disappeared. Sunlight engulfed them. According to the weather people, tomorrow was supposed to be an idyllic day.

'Are you busy for dinner tomorrow night?' she asked on impulse. *Why am I doing this?*

'No—' His face brightened.

'Let's have a cookout on the deck,' she invited. *This could be our last weekend together. How much longer can I stall on outrunning Marty?* 'Provided you have a grill?'

'I have a grill. It needs some cleaning up, but I can handle that.' His smile was charismatic. Hannah had confided, Caren recalled, that 'every unattached woman in town has tried to take him to the altar.'

Does Brian think I'm in pursuit of him? No! He realizes there can be nothing for us.

Caren willed herself to be casual on Saturday. Again, Danny went to the soccer game with the Bernsteins. Brian had driven away early in the morning. Sitting on the deck to read the morning's *Sentinel* – passed on by Brian, she remembered his parting words.

'I'm crammed with meetings today – but I'll be back around four o'clock. Plenty of time to clean up the grill. And I'll bring a shrimp salad and dessert.'

In the afternoon Laurie and Cindy joined Danny at the basketball hoop. Caren brought out plates of fruit salad topped with low-fat frozen yogurt for them. For a little while she could brush aside the fear that was constant in her life since the flight from Iran.

Brian came home, delivered shrimp salad and three chocolate eclairs.

'Low-fat eclairs,' he pointed out. 'We fight obesity in this house.'

'Right,' she agreed. Cherishing this light mood.

Brian went down to the basement, brought up the grill.

'I might as well clean it out here and enjoy the sun,' he said exuberantly.

Laurie and Cindy had been summoned home. Danny focused on Brian's grill-cleaning efforts. The portrait of serene family life, Caren taunted herself. Watching Danny with Brian, she realized she could go inside the house for a few minutes. To the computer and Janis's website. There would be no new letter today – but just to read the most recent was to feel in touch with Janis. To feel less alone.

She brought up Janis's website on the monitor – and all at once tensed. Janis began with the usual tidbits about their family life. New tidbits – new letter, Caren realized. She scanned casual news about family, then hit what Janis would call 'pay dirt.'

> I ran into Nadine about an hour ago. She was beginning to feel relieved – no e-mails from that PI for two days. Then she and Al drove up to San Francisco for the day. Al said they needed a change of scenery. They were in one of those news-stands that carries papers from all over the country. Al glanced through a couple of papers. There in a Kansas City newspaper was the weird ad again – offering a $20,000 reward now for information leading to his locating his wife and his two daughters.

Caren sat back in her chair. Dizzy from shock. Already Marty was moving on. Always so impatient. He'd receive no results from the Kansas City newspaper ad. How long would the ad run in that Kansas City newspaper? How long before he moved on to a supermarket tabloid? Into a Primrose supermarket.

Thirty-Four

B rian sat at his school desk on this Monday morning and tried to focus on his phone conversation with an angry member of the school's PTA.

'I know you're on our side,' his caller conceded. 'But when I heard the distributor controlling those awful soda and candy machines was fighting to install them in our elementary school, I was outraged. I don't want my kids exposed to that junk food.'

'I know they're in the middle school and high school cafeterias here – but we won't allow them to invade our school.' His laid-back voice, yet firm. 'It's not going to happen.'

His mind was still reeling from what Caren had confided to him yesterday afternoon. About her sister's website. Her husband's frenzied efforts to take back Danny. His ads – the offer of a reward. Caren's sense of being on the run.

It unnerved him to realize that in a matter of days – once Caren suspected her husband was close to locating Danny – she and Danny would disappear from his life. And he knew – without their exchanging words – that his feelings towards her were reciprocated. He was overwhelmed by a sense of helplessness.

'I wasn't sure who was in control of the situation.' His caller brought him back to the moment. 'Whether the elementary school could handle this – or if it goes all the way up to the mayor's office.'

'The machines won't come into our school,' Brian reiterated. 'We'll stop the delivery at our door if necessary. And I'll talk to the *Sentinel* about making this a front-page story.'

In another few moments he was able to get off the phone. He heard sounds in the halls now. Lively chatter, laughter, a teacher's voice remonstrating – as usual – about the noise level. The lower grades en route to the cafeteria for the first lunch period. Was it that late already? Where had the morning gone?

In line with his class Danny waited to be ushered into the cafeteria. His eyes – slightly anxious – were skimming the class ahead. Yes, Cindy was here, he saw with relief. Laurie ate with the next group.

'Hi, Danny—' Cindy had spotted him, waved.

'Hi—' It felt good to know Cindy was here.

His class lined up with their trays, made their choices, paid at the register. As usual he headed for the long table occupied by his classmates. At the next table sat the group of second and third graders who were in bilingual classes. Last week he'd been startled to hear one little boy trying to translate from Farsi to English.

Two older boys carrying trays – sixth graders – were arguing with the teacher on duty.

'You're not supposed to be in the lunch room at this hour,' she reproached them. 'This is for lower grades only.'

'We got permission,' one said with an arrogant smile. 'We have trouble with the pollen – Miss Brown said we could come and eat now.'

The two swaggered past the teacher, scanned the room, exchanged a whisper. They strolled down the aisle that divided the tables, paused at the table occupied by the bilingual class – just behind the table where Danny sat.

Danny turned around in his chair, watched. Sensing they were troublemakers.

'Well, whadda you know – more foreign kids here,' one remarked to the other. The eyes of the bilingual students cast downward. 'Do we wanna sit here?' he asked his companion, though every chair was occupied.

'This is our table,' one second-grader sitting directly behind Danny said with shaky defiance. The one who spoke Farsi.

'Why don't you and your old lady and old man go back where you come from?' the other demanded. 'You don't belong here!'

The second-grader lashed back in Farsi.

'Watch out!' Danny yelled in Farsi. He pushed back his

chair, leapt to his feet as one sixth grader attempted to dump his plate of soup on the little second grader.

Danny diverted the tray. The soup landed on the floor. Infuriated, the sixth grader reached to pull his target from his chair, while the other sixth grader began to punch him. Danny pummeled one sixth grader in rage. The teacher – involved with a pair of students across the room – blew her whistle, rushed to separate the four boys.

The other students watched – mesmerized – while the second-grade teacher – Miss Lockhart – tried to separate the four. The two sixth graders as tall as she. Brian charged into the room. In moments he separated the fighters, clamped a hand on a shoulder of each of the sixth graders.

'All right, you two!' Brian dared them to defy him. 'Miss Lockhart will take you to Mr Hanson's office. I'll be with you shortly. You're not getting off with just a warning this time!'

Danny was trembling. Furious. He and the boy who spoke Farsi had been attacked by infidels! All at once he felt himself in enemy territory.

I want to go home! I won't stay here!

'Move, you two,' Miss Lockhart ordered the two sixth graders. 'To Mr Hanson's office.'

Now excited young voices rushed to tell Brian what had happened.

Danny cowered, fearful of being punished. He remembered punishment back at his religious school. Would he be flogged? How many lashes?

With an encouraging smile Brian reached for the hand of the young bilingual student, then for Danny's hand. 'Everybody back to lunch now,' he called out to the others. 'You two,' he told Danny and the Farsi-speaking boy, 'you'll have lunch in my office with me.' He stopped to talk with the woman at the register, gave orders to send lunch for three to his office. Consulting with each startled boy about what he would like.

In obvious reluctance – while the other little boy seemed encased in shock – Danny allowed Brian to conduct them to his office. *Why are we to have lunch in Brian's office? What's Brian going to do to us? We started a fight in the lunchroom. What's the punishment for that?*

Brian instructed the two little boys to sit in chairs before his desk. He sat behind the desk. Danny shifted in unease.

'I was very proud of you, Danny—' He smiled as Danny gaped in disbelief. 'You're a hero. You went to the defense of a student who was being attacked by bullies. Neither you nor Hassan – ' he turned to the little Iraqi boy – 'was responsible for what happened.'

'They follow me home from school—' Hassan stammered, reaching for words. 'Say they beat me—'

'You won't have to worry about those two any longer,' Brian said. 'We live in a democracy. We don't accept such action.'

'They are infidels.' Danny's eyes were accusing. His father's words – drilled in him for five years – darted across his mind. *'Only true Muslims will go to Paradise. Infidels will die a terrible death.'*

'The word "infidel" means a disbeliever.' Brian spoke slowly. Like he was teaching a class, Danny thought. 'But in this country – in a true democracy – everyone has a right to follow his own beliefs. Or her own beliefs,' he added. 'We have all kinds of religions followed in this country. People who are Christians, Jews, Muslims, Buddhists – oh, a lot of religions. And that's the wonderful part about living in the United States. You can follow the religion you wish.'

'But those – they're—' Danny searched for a despicable word, settled on a Farsi epithet, which brought a fast nod from Hassan.

'They'll be punished,' Brian promised. His face grim.

Danny's eyes widened. 'How many lashes?'

'Danny, in this country no one is flogged. Those two will be expelled,' Brian explained. Danny and Hassan exchanged a puzzled glance. 'That means they can never come to this school again. If they try to come back – and to start trouble, the police will take them off for a hearing in juvenile court. They will be held in juvenile facilities. Like in jail,' he explained.

Danny's face was set in stubborn disbelief. *Brian is just making up stories.*

'Mr Woods—' Hassan hesitated. 'What is-is juvenile court?'

'You two must understand – in this country bad kids are punished, as they should be. But no floggings,' Brian emphasized.

Danny listened with mixed emotions while Brian explained how juvenile offenders were handled in the United States. But how could he know if Brian was telling the truth? Troubled, he turned to Hassan, who – like himself – seemed skeptical.

'Here's lunch,' Brian said, smiling. A cafeteria server had appeared with a tray. *He's not mad at us.* 'We'll eat, then I'll take each of you back to your classroom.'

Danny ate his lunch, but – like Hassan – contributed little to the conversation. *Did Brian mean what he said? Hassan and me won't be punished? We're heroes?*

Still, he was scared when he and Brian approached his classroom. The door was open. At his appearance twenty-two pairs of eyes swung in his direction.

'Hi,' Brian said with a wide smile. 'I've brought back your hero—' And twenty-two pairs of hands applauded.

Danny was light-headed in astonishment. *I did all right. Mommie will be glad.*

Thirty-Five

Walking home from the Loveland offices, Caren was conscious of a sharp chill in the air. Earlier the day had been late spring warm. The sun dazzling. Now huge clusters of dark clouds hovered above, threatened imminent rain. Thunder rumbled at disconcerting intervals. She should have packed a small umbrella in her purse, she reproached herself.

She'd been haunted by fearful images since reading Janis's website letter on Saturday. She couldn't stay in Primrose – she and Danny must run again. For the next few days they were safe – until Marty realized he'd have no response to his ad in the Kansas City newspaper. But this must be their last week in Primrose.

She felt sick at the prospect of uprooting Danny again – when he was beginning to accept living here. She knew that Marty would send thugs from Iran to snatch Danny away once he knew where they were. Brian talked about local protection. He didn't know Marty.

'How about a lift?'

Caren started at the sound of Brian's voice. She hadn't realized a car was approaching.

'Oh, yes—' Caren managed a smile. 'I was asking myself if I could make it home before the storm hits.'

'I figured I'd catch up with you.' He reached out a hand to squeeze hers in reassurance as she sat beside him.

'Not much happened at the office today,' she began her usual report. 'Nothing to be followed up—' She hesitated, for the first time voicing a concern about the job. 'I'm sure they haven't connected me with you as yet. I'm just a stranger in town, who needed a job.'

'If they discover you're living in the apartment, consider

you a hazard and fire you, the group will jump in to locate a replacement job for you.' *But I won't be here.*

For a few moments they rode in silence. Caren sensed that he was in some inner debate. Was he concerned that she'd lose the job?

'Caren, there was an incident at school today—' Brian began.

Alarm surged in her. 'What kind of an incident? Something to do with Danny?'

'It worked out all right,' Brian rushed to reassure her, then launched into a full report. 'Danny and Hassan appeared doubtful about those creepy bullies being expelled – but an announcement will be made at the school. They'll realize it's true. Still, it was a traumatic experience for Danny. He was afraid he'd be flogged.' Brian's eyes were angry. 'A routine in Iranian schools, I gather.'

'This threw him back into the old life.' Caren closed her eyes in anguish. 'I thought he'd put that behind him.'

'He went to his after-school group. I looked in on it. Later he'll play with Laurie and Cindy – and he'll snap back.' Brian exuded optimism. *Or is he just trying to comfort me?* 'You should have seen his face when his whole class applauded when I brought him back there. He was astounded. And I think – I suspect the difference between Primrose and Tehran was engraved on his mind in that moment. Yes,' he added with conviction, 'Danny can handle this.'

When Caren saw Kathy's suburban approaching the Bernstein driveway, she hurried forward with an oversized umbrella she'd discovered in a closet.

'What a rotten day it's become,' Kathy mourned, handing umbrellas to Laurie and Cindy. 'No outdoor play before dinner. But tomorrow's supposed to be nice again,' she reported. 'Let's hope they're right.'

'Mommie, there was a big fight in the cafeteria,' Cindy bubbled. 'Brian came to our class to talk about it.' She beamed. 'He said Danny was a hero.'

'I didn't do anything—' Danny stammered.

'I heard about it,' Caren rushed in with a smile, managing

to shelter Danny under the huge umbrella as he emerged from the car. 'I'm so proud of you, Danny.'

She wasn't surprised that Danny seemed troubled – silent – when they sat down to dinner. He'd been thrust back into the old life with ugly suddenness. Immediately after dinner he excused himself to go to his room to do his homework. No computer tonight.

An hour later the phone rang. Caren froze for an instant. Who would call them here? A wrong number, she told herself, and reached for the phone.

'Hello—'

'Hi, it's Laurie. Can I talk to Danny?'

'Sure, Laurie. Just a minute.'

She went to the door to Danny's tiny bedroom. 'A phone call for you, Danny—' He stared back in astonishment. 'It's Laurie.'

She pretended to be busy in the kitchen while Danny talked with Laurie. Something about a birthday party, she interpreted. Now Danny was calling to her.

'Mommie, Laurie's going to a birthday party on Sunday afternoon. I'm invited, too. It's a girl from my class – her mommie didn't know where to reach you. Can I go?' Yet an odd doubt coated his voice. He'd attended no birthday parties since leaving his preschool group in Tehran. He was eager to go because Laurie would be there – but wary, Caren interpreted. Another new experience.

'Of course, you can go to the party,' Caren told him tenderly. 'I'm sure her mother will call me, too.'

We'll be here for the party – leave the following Monday. Late at night. Marty understands it takes time for letters to reach him in response to the ad. We're safe till Monday.

As the weather people had promised, the rain that had pounded Primrose throughout the night gave way to another glorious spring day. Lawns were lush. Flowers bursting into bloom. But walking to Loveland this Tuesday morning, Caren knew she must cement her plans.

She'd spent every possible moment at the computer – on Google – in search of information about Canadian cities.

She wouldn't allow herself to ponder about the legal problem of remaining in Canada. Just live one day at a time.

At the office Caren realized within minutes that Carl Watson was in a triumphant mood. Not until late in the day did she realize he was about to cement a deal with Mayor Davis. Cash would exchange hands.

She was impatient to report this to Brian. But it must wait until they could talk in person – no phone calls. Here was the action Brian's group needed to kill Davis's chances at re-election. Action that would force the town council to reject Loveland's plans to take over those houses on the lake.

This was one of the two days each week when she had to pick up Danny at the after-school center, Caren reminded herself. Watching the clock. Carl knew she must leave on the dot of 5 p.m. today.

On schedule Caren was at the after-school center. She headed home with Danny, listened to his report of his day's activities. Brian was right – Danny could handle what happened yesterday.

'Hi!' Laurie's exuberant voice came to them.

Moments later Kathy drew up beside them in the suburban. 'I picked up Laurie at her ballet class and dropped off Cindy for a sleepover with her new best friend. First time,' Kathy confided. 'And in the middle of the week. But they'll get to school all right in the morning. I'm such a worrier,' she jibed at herself.

'The grass smells so good,' Laurie said and sniffed with pleasure.

'Grass always smells wonderful when it's just been cut.' Caren smiled when the crew trimming the lawn to the right of the Bernstein house turned down their overloud boom-box as Kathy turned into her driveway.

'It's too beautiful a day to stay indoors until we have to. I'm going to collapse on a chaise and read for a bit.' Kathy turned to Laurie and Danny. 'Why don't you two play on the lawn until dinner? OK, Caren?'

'Sure. Send Danny home in about an hour.' Plenty of time to prepare dinner for the two of them – and sneak in a few minutes at the computer again. Touching base with Janis.

Caren crossed the road with an unexpected sense of peace.

For the moment, she scoffed at herself. It was just that the day was so beautiful – and for the moment life seemed to stand still.

She sat at the computer and read with a feeling of closeness to Janis and Ira and the kids. Dwelling on minutiae about their daily lives. With reluctance she signed off on the computer, began dinner preparations.

Danny came into the apartment. Why so somber? she worried. But kids – even little ones – were complex.

'Dinner will be ready in a few minutes. Are you hungry?' She was solicitous.

'I guess so—'

'All right, you can set the table for me.' That craziness at school still bothered him at intervals, she suspected.

Danny set the table, brought out the pitcher of orange juice. Caren was about to bring the casserole out of the oven when the phone rang. As usual, she stiffened for an instant.

'Danny, answer that, please.'

'It won't be for me,' he hedged.

'It could be.' But she went to the phone. 'Hello—' Her own voice strained because each time the phone rang, she was fearful.

'Caren, is Laurie there with you?' A hint of anxiety in Kathy's voice.

'No – Danny came home alone.'

'I went inside to answer the phone. I was there just a few minutes. I came out – and the kids were gone.' Her voice strident now. 'Ask Danny where Laurie went!'

'Hold on—' She understood Kathy's alarm. All those little girls who disappeared these last months. 'Danny, where's Laurie?'

'I don't know—' He appeared to be searching his mind. 'When I left her, she was playing out front with Daisy.'

'Kathy, Danny said he left her on the front lawn. She was playing with Daisy.'

'She's not there. I don't see her anywhere—'

'She's probably at another house on the road—' Caren sought for an explanation. 'You know how friendly she is with people.'

'Howie's away on business again.' Kathy was battling panic. 'I don't know what to do!'

'I'll be right over. We'll start looking for her – she probably popped into somebody's house.' *Nothing bad could have happened to Laurie – not in quiet little Primrose.* 'You know how she adores dogs and cats – she probably went to—'

'Something terrible has happened!' Kathy broke in. 'Laurie never wanders away! She knows not to do that. Where is she, Caren?'

Thirty-Six

For an instant Caren froze. *This isn't happening! This is a nightmare!*

'I'll be right over,' she told Kathy again. 'We'll find Laurie.'

Caren switched off the oven – the casserole would wait. She turned to Danny. 'Let's go over to Laurie's house.' *Nothing terrible has happened to Laurie – there's some explanation for this.*

Danny's hand in hers, Caren hurried from the apartment. 'Danny, did you see Laurie talking to anybody when you left her?' she asked while they darted across the road.

'No.' He shook his head. 'Nobody.' *Poor baby, he looks so scared.*

Kathy was on the deck – cordless phone in hand. 'Please, if you see Laurie, tell her to hurry home. I'm so worried.'

While Caren stood by – and Danny fondled Daisy, who seemed aware that something was not right – Kathy phoned house after house. Her eyes were frantic.

'Nobody's seen her,' Kathy whispered. 'Nobody.'

Caren saw Brian's car swing into their driveway. 'Let me call Brian—' Without waiting for a reply, she rushed from the deck. 'Brian! Please come over—'

Brian sprinted across the road. The urgency in her voice had reached out to him, Caren realized.

'Problems?' Brian was calm. Reassuring. *Brian will know what we must do.*

'Laurie's disappeared—' Kathy's voice was hoarse with terror.

Caren explained the situation. His voice gentle, Brian questioned Danny.

'Danny, you were with Laurie. Tell us what happened.'

'Laurie and me were playing with Daisy – and I figured

it was time to go home for dinner. I was getting hungry. Laurie went up on the deck with Daisy.'

'You didn't see anybody on the road?' Brian pursued.

'Nobody. Just Rusty,' Danny recalled, 'chasing a squirrel.' Rusty was the Irish setter living three houses down.

'Maybe Laurie's at Rusty's house,' Caren said hopefully.

'I called – she's not there.' As though to bring Laurie closer, Kathy reached to pick up Daisy.

'We'll find Laurie.' *Brian sounds so laid-back – but I know he's upset.* He reached for Kathy's cellphone. 'There's some logical explanation for this,' he soothed Kathy, 'but meanwhile we'll look for Laurie.'

The two women stood by while Brian made several calls. In minutes a police car pulled up before the Bernstein house. Brian talked with the two police officers, discussed strategy. Minutes later neighbors were approaching the house.

'You say Laurie's crazy about dogs,' the policewoman pinpointed. 'Like my two kids. Laurie may have followed one home. Let's call at every house within a four-block radius. Brian, you organize these people—' She nodded towards the cluster of neighbors walking towards them. 'Bert and I will go back to the station house, do some checking on the computers.' Meaning they would check on possible sexual predators in the neighborhood, Caren thought and felt dizzy at the implication. She reached for Kathy's hand. They both feared the same thing, she guessed.

Brian was to remain at the Bernstein house to coordinate efforts. More people were arriving – from beyond their own neighborhood, Brian said. The dinner hour forgotten. What had happened in other towns was happening here. One of their little girls was missing.

Laurie's teacher – Joan Harris and her husband arrived.

'We'll find Laurie. She'll be all right.' A comforting arm about his wife, Harris was grim. 'You hold on to that thought, Kathy.'

'Show me to the kitchen and I'll put up coffee,' Joan told Kathy. 'We brought over a roast—' She indicated the insulated bag her husband held. 'You have to eat.'

Each minute seemed an hour, Caren thought while she watched Brian make calls for more searchers. Danny sat cross-legged on the deck, holding Daisy. Earlier he'd taken Daisy into the kitchen and fed her, as per Kathy's instructions. He was somber, frightened for Laurie.

Kathy had reached Howie at his hotel. He was flying home, should be here by midnight, Kathy reported.

'It's best for Cindy to stay with her friend—' Kathy struggled for composure. 'She doesn't know what's happening.'

Brian left to join the searchers. The two women made a pretense of eating – to please Joan Harris and her husband. Danny refused to eat. Now the Harrises took off with a new group of searchers – quiet, determined to be optimistic. But reality was frightening.

'We'd better go inside,' Caren said at last as dusk blended into night. 'The temperature must have dropped ten degrees.'

'Laurie was wearing just a tee shirt and shorts because it was so warm earlier—' Kathy's fragile hold on calm was eroding. 'She must be cold.'

Not a star in the sky, Caren noted while they walked into the house. The moon hidden behind clouds. A feeling of imminent rain permeated the atmosphere. Caren fought against an urge to join the search. She knew Kathy needed her here.

At intervals Brian called on his cellphone to report on where they were searching. Nothing yet. Not a clue. Still, the searchers were determined to forge ahead – even when the rain began.

At shortly before 10 p.m. Howie phoned from the Saratoga Springs Airport, where he'd left his car when he took off for his meeting in New York. He'd be home in less than an hour, he promised.

'We'll find Laurie,' he told Kathy, while Caren listened on the cordless phone. Danny asleep in a corner of the sofa. 'She'll be all right.'

Howie and Brian arrived at the house at the same time. Caren saw them in somber conversation as they walked up to the deck while rain lashed them and lightning flashed across the sky.

'Oh, Howie, thank God you're here—' Kathy rushed into his arms. 'I don't know how it happened,' she sobbed. 'I went in to answer the phone – I was gone a few minutes.

I came out of the house – expecting to see Laurie and Danny playing on the lawn.'

'We'll find Laurie,' Howie insisted – but his eyes revealed his fear. 'Brian says hundreds of people are out there searching for her—'

'We've had to call off the search because of the storm.' Brian was apologetic. 'But at daybreak we'll move out again.' He reached down to pick up Danny, coming awake now. 'I know it sounds awful – but we all need to get a couple of hours sleep before we start off again.'

With Danny half-asleep in his arms, Brian walked with Caren to her apartment door.

'Stay with us – for a while?' Caren reached to take Danny from him.

'Sure.' Brian pulled the door open.

'I'll get Danny into bed – and we can have coffee—'

'Don't wanna go to bed,' Danny grumbled but allowed Caren to carry him into his room.

'Pajamas, Danny,' Caren said, lowering him on to his bed. Undressing him, she was startled to see both knees scraped and bloody. 'How did you hurt your knees?'

'I jumped off the deck—' he mumbled, fighting yawns. 'It's OK.'

Caren hurried out to the bathroom for a wet cloth and wide Band-Aids. Brian emerged from the kitchen, where he'd been putting up coffee.

'You ground beans earlier,' he guessed. 'That's great.'

'Danny scraped both his knees,' she reported, exuding concern.

'Caren, it's part of the territory – nothing to worry about.' His eyes reassuring.

'Danny hadn't said a word about it to me.' *Am I becoming an overly protective mother?* 'I'll clean up the scratches and he'll be off in minutes.'

With Danny under a light blanket and oblivious to the world, Caren joined Brian at the table in the tiny dining area. It felt so good – having Brian here, she thought in gratitude.

'I found slices of turkey in the fridge,' he told her – carrying a tray to the table. 'I threw together sandwiches for us. And you eat,' he ordered.

Though the door to Danny's bedroom was closed, they talked in whispers. Only now did Caren realize that she was hungry. How could she be hungry when they didn't know where Laurie was at this moment?

She was startled at the sudden outcries that emerged from behind Danny's bedroom door.

'He's having a nightmare!' She rushed to his room – Brian beside her, pulled the door wide.

'No! No!' Danny shrieked. 'Put her down! Leave her alone!'

'Danny, wake up—' She was trembling. *Danny knows something. He was there when Laurie was kidnapped!* 'Darling, you're having a nightmare—' But it wasn't a nightmare. It was real.

Thirty-Seven

'Mommie, Mommie.' Danny clung to her. 'I couldn't tell! He said he would kill you if I told—'

'Nobody's going to hurt your mommie,' Brian said, hovering above them. 'We won't let that happen.' Danny gazed up at him. Only half-convinced. 'I promise you, Danny!'

'We must find Laurie. Before he hurts her. Danny, tell us what you know,' Caren implored.

'Laurie and me – we were playing with Daisy. And this – man – came up and grabbed Laurie. He put something over her mouth. I yelled at him to put her down – and he pushed me on to the road and ran to his car—' *That's when his knees got scraped.*

'What kind of car?' Brian asked, reaching for the cellphone in his jacket.

'Old – beat-up. A blue pick-up truck—' Danny remembered.

'Did you see the truck earlier?' Caren prodded. 'Do you know that man?'

'He was mowing the lawn next door to Laurie's house – when we first got home.' Danny was struggling to recall those moments. 'He and another man were mowing—'

'Then you'd recognize him if you saw his picture?' Brian probed.

'You won't let him hurt Mommie?' Danny was still insecure.

'We won't let him hurt Mommie,' Brian insisted. 'But we must find Laurie before he hurts her.' Now he was punching numbers into the cellphone.

'This is Brian Woods.' Brian was brisk. 'We've got a lead on the kidnapper—'

'I'll get Danny dressed – we'll be ready in a few moments,' she told Brian at a break in his conversation with an officer on duty at the police station. She hesitated. 'Shouldn't we tell Kathy and Howie what we've learned?'

'Not yet,' Brian said after a moment. 'Not until we have something definite.'

'Please God, let this lead us to Laurie.'

'We're getting quick action—' Brian hovered in the doorway while Caren helped Danny into clothes. 'Detectives are tracking down the lawn-mowing crew. They'll pick up the guys who were mowing there this afternoon.'

Caren knew the entire police force was on active duty. Never in living memory had a child been abducted in Primrose.

They were determined to find Laurie. Find her unhurt. Several had small children of their own, vowed not to sleep until Laurie Bernstein was found.

The rain had dissipated to a drizzle. The three of them hurried to Brian's car, parked in the driveway because the search was to begin again at daybreak. Brian slid behind the wheel. Caren held Danny in her arms on the front seat.

Every minute counts. Laurie has been missing for almost five hours.

At the police station they learned that a squad car was picking up the two men who'd been mowing at the house next to the Bernsteins' house. Moments later two detectives strode in with a pair of frightened workers, escorted them to an interrogation room.

'Danny, we want you to tell us if either of these men carried off Laurie,' a deceptively soft-voiced detective told him. 'They won't see you,' she soothed. 'But take your time—'

Caren and Brian followed the detective and Danny. The detective talking with the two suspects walked out of the small interrogation room. Two men – appearing dazed and frightened – sat there in silence.

'We dragged both out of their beds,' the detective reported. 'No sign of Laurie—'

'Danny,' the other detective began, 'look at them carefully. 'Was either of them the man who took Laurie away?'

Danny stared through the separating wall of glass. He frowned, shook his head. 'It wasn't them—'

'We have some checking to do,' the detective told Caren. 'This could be the wrong crew.'

Caren and Danny – along with Brian – were then led to a room where they were to wait.

'There's an all-night diner across the way.' The Chief of Detectives who'd arrived while Danny was viewing the men approached them. 'Coffee for you two? And hot chocolate for you, Danny?'

'OK—' But Danny seemed disinterested.

Caren and Brian were sipping their coffee, Danny showing desultory interest in his hot chocolate when another detective charged into the room.

'We're bringing in another man,' he told them. 'Those two you saw earlier, Danny – were the two who were supposed to be mowing this afternoon. But it seems one of them was sick – he sent his cousin to fill in for him. He'll be picked up any minute now. You'll tell us then if he's the one who kidnapped Laurie.'

Caren reached for Brian's hand. Would they find Laurie with him? Was she all right?

Minutes before midnight a loud, exultant cry circulated through the police station:

'We've found Laurie! She's all right!'

Caren and Brian leapt to their feet as a detective charged into the small room where they waited. Danny asleep in his chair.

'It's true – Laurie's OK!' The detective glowed in relief. 'This creep – the one who was filling in as a mower – was holding her in a beat-up trailer. She's OK, but she'll be checked out at the hospital. It's routine. The Bernsteins are on their way over there now!'

'Oh, thank God!' Caren felt herself swept up in Brian's embrace, clung to him in relief. 'We'll take Danny home now – put him to bed. Poor baby, he's had such a rough night.'

'Don't rush away,' the detective admonished in high spirits. 'The newspaper reporters – the TV crew waiting outside – they'll want to talk to Danny. He'll be the hero of the day!'

'No!' Caren gasped. *Danny's face on newspapers throughout the country? On TV screens everywhere?* She turned to Brian in panic. His eyes reflected her own alarm. 'Danny mustn't be interviewed—'

'Please, show us to a side exit,' Brian ordered the detective. 'We—'

'But he's a hero,' the detective interrupted. 'He's led us to a kidnapped child. People—'

'No.' Brian was brusque. 'Danny's mother doesn't want him brought into this story. She feels it would be detrimental to his mental health. It was enough that his mother's life was threatened – and he had to deal with that—' He shot a warning glance at Caren. *He's going to handle this – I must be quiet.* 'Tell the news people that a small local boy was instrumental in finding Laurie. But his family doesn't wish him to be exposed to national scrutiny. Let nobody reveal his identity. Nobody knows except members of the police department,' he pointed out. 'His name does not have to be released.'

'Whatever you say—' The detective's smile was compassionate. 'Yeah, I wouldn't want either of my kids exposed to a media circus. There's a back entrance. Just follow me.'

The rain had ceased. Danny was asleep in his bed. Laurie – dismissed from the hospital within an hour of being found – was asleep for now in Caren's bed while her parents talked in low tones with Caren and Brian. Kathy and Howie had come here before going home – to express their gratitude for Danny's leading the police to Laurie.

Kathy and Howie had listened in stunned silence while Caren haltingly explained her personal situation – without mentioning her fear of ads in a supermarket tabloid.

'I couldn't stay in Iran – seeing what Marty was doing to Danny. And in the last weeks there I was terrified Danny and Marty would both be killed. They went nowhere without security guards. There's such violence in Iran.' Caren shuddered in recall. 'Each morning when Danny went off to school, I was afraid for him.' She drew a deep, anguished breath. 'I can't let Marty take Danny.'

'The police understand that you don't want Danny involved,' Brian rushed to reassure Caren. 'You're safe here.'

'For now.' Her smile was wan.

'This is a small town—' Kathy was searching for answers. 'If Marty—' she stumbled over the name, 'if he discovers you're here – and that's unlikely – and sends his goons for Danny, everybody would fight for you.' Except some greedy monster determined to collect that $20,000 reward.

'It's been a long night.' Howie rose to his feet. 'I'll go pick up Laurie – we'll take her home.' *He makes it sound like a benediction.* 'She won't even wake up,' he predicted.

'The elementary school will be closed tomorrow,' Brian told them. 'I've already sent the word out to the radio and TV people. Announcements will start at 6 a.m. Let's all try to get a little sleep.'

No wall between Brian and her tonight, Caren thought exultantly while he pulled her close. But no future for them either . . .

Thirty-Eight

At moments past 9 a.m. – after three hours of troubled sleep – Caren called in to the Loveland office to explain she couldn't come in today.

'My son's school is closed for the day. We learned this too late for me to arrange for babysitting,' she apologized. 'I'm terribly sorry. I'll be in tomorrow morning as usual.' A hint of question in her voice. Would she be fired for not being able to handle this situation? What would it matter? In six days she and Danny would be headed for Canada.

'We know about all the excitement last night.' Carl Watson's voice was coated with sarcasm. 'What do people expect when they let all these immigrants into the country? Nothing like that will ever happen in our new community.' He chuckled. 'But then there'll be no kids except as visitors.'

Off the phone, Caren checked on Danny again. Still asleep. What a rough night he'd had! And now, she tormented herself, she must put him through more turmoil.

They'd leave Monday morning. She wouldn't wake Danny as usual – he'd sleep past the school bus pick-up. Brian would be at school. On Monday mornings Kathy went for an early workout at the gym. Nobody would see them leave.

They'd take a bus to Saratoga Springs, then the train to Montreal. The Adirondack left at 11.47 a.m. – even if the bus was slow, they'd make it. They'd arrive in Montreal at 6.30 p.m. She wouldn't allow herself to think beyond that.

Their passports were in order – they'd have no problem entering Canada. *But how am I to explain this sudden –*

surreptitious – move to Danny? What excuse will I give him?
He'll be bewildered, frightened. But take one day at a time.
That's the road to survival.

Danny would miss Laurie and Cindy – and Daisy. He'd
miss Brian. In such a short span of time the three of them
had become close. Like a family. And now she must uproot
Danny again.

Kathy and Howie were sure Laurie would be all right
despite the trauma of last night, Caren told herself. Always
so bubbly, Laurie had been subdued then – but Kathy was
convinced she'd bounce right back.

Laurie didn't understand what had been in store for her
if the police had not arrived when they did. Caren flinched,
remembering a detective's words:

'That rotten sicko was released on a child molesting charge
just seven months ago. In another state. He'd planned the
same routine here. Presents, semblance of a party, then at
midnight – surrounded by endless candles – rape.'

Detectives – with much backup – had arrived at his broken-
down trailer at 11.56 p.m. Laurie had been very solemn.

'I woke up in this ugly little trailer – and my clothes had
been changed. I was in a pretty party dress. I think he must
be very lonely – but he promised to take me home in the
morning.'

Brian had warned her – it would take time for Danny to
recover from this experience. Danny had been so frightened
for her – and for Laurie. So torn. So young to have been put
through such torment.

Danny awoke as Caren came into his room to check on
him. He was startled when he realized the time.

'I missed the school bus—' And then memory of last night
assaulted him. 'Oh—'

'No school today,' she soothed. 'And everything's fine
now—' Not fine, but last night's nightmare was over. 'What
would you like for breakfast this morning? Strawberry
pancakes?' A special treat.

'OK.' But he was solemn. 'Mommie, you're not mad at me?'

'Darling, no. Why should I be angry?' She sat at the edge
of the bed and reached to pull him close. 'You told the

detectives how to find Laurie. You're a hero. I'm proud of you.' Words that Marty had never uttered to his small son. A little boy shouldn't have to fight for his father's love.

Caren was relieved when Laurie and Cindy came over to the apartment right after breakfast. She saw Kathy watching from her deck. Still unnerved by Laurie's kidnapping.

'Can Danny come out and play?' Laurie asked when Caren opened the door.

'Of course, Laurie,' Caren told her. 'Danny, Laurie and Cindy are here.'

Life seemed almost normal again, Caren thought as the week rolled on. As normal as it could be when she lived in constant fear of Marty's discovering their whereabouts. It was clear that she would not be fired for staying home when the elementary school was closed for the day. Her job, at least, was secure.

After a flurry of news stories – none of which mentioned Danny by name – the town was settling down. Again, the major story was the proposed Loveland Development complex. Brian and his group were convinced that Loveland would be denied the right to oust the homeowners along the lake. And that in the coming elections Mayor Davis would be ousted.

But Caren lived each day on the edge of panic.

Saturday morning was unseasonably cool. A hint of rain in the air. Brian was in his car and headed for the IGA a few minutes before 7 a.m. The store opened at 7 a.m. – and as long as he was awake, he'd told himself, he might as well do the Saturday morning shopping before the mad rush.

He'd spent a night of broken sleep, punctured by worries about Caren's plight. He recoiled from the prospect of her moving out of his life. They were both eager for more – but for now he clung to what they could share. How was she to free herself of her monster of a husband?

He turned into the IGA parking lot. Only a few cars there. Mostly employees, he suspected. Pushing a shopping cart, he strode into the supermarket. Only one cashier on duty thus far. One shopper in the produce section. He'd be out of here in five minutes, he congratulated himself and made a fast foray down the aisles.

He hurried to the one checkout counter open at this hour, took his place behind the other early morning shopper – in lively conversation with the cashier. His eyes scanned the supermarket tabloids. He'd checked earlier in the week – no ad placed by Mohammed Mansur. Then all at once he realized there was a new tabloid on the stand.

He reached for the unfamiliar tabloid. A new one – coming out on Saturday mornings. Wary yet deriding his fear, he flipped through the pages. He froze. His eyes focused on a small ad. The reward Mansur was offering had risen to $25,000.

Brian swerved his shopping cart around, charged in the direction of the manager's cubicle. No time to lose! He had to get Caren and Danny out of sight.

'Chuck!' he called out, banging on the door.

'Hey, what are you doing up at this hour on a Saturday morning?' Chuck joshed.

'Chuck, I need a favor.' No time to waste. 'That new tabloid rag you have on display – I want to buy up the lot. And I want you to promise not to order any more!' Sure, there would be others on sale in other supermarkets – but make sure these were gone.

'OK—' Chuck was bewildered. 'That's a bundle of cash.'

'I'm in a rush – put it on my tab. I'll—'

'I'll take the lot of them out to your car. You're still driving that antique Ford?'

'Yeah, do that, please. Meanwhile I'll check out with the cashier.' Chuck knew him well enough not to ask questions.

He headed back to the checkout counter. Chuck was already charging towards the back of the store. Damn, every minute counted now!

On this Saturday morning Caren awoke almost as early as on midweek days. Barely 7.30 a.m. Instantly she realized this would be their last weekend in town. She fought against an urge to confide in Brian. No! He'd persuade her to stay. He was sure they could handle the situation. But he didn't know Marty. To stay would be a horrible mistake.

She was startled by a sudden staccato tapping on her window. Light yet urgent. Alarmed, she hurried from the bed to the window, opened the drapes.

'I have to talk to you,' Brian mouthed the words. 'I didn't want to wake Danny just yet—'

She nodded. Alarm surging through her, she reached to pull on her robe, hurried to open the door.

'Brian, what's happening?'

'Stay cool, Caren – we can handle this,' he whispered and rushed to close Danny's bedroom door. 'We need to move fast – I'm taking you and Danny to my cottage in the mountains. I was at the IGA – they're selling a new tabloid that comes out on Saturday mornings. Marty's ad is there – with the reward and a collect phone number to call.'

Caren's face was drained of color. 'I knew it would happen—'

'You'll be all right.' Brian pulled her into his arms. 'I bought all the papers – the manager promised not to order more. He owes me—'

'But they'll be in other supermarkets – here and in towns all around us!' *Danny and I mustn't be seen!*

'The ad will run just so long. You and Danny will stay in the cottage until the ad stops showing up. I'll ask Kathy to call Loveland and say you've been called out of town on a family emergency. Outside of the people there, few people in town know you,' he reminded.

'But the kids at the school know Danny!'

'The kids don't read the tabloids. But we'll play it safe,' he soothed. 'You and Danny will stay at my cottage. Now wake him and get him dressed.'

'Yes—' Caren drew away from him. Willing herself to appear calm. For Danny's sake.

'And pack a bag – whatever you'll need for a while.' *How long?* 'Danny will love it up there – deer running across the property, rabbits and opossums and squirrels everywhere.'

'I'll tell him we're going on a holiday in the mountains—' Caren opened the door into Danny's bedroom. 'Danny, time to rise and shine,' she said with contrived high spirits. 'We're going to have a wonderful weekend!' But it would be longer than that, she warned herself. *How long will Marty run that ad?*

In a few minutes Danny was dressed – 'You'll shower at the cottage.' Caren had packed a valise. Brian emptied the contents of the refrigerator into an insulated bag.

'We'll have breakfast on the road,' Brian told Danny. 'It'll be fun. You and Mommie get in the car – I have to bring some things from the house.'

Caren and Danny settled themselves on the back seat, waited for Brian to return. Danny was fighting yawns.

'OK, we're all set.' Brian deposited his laptop and a cell-phone on the front seat, circled around to slide behind the wheel.

'You'll like to have these,' he told Caren. Meaning, she interpreted, he'd call her on the cellphone. She'd have the laptop to entertain Danny – and to keep in touch with Janis.

Early Saturday morning traffic was very light. Every motorist – including Brian – exceeding the speed limit. Twenty miles out of Primrose, Brian stopped to shop at a roadside diner for breakfast. They ate in the car. Caren and Brian made it a festive occasion.

Only a handful of cars on the road as they drove up the side of a mountain. Long stretches of towering evergreens rose on either side of the road. An occasional house appeared. Now civilization seemed to be left behind. No car in sight behind them.

'The cottage and its two acres are just ahead,' Brian said. They'd been on the road about seventy minutes, Caren noted. 'It's tiny – three small rooms and a porch – but you'll be surrounded by nature. The property's wedged in between a ninety-four-acre deer preserve and a forty-acre hideaway owned by some New York millionaire who never comes up before June each year.'

'A deer!' Danny shrieked. His face transfixed. 'I just saw a deer running that way!'

The cottage was surrounded by wild flowers, trees bursting into bloom. They left the car and walked to the porch. Brian reached into his pocket for the key.

'Nothing fancy,' he cautioned. 'I keep the electric running

year-round. The heating's electric. No phone – but you'll
have the cellphone. No television. Two radios – in case one
conks out.'

Caren and Brian walked into the cottage. Danny remained
on the porch – entranced by the view, hoping to see another
deer.

'It's cozy.' Caren struggled to relax. 'Oh, you have a fireplace!' And stacks of logs at either side.

'You and Danny will be all right here,' he promised, pulling
her close for an electric moment.

'What would we have done without you?' she whispered.

By early evening the temperature had dropped. Brian built
a fire in the grate, involving Danny in this activity while
Caren prepared an early dinner. With dinner simmering on
the electric range and Danny engrossed in helping Brian
with the fire, Caren took the laptop into the bedroom, brought
up Janis's website. Her heart pounding she read the new
letter.

> 'Hi Bobbie,
>
> Everything about normal here. Jimmy's still excited
> about his e-mail pen pal in Iran. Nadine more upset –
> though Ira and I try to calm her down. She called to
> tell me she'd gone shopping at her supermarket – and
> she saw this new tabloid there. Her niece's husband's
> ad somewhere in back – and she knows it's probably
> sold nationwide. But I pointed out that her niece was
> watchful – she'd know. Probably by now she's on a
> train to some distant town. Not by plane because that
> would leave a trail.'

Janis was telling her to run. She didn't know about Brian
and the cottage. *We're safe here.*

Danny was startled when Brian prepared to leave after
dinner. 'You won't be here with us?' He was disappointed.
Brian's become important in his life.

'I have a meeting in town tonight,' Brian explained. 'But
I'll be back out tomorrow morning.'

When he said he'd bring up more groceries, Caren remembered. How long would Marty run the ad in the tabloid?

A new one – probably offering low rates to advertisers. Would Marty run the ad longer than two weeks?

Will someone in Primrose buy a copy at another store? Someone with a child in Danny's class? Someone hungry to collect that reward?

Thirty-Nine

Caren and Danny sat before the fireplace, where most of the logs had been reduced to gray ash. One small chunk – still burning – cast a soft, red glow. Music from a classical radio station lessened Caren's sense of isolation from the world. But as always – when a brief news report began, she silenced the radio for a few moments. Danny must not hear or watch the news. Any word of Iran was to be avoided.

'What's that?' Danny tensed at unfamiliar sounds outdoors.

'Animals in the woods,' Caren explained. 'Maybe a bear—'

Smothering a series of yawns, Danny considered this. 'They won't come in here?' Simultaneously intrigued and alarmed.

'No, darling. And I think it's time we go to bed. You'll sleep in the bedroom – I'll take the day bed in here.'

'Mommie—' Danny seemed in some inner debate. 'Can I sleep with you tonight?'

'All right—' Her smile reassuring. She understood – night-time in such a deserted area was intimidating. 'Go brush your teeth – we'll get ready for bed.'

For Caren sleep was slow in coming. All it required to destroy her life and Danny's was for one person to read that ad, bring Marty's goons to Primrose. They'd track her down. They would have no respect for the laws in this country. They would grab Danny and run with him.

In sleep Danny clung to her. Her precious baby, whom she was putting through such chaos. But with Marty's ad in a tabloid that was circulating throughout the country, she didn't dare emerge from the cottage. To try to move to Canada was too dangerous now.

They both awoke to a magnificent sunrise that showed through a chink in the drapes.

'It's so quiet,' Danny said in awe, then laughed as the noisy clatter of birds refuted this.

'Hungry?' she asked, striving to sound casual. Her perennial question. *This is supposed to be a weekend holiday. How will I explain to Danny when we stay on? For how long?*

After breakfast she and Danny went for a walk. Careful not to lose sight of the cottage. What beautiful country, she thought, lulled into moments of serenity. The trees bursting into bloom. Birds singing in appreciation of a gorgeous morning.

'Mommie, look at that red bird!' Danny pointed. 'Wow!'

'That's a cardinal. Isn't he beautiful?'

After their walk they sat on the porch and watched the small animals that scurried about in the morning sunshine. Danny squealed in delight when a faint rustle in the woods just beyond revealed a pair of deer foraging for food.

Earlier than Caren expected – it was minutes past nine – they heard a car approaching. She was confident it was Brian.

'Hi, it's a great day,' he greeted them, emerged from the car with a bag of groceries. 'See any more deer, Danny?'

'Yeah!' Danny glowed. 'Two more.'

'You take this and put it in the fridge pronto,' Brian told him – pulling forth a quart container of frozen yogurt from the loaded supermarket bag.

'That's cool—' Danny took the yogurt and darted into the cottage.

'What do you hear in town?' Caren asked Brian while he pulled her close. Danny in the kitchen now. 'Anything?'

'Not a word,' he comforted.

'Marty will have the ad running again next week,' Caren predicted. And maybe longer. 'Nobody followed you up here?' she asked in sudden terror.

'Honey, don't let yourself become paranoid. Nobody knows how we feel about each other – except possibly Kathy. Nobody will expect me to lead them to you.'

'My head's in such a whirl,' she admitted. 'I try to tell myself – live one day at a time—'

'You'll be all right here,' he repeated for the dozenth time.

'You can outsit Marty and his ads. I was tempted so often to sell this little place, but I couldn't. It's as though I knew that someday it would be terribly important to me.'

'Brian—' Danny came charging out of the cottage. A baseball in hand. 'Look what I found!'

'You want to play catch?' Brian invited.

'Yeah—' Danny was jubilant.

Marty never once played 'catch' with Danny. That was too American. Maybe twice a year he took Danny for a day of skiing. But Marty was never a real father. Not once we were living in Tehran.

Caren sat on the porch and watched while Danny and Brian played 'catch.' Then Brian talked about a little pond – where usually there were several ducks – that was a short walk through the woods.

'OK if I take Danny off to the pond?' Brian asked Caren.

'It sounds like a great trip. Go. We'll talk about lunch when you get back.' *I don't want to move out of Brian's life. I need him to make my life whole. Danny needs him.*

Caren went into the cottage, plotted a lunch menu, set the table. Wishing now that Danny and Brian hadn't gone to the pond. Her mind trying to deal with the days ahead. Danny would be upset that he wouldn't be back at school in the morning, she warned herself. Her job would be gone.

It was silly to go to the laptop again. Janis could have nothing new to tell her. It was still early morning out there. But with a compulsive need to feel in touch with her sister, she brought out the laptop.

In her rush she hit the wrong keys. *What does this stupid machine mean? No such website.* And then she realized her error. A period, stupid – not a comma! She sighed with relief when Janis's website surfaced.

Caren, it's over! The nightmare is over! Our mail comes early – I just brought it in from the mailbox. Including Jimmy's first airmailed copy of the *Tehran Times*. Four days ago Marty and his bodyguard were ambushed on their way to a meeting. Both were killed.

Caren gasped in shock. If she and Danny had been in Tehran, Danny might have been with Marty! Her eyes clung to the computer monitor:

'*Both were killed.*' Caren felt encased in ice. This was not the way she wished for freedom to come to Danny and her. Marty overreached in his greed. In Iran assassination was too often a response from enemies.

> Fate took a hand. I know – Danny's lost his father. But his life will be better now. Call me, Caren – I'll be waiting by the phone. Love, Janis.

The running was over – Danny was safe. But shock waves swept over her now. Cold and trembling, she sat before the computer, reread Janis's words. Thank God, Danny had been here – not with Marty. Danny would have been killed, along with Marty and the bodyguard!

Her mind in chaos, she fought for calm. Danny had lost his father – and that was tragic. No, she rejected this – Danny lost his father a few months after they arrived in Tehran. For almost three years of his young life Danny had a father. Marty killed that man.

She mustn't tell Danny right away that his father had been assassinated. He'd been through so much in these past few weeks. He was accepting the separation from Marty. Brian was more a father to Danny than Marty had ever been since he was three.

It was sad that she could feel this relief that Marty could never again terrify her with efforts to take Danny from her. She didn't mean for it to happen this way – but all at once she saw a fine new life ahead for Danny and her. *We don't have to be afraid! We don't have to run!*

In a burst of impatience she darted out on to the porch.

Where were Danny and Brian? She stood at the railing. Too impatient to sit. Her face luminescent. Why don't they return?

And then she saw them. Danny ran ahead of Brian – eager to report on this adventure.

'We saw a mommie duck and six little baby ducks in a line behind her. Brian says we can go back later and feed them bread crumbs!'

'Oh, how exciting, Danny—' Her eyes sought Brian's as he approached. 'Perhaps we can come here again other week-ends.' *Brian realizes something has happened.* 'Danny, pick a bunch of flowers for us to take back home with us.' *It is home now. A blessed word.*

'Danny, over there—' Brian pointed to a cluster of deli-cate blue flowers about thirty feet away. 'They're very pretty.' His eyes clung to Caren's. Asking questions.

'OK—' Danny hurried in that direction.

Softly – when Danny was out of hearing – Caren told Brian about the message on Janis's website.

'I feel guilty that I'm so happy,' she whispered while Brian pulled her close. 'Marty was assassinated four days ago – but how can I grieve for him?'

'Don't tell Danny just yet,' Brian cautioned.

'I won't,' she said quickly.

'This isn't the time to talk of such things,' Brian began, searching for words, 'but I see a good life ahead for the three of us. I know – you'll feel we must wait a while. I hope – when we're married – you'll agree to my legally adopting Danny.'

Tears filled her eyes, spilled over. 'I'll agree,' she whis-pered. 'Danny will have a real father again—'

'Hey,' he joshed, 'is that why you're willing to marry me?'

'I want that so much. Soon,' she promised. 'I feel reborn.'

'You realize that Danny probably stands to inherit a fortune.' Brian was somber now.

'He doesn't need a fortune.' Her face was resolute. 'It's tainted money – and he'd have to live there to inherit. We'll be rich – in the ways that count.' All at once she remem-bered Janis – waiting by a phone in California. 'Oh, let me call Janis!' She frowned for an instant. 'Can I call California on a cellphone?'

'You bet you can.' He brought her hand to his mouth for an instant. His eyes making passionate love to her. 'It's going to be hell to wait for more.'

'Oh, you're an imaginative one,' she murmured. 'We'll find ways.'

'Go call my future sister-in-law,' he ordered with mock sternness. 'You mustn't keep her waiting.'

*   *   *

With Danny asleep on the rear seat, Caren sat with her head on Brian's shoulder while they headed back for Primrose. Yesterday morning she'd been running in terror. Now the three of them were returning to another world.

The night sky was aglow with stars. Moonlight caressed the car. Few cars on the road thus far, Caren noted. Traffic would pick up when they neared Primrose.

'You may be out of a job soon,' Brian joshed tenderly. 'Loveland will fold up their tent and leave town, the way I see it. But I predict a summer school job ahead for you – if you'd like it.'

Caren sat upright. 'I'd love it!'

'We'll have a fight on our hands to oust Mayor Davis – but the anti-Davis campaign is growing stronger by the day. A lot of people in this town think that Howie Bernstein is just what Primrose needs.'

'You never told me that—' Caren was surprised but pleased.

'You know now – so prepare to do battle.' A hand left the wheel to squeeze Caren's for a moment.

'I'm ready.' Her smile tremulous. This was familiar – comfortable – territory.

But now her thoughts grew tumultuous. She remembered Pari, who taught at the university under such restrictive conditions. Always fearful. Andrea, who fled Iran.

'I pray that the people of Iran will win their freedom soon. The young are often open about their rebellion. The older are more cautious. They remember that over 120,000 Iranians have been executed since the Mafia clerics have ruled the country – and nobody knows how many more have been maltreated. They live in fear of the next massacre.'

'May their freedom come soon.' Brian, too, was somber.

'I can call Pari!' Caren realized all at once. 'I was afraid to write her – she understood.'

'Don't call her as soon as we get home—' Brian tried to dispel the somber mood. 'What's the difference in time? Eight hours?'

'There are two centuries between us.' Caren's eyes were compassionate. 'And many Iranians are fighting with such desperation to bridge that gap. Let's pray they make it soon.'

'Amen,' Brian said quietly.

'Freedom – it's such a beautiful word.' Caren's face was luminescent. 'Danny and I have truly come home now.'

'Mommie—' Danny's voice came to them from the rear seat. 'Can we go out to that little house in the woods again? Can we, Brian?'

'You bet, Danny,' Brian assured him.

Caren's hand reached out to touch Brian's for a moment. Danny and she had truly come home.